MW01713576

KARONTEON

Dennis Marshall

PublishAmerica
Baltimore

First printing

ISBN: 1-4241-6260-2
PUBLISHED BY PUBLISHAMERICA, LLLP
www.publishamerica.com
Baltimore

Printed in the United States of America

To my wife, Mary Jo,
your belief in me kept me going,
I miss you.

To my best friend, Rachelle,
you being in my life inspired me to reach for the stars.

To Susan & John
Thanks for your
friendship + support!
Enjoy!

I would like to send a sincere thank you to the staff of the Detroit Free Press who compiled a book called the *Detroit Almanac* for the city's 300th birthday. You gave the world a great source of history of the Detroit area.

Also, thank you to author, Clive Cussler. Your advice and encouragement on how to develop my style was an inspiration to me. I will never forget it.

Thank you to the family and friends who never stopped believing.

Finally, to God who never stopped loving me.

CHAPTER 1

AD 1285

The plaza swarmed with artisans and their families busily perfecting their wares for the upcoming bazaar two days hence. Pottery makers fired their coils while others molded the pottery, adding intrinsic clan etchings and paint before placing it on coils to be fired. Basket makers wove dried Yucca leaves and turkey feathers into headdresses known throughout their world. The Sipapu had blessed their people with good weather as silky white clouds floated graciously through the blue afternoon sky. The Anasazi had thrived on the Mesa Verde for centuries with a population as large as many of today's mid-sized cities. Several droughts, over the last decade, were forcing families to relocate to the south. Local shaman fueled fears by preaching that frequent lunar and solar eclipses happened because the gods were angry. Raids by the Athapascans to the south also fractured their lives. Naked children romped throughout the bazaar, no fears about their world. All the bustle failed to disturb four men standing high above the Cliff Palace involved in a very animated discussion.

The tribal council was actively arguing about the current problems affecting their lives. Standing Deer, their strongest leader, watched intently while his tribal brothers vied for attention. Oblivious to their words, the chief perpetuated a semblance of listening while unifying answers to their problems independent from the council, a trait that made his tenure as chief unique.

They were losing more and more families every week, an exodus with no end in sight. Wild dogs raided villages at night, stealing their small animals for food. For every acre of terraced farmland lost or every inch of deforestation on the plateau, life became harder for the tribe to live day by day. As incidents increased, medicine men became more concerned about the imminent future. Standing Deer found it hard to concentrate on the conversation that encircled the kiva. Running Bear of the Square Tower clan spoke about fulfillment of a prophecy by the Ancient Ones. It was passed down for generations that a warrior would come from the south to lead their people to a better life. He never believed that prophecy, but as chief, it would be hypocritical if he denounced it. Snapping back to reality, he listened intently as Jumping Wolf spoke sternly to his blood brothers.

"The Great Spirit is very angry with us," said the leader of the Oak Tree clan.

"Strong leadership is needed to please him and bless our people again."

Strong Beaver, leader of the Spruce and the Cedar Tree clans and the eldest of the group, spoke softly and silenced the others with his words of guidance.

"For years, we squabble over work, but still see a light over the horizon. Many of our people suffer from lack of food and water. We have overcome many trials before. Let us do so again. Go, commune, with your loved ones tonight and gather, as the Great Spirit leaves us the next day, at the ceremonial kiva at Sun Temple. There we will do what we must do." With that wake-up call, Standing Deer spoke firmly to the council.

"Strong Beaver speaks truth. Meet at Sun Temple tomorrow after the gods retire. Decisions will be made then." Quickly dispersing, the council members slipped into obscurity as the tribe prepared for the bazaar.

Bats fluttered from their caves, using their inborn radar to search for breakfast. A lone coyote howled forlornly, spreading fear into the night animals searching for their nightly snacks. Mother Nature's sure-fire plan worked like clockwork as the night enveloped. The Cliff Palace was a masterpiece of architecture. A five story adobe apartment-like building, built into the wall of Fossil Canyon, it stimulated this style of building throughout the community. Designated by the council to be the residence of its tribal leader, construction began around 500AD finishing some twenty two weeks later. It had a single path leading to the upper mesa, used mostly for defensive posturing, with well-defined stairways leading to the canyon bottom and the terraced farmland. The main building was one hundred meters long, with a five story central tower that showcased a communal room on the fifth floor for the reigning chief of the tribe. The bottom four floors were designated living quarters for the families of the chief's clan. All family gatherings were held around the central hearth on the first level. Women prepared the meals as well as directed every aspect of family life, except for hunting. Women anchored the tribal household.

Straight Heart fussed from pot to pot, toying with the nightly meal while teaching her new daughter-in-law the joys of marriage. As matriarch of the tribe, it was her job to show future maidens what would be expected of them as they come of age. As the daughter of a famous brave, who lost his life during the great battle against the Ute Indians in Crow Canyon a few years before, she has seen the face of her people change from the flourishing community that it was just twenty years ago, to a weakened cell of people fighting shriveling land and shortages of food and water. If not for her husband, Standing Deer, she might not have had the tools to deal with this crisis. He was the perfect mate to lean on in a time of need. Members of the tribal community looked to them with great admiration and respect for consistent guidance and leadership.

The climb down from the mesa seemed more tedious than ever before. Every step made his spirit feel heavier as he got closer to the bottom of the stairs. The chief dragged his tall torso through the front door of the palace like he was dragging two four-ton boulders behind him. The shadows of dusk sequentially enveloped the canyons as the people prepared for the night. Standing Deer stepped through his doorway looking unusually tired and worn from the days problems. Straight Heart walked over to him with that caring look she always gave the chief when he came home from council meetings. He kissed her on the forehead and held her tight. Straight Heart met her husband and led him to the hearth.

"Your spirit is heavy with trouble my husband. Let us eat before we talk about them."

As the family gathered around the hearth, Standing Deer carried the face of a man who just lost his best friend. He put some beans in bowls, passing the food to the rest of the family while he pondered what he needed to do. The family ate quietly, sensing the tension that had enveloped their family room. The chief's daughter, Red Deer, and her grandma, Sparkling Dove, cleaned up the meal. Straight Heart led her husband to the area called their "kiva." After crawling in, the chief began to relax. Stroking his neck, Standing Deer finally unloaded his suitcase of trouble to her.

"Three groups are fighting for supremacy in this community. One preaches about a warrior who will come from the south to save our people. Another accuses me of creating the water shortages and the droughts that have hurt us for years. The third group blames the large population as causing of our problems. All I know is how I feel in my spirit. This land has run its course for our people. We must look to the future. Moving south to a new land is the only possible solution. To save our people, we must join with the other tribes that live on the Rio Bravo. It will take all of us standing together to avoid a split in our people. There is no other way" With that, he began to gently stroke her face and hair, paying particular attention to her prominent cheekbones and chin. Tilting her chin towards his face, their lips locked in such a passionate embrace, their love quickly soared to its highest peak before they slowed to rest for the night. As he turned to cover his loved one for the night, Standing Deer noticed two bright eyes with a wide smile glaring at the two of them. His father, Chief Running Dog stood at their door and was pleased to see his family strong as ever. Standing Deer smiled back sheepishly and they both settled down to a peaceful sleep.

Smoke swirled throughout the city of Veracruz. Local farmers swarmed to the temple preparing to roast the High Priest of the Tribe named Amozeltec. An orphan from a poor farming province known as Quintana Roo, tribal priests took him to their capital at the robust age of five. The priests also trained him voraciously as a warrior in the aggressive ITZAS tribe. Through all of his reign as High Priest, his teachers never lost track of his training, something that had been prophecied centuries ago. He became well versed in mathematics and astrology, specializing in weather forecasting. Success came swiftly for the fledgling priest, bringing men from miles around seeking his wisdom and insight crops. Communing with the great snake god, Kulkukan, he guided them to complete their planting now with plenty of rain on the way. Unexpectedly, a hurricane thrashed the gulf coast. Fields were thoroughly flooded, leaving the natives totally outraged. They merged together and marched on the city with the intent of avenging the calamity.

The many steps of the Great Temple rose high above the farmers as they entered the city. Built over the last hundred years from stones cut from nearby mountains, they were put in place with the toils of slave labor. Artisans chiseled out statues to add character to this sacred structure. Farrmers gathered outside, torches in hand, chanting "Death to Amozeltec", while the high council assembled to discuss what to do about their embattled priest. Amozeltec sauntered casually into the subterranean meeting room.

"My brothers, these are menacing times. But our question may already have an answer. The body of a young man who was sacrificed last night is still within our walls, a physique very similar to my own. Let us switch his body for mine and offer him up to the crowds. We will tell them that I sacrificed myself and will permit an escape through the catacombs and the jungles to the south. Do we agree?" Heads nodded in agreement in the council chambers. Amozeltec took three volunteers deep in the bowels of their sacred ground to make their masquerade a reality.

The temple doors opened with slow, magnificent grandeur. The council of priests carried the lifeless body of the High Priest's surrogate, offering him to the maddening crowds for their sacrifice to the Great Kulkukan. A tumultuous roar erupted from the plebeians. The crowd moved away from the temple, reveling as they marched through the city with their sacrificial lamb. The priests were relieved as they watched their troubles drift away. Fifty feet below the temple, Amozeltec slipped through ancient catacombs, out of the city and into the thick brush of the coastal jungle. He would establish a new identity the minute he emerged from the caves. His plan was simple; get as far away from the capital as possible. To accomplish this, Amozeltec headed south to the city of Uaxchun, a thriving metropolis for his people but far enough away to grant him some sense of anonymity. Blending into the populace, he assumed the image of a widowed farmer. No one was wiser. Years later, a traveler straggled into the village, asking many suspicious questions. Quickly leaving, he traveled through four cities before his disguise had worn off. After twenty-five years, the time had come for the little priest to leave the land of his forefathers forever.

Amozeltec traveled straight to the mountains above Contreras. After jumping from cave to cave for months, he wandered to a small village well isolated in the bowels of a mountain valley, away from the rest of civilization. A place that would soon reveal his ultimate calling. A tribal sage befriended the little adventurer as he entered the village at nightfall. Considered a man of great wisdom, the shaman brought Amozeltec to his tent to prepare to tell the young warrior's future. Stunned by the pungent odor of incense as he entered the tent, Amozeltec stared at a mask/headdress that contained some very pale, luminescent blue stones. Hypnotized by their penetrating colors, he sat by the shaman's fire to await his future.

Bazaar day was abuzz with activity. Tribesmen traveled from as far as Hovenweep and Yellowjacket to ponder, barter and trade their wares with their fellow Anasazi. Many different kinds of pottery exchanged hands as people shared ideas as to their creation. From the south, people from Aztec and Pueblo Bonito, brought baskets of jewelry made with the little stones that sparkled as blue as a crystal clear ocean. A shaman from Aztec took two of blue stones and began to slowly rotate them in her hand, absorbing the vibrations that emanated from them. She began to chant something unrecognizable to the other members of her tribe. Her chestnut brown eyes suddenly popped open and she looked around for a brave. Grabbing Jumping Wolf immediately, she demanded "Take me to your chief."

Jumping Wolf led her to Standing Deer like he was following a script. When they arrived, another solar eclipse was beginning. Scattering to all corners for safety, some stragglers stayed in the plaza to witness the third celestial event in the last ten years. They were not worried about the potential blindness that occurred when watching the eclipse. The mystic looked at Standing Deer and registered a tone of danger in her voice.

"Oh wise leader of this great tribe, we must speak immediately. Your people are in grave danger." Standing Deer took her by the arm, leading her up the ladder to the Cliff Palace. Once inside, he gave her permission to speak.

"Speak now, ancient shaman," he said.

"The blue stones, that come from the land of the great river, have shared with me some very grave news. Your people will die, if you do not take action immediately. Many forces are attacking this plateau to destroy your tribe. You must act now before it is too late." She took a deep breath as she finished, searching Standing Deer's eyes intensely as she awaited his reply.

The chief stared at her in disbelief. His brain absorbed the information as he attempted discern what was said.

"You come at a troubled time with a message for my people. I thank you. May the sun god guide your way through this treacherous land." With that, the woman bowed her head and left the Cliff Palace to return to her village. Standing Deer quickly returned to the plaza, searching for his friend, Strong Beaver, while his followers returned from their kivas as the eclipse began its farewell pass over the village. Over a hundred members of his tribe lost their sight during the last eclipse. He must to talk to Straight Beaver before tonight's council meeting.

The shaman shifted his chant with ease. The priest, thoroughly comfortable thanks to the aroma of incense all over the hut, sat at peace.

"Oh Great and Mighty Kukulcan. Give me the power to see what you hold for your benevolent servant here in your presence." Amozeltec watched as the smoke revolved around him. Thanks to the incense, his body felt like he was flying through the clouds with the gods.

The ancient one suddenly shed his silence, stared into Amozeltec's waiting eyes, and spoke."Your journey is long but not. Your destination is a valley of peace and tranquility. There your destiny will be fulfilled. Tomorrow, go north to the great road at Casas Grande. On that road, your journey will complete." The shaman brought his hands together and then bowed his head. On that note, Amozeltec left for the night.

The waning stars blazed like a thousand searchlights as the sky prepared the transformation from velvet dark night to gloriously clear day. From over 8,000 feet in the sky, Amozeltec rose to prepare for an early start to completion of his destiny. His warrior resolve gave him strength to handle the perils of the treacherous terrain. Casas Grande appeared after two weeks travel with only two nights rest. Rest was short lived with a local family before completing the final part of his life journey.

The Great Kiva sat on the grounds of the Sun Temple, adorned simply the way other kivas had been. About forty feet wide, this kiva was built to handle all large meetings, with the tribal council its most frequent user. In the center sat a circular bench with a hearth or fire pit in the middle of this center of Anasazi life. Incorporating a sufficient ventilation shaft for air and cooking, the kiva proved it could serve the tribe in many ways.

The council arrived in solitary order. Strong Beaver was the first to arrive. The northern settlements at Spruce Tree and Yellowjacket selected him because of his reputation as a fair leader. Jumping Wolf followed appearing very agitated. Coming from the area of Square Tower, Jumping Wolf was known as the hot-head who nearly caused several disasters in the community. His was the leader for those fighting for change. From the House of Many Windows came Red Knee. The youngest of the council members, Red Knee was known as a motivator, able to swing people's support one way or the other. The last member was Cottonwood Leaf, representing the people at the house at Oak Tree. A proponent of peaceful resolution, he consistently led the drive for alternative solutions. Standing Deer stood between the workbench and the impatient council, surveying them critically.

"My brothers, I stand before you with a burden on my soul that just being here has been one of the hardest things I have ever done.

"Our water dries up no matter what we do to save it. Raids from nearby enemies add to the internal strife our people are feeling. And losing our large animals to hunt has led to starvation with many of our community. And problems continue to grow with no end is in sight.

"For years, many of our people have migrated south to live with our brothers on the Rio Bravo. After careful thought, I, too, share those desires. I recommend that we disband our communities immediately and relocate in Chaco Canyon at Pueblo Bonito. Your thoughts."

Jumping Wolf quickly chimed, "We have always followed you as our leader without any reservations. But now many braves voice their unrest in seeing these events chase us away from our land because they believe the prophecy of the ancients will be fulfilled. To leave now would blacken the honor of our tribe."

Standing Deer stood stoically as he judged the faces of his fellow tribesmen. After a few moments, the chief spoke.

"Is that the way the rest of you feel? Let me see a show of hands." Of the four people sitting on the bench, three responded to his query. Deeply, his heart sank. This definitive blow pierced him like an arrow piercing a heart. He would have to push for the people to have an opportunity to decide.

"Then I would hope that we all agree that a choice must be offered to our people, with the advent of the full moon in a few days as our date for decisions." With that said, Standing Deer left the Kiva, walking briskly to his soon to be former home at the Cliff Palace.

Amozeltec traveled north on the Great North Road, constantly admiring the handiwork of the engineers as he walked down its wide expanse. Two days passed before he arrived at the Pueblo Bonito community in Chaco Canyon. The town square was active with artisans showcasing their wares. One booth caught his eye. It showcased many headdresses made with pale blue stones that he had seen in the shamans tent in his homeland. He approached the vendor cautiously.

"Your gems interest me, my brother. I see that you have made them into magnificent headdresses."

The vendor looked pensively and spoke.

"The adornments are here to give our chiefs the power and foresight to lead their people. The blue stones give them that power." Amozeltec carefully examined each symbol of authority recognized on the headdresses. One had four of the mesmorizing stones woven into numerous yucca leaves and topped off with a dozen eagle feathers. Dreams of coronations flooded his brain as he gathered the courage to speak.

"The gods have brought me to you, my brother, as I complete a long and arduous journey. Please select the one with the four stones for me." In his knapsack, the priest grabbed a silver chalice, taken from his former jungle temple, gave it to the vendor, and continued on his way.

Standing Deer stood on block of obsidian stone in the center of the market square with a heavy heart. Family and friends, some that he had known for decades, slowly filled up the square to hear their leader at this momentous event. Straight Beaver brought his people up close to the make-shift podium, staying close to his boyhood friend and confidant. Straight Heart, Little Feather and Red Deer stood to his left, showing solidarity in this time of crisis. Other council members led their followers into the square, anxiously anticipating their chief's words. At last, Standing Deer began to speak.

"Blessed family. For many moons, we have been one with this land on both physical and spiritual levels. We have weathered stinging droughts, invasions by new found enemies, internal strife within ourselves and even pestilence. Your council has been giving the people a voice and today they have spoken. Oh Great Kachinas, we come to you in unity for the good of your people. Take your hands and guide us safely as we embark on this unknown journey." The people broke into a wild chant, dancing together in a wild and joyous fashion, just like the rituals they did to bless the hunters before going hunting for meat for the tribe. The celebration continued for about an hour before the chief raised his arms to quiet the masses.

"My friends, the time has come. Your spirits will be missed." He grabbed Strong Beaver's forearm and said, "Lead them well." He turned, leading his family and followers away from the Mesa Verde for the last time.

A phalanx of thunderclouds broke free from the top of the mountains, whisking swiftly towards the Upper San Juan Valley, directly at the little traveler. Terrain became challenging with very steep canyons and glass-like walls dotting the landscape. The canyons, some wide enough for an army and others small enough for a snake to slither through made every journey an adventure.

Amozeltec saw the storm coming towards him, eager for the clash of thunderous titans with ardor and enthusiasm. Suddenly, a faint little hiss in the wind found its way to his ears. Stopping abruptly, he crept around the rocks and peered into the narrow canyon before him. One hundred rattles struck his ears as the slithery squatters blocked his journey. The King of the snakes slowly slithered towards the stocky, little priest to protect his flock. As he coiled for an attack when he closed the distance, something stopped the snake. Amozeltec raised his arms to the sky and began to chant a prayer to his great snake god, Kukulcan.

"Oh Great Kukulcan, speak to your servants as we journey through their home. Let them know that I am a friend, not an enemy." The snake rested in his coil, primed to strike from the top of a boulder while Amozeltec performed his sacred dance. The priest's eyes were filled with waves of fire, sending tons of fright through the slippery occupants impeding his progress. Suddenly, two cumulonimbus thunderclouds cracked open with two great bolts of lightning sending a thousand volts of electricity into the canyon, charging the walls in a bright florescent orange glow. Sliding down the canyon walls, the electrical phenomenon hit the snakes with the full charge, sliding up to the entrance where Amozeltec stood.

The full power of the physical phenomenon hit Amozeltec in the soles of his feet with a colossal slap. It traveled through each cell of his body so fast that he glowed like he was on fire. The priest accelerated his dance so fast that he ultimately mesmorized the slithery attackers. The king snake was so frozen by his dance that the priest reached down and picked him up to participate in the dance. Holding the king high above his head, Amozeltec screamed at the top of his lungs, "Great God of my ancestors, deliver us from this peril that we now go through. Open your vessels to baptize the children you see before you."

The heavens opened with torrents of water swooping down on the unsuspecting mesa. Thousands of gallons of water toppled on top of the unsuspecting ophidians. Trepidation flowed through the ravine as the water began to collect at the floor of canyon. The reptiles began to panic since no escape was evident. Amozeltec suddenly stretched his arms to the sky and screamed loudly at his god.

"Guide our path, Oh great one. Deliverance from this affliction as we journey to safety." His dance increased as he walked off the boulder, the king snake following close behind. Slowly the trek moved through the rising waters leading to a path that raised 45' to the top of the canyon. One by one, each reptile slid out of the swelling river and onto the slippery pathway. The priest continued his chant and dance turning to encourage his followers to continue. Out of the one hundred rattlesnakes that met him in the canyon, he would be able to save only ninety.

The trail from the plateau went from dry to a mud bath in a flash. Standing Deer pressed his regiment hard so that they could reach shelter before they were washed away. Lightning struck many times around them, burning many trees and shrubbery around them. One big flash caught the eye of one member of Standing Deer's ensemble, his daughter, Red Deer. She broke from the enclave and walked towards the flickering orange light. Spellbound, she moved slowly and deliberately towards the light. Quickly, she stopped in her tracks standing amazed at what was before her.

A small figure, dancing wildly while chanting a song, headed towards the rim of the canyon. Walking to the top of the ravine, he carefully placed his steps as he touched the mesa for the first time. To her astonishment, the man glowed bright orange, like the great celebration bonfires the village always had when she was growing up. One by one the snakes followed this unique man onto the mesa. Red Deer stood frozen at the site of dozens of venomous rattlesnakes laying in the rain so peaceful and placid, they acted like garter snakes. By this instant, the rest of the tribe had returned to find her but found more than they bargained for. Standing Deer walked up to his daughter and put his coat on her shoulders to help protect her from the rain.

"Are you OK, my daughter?"

"Father, that is the man I am to join with. Please help me meet him." They trudged together through the thick, sloppy mud to the slippery rim of the canyon to meet this enigma to their land. Amozeltec slowed his dance as he gazed at the approaching maiden and her escort. Red Deer spoke first.

"The gods have brought me to you, divine one. I am your chosen one." The little vicar gazed into her lime green eyes as she stood before him awaiting his response.

"I have been expecting you, my dear. The future awaits us. Come." The couple looked at Standing Deer, who was overwhelmed with emotion, piggybacked with fear for his daughter and this totally unknown human being. He questioned whether his blessing should be given or pull her back with the rest of the tribe and continue to the Rio Bravo. Quietly, Straight Heart slipped in beside him. Her eyes met his and gave him the answer. Clasping each others arms, Standing Deer turned and walked towards his daughter and the stranger. He looked affectionately in Red Deer's eyes before he spoke.

"Go with our blessing, dear daughter. Give us many grandchildren." With a kiss on the forehead, Standing Deer turned back to resume his trek. Amozeltec and Red Deer gathered themselves and returned to her home on the Mesa Verde.

Months later, Standing Deer was in the plaza at Pueblo Bonito when a movement far in the distance caught his eye. Patiently, he stood with eyes glued as the movement slowly took shape and became a swarm of people. The travelers became more visible to him as weary men, women and children entered the village very tired after their long journey. Staring at their images for what seemed like hours, unexpectedly the situation changed like the flip of a coin. Faces began to look like people he knew from the mesa. The closer the crowd came, the more people Standing Deer recognized. He took off running, not stopping until he reach the lead person of the group, Running Wolf. Standing Deer, panting slightly after the run, quickly questioned Running Wolf.

"What has happened? Why are you here? Is everything all right at the village?" Running Wolf raised his hands to cue the troupe behind him to halt. He carefully looked into Standing Deer's eyes, as he fought to hide the sorrow he would now express.

"My friend, we have traveled many days and lost over a dozen members of our family. The land finally gave out leaving many families near death. When Amozeltec arrived with Red Deer, Jumping Wolf proudly proclaimed him our new chief. His first order was to have a headdress made for him that included two very bright blue stones woven into it, just above the eyes. His reason was as leader, he wanted something to set him apart from the crowd. The stones, he said, would give him the power to see into the future and be able to better lead us as a tribe. He directed the men to create weapons because the gods wanted us to expand our territory. After many weeks of training, he led our braves against the Ute tribe to take over their lands. Twice we attacked and twice we lost many of our young men. Coal Canyon was just flowing in blood.

"Next, the Ute dammed up the reservoir and cut off our water supply to the crop lands. Food started becoming so scarce that Amozeltec ordered that any of our older members that died off were to be used as food to feed the tribe. We obeyed, quietly resenting this order from our new chief.

"Consistently, he came out to do a dance to bring rain to help our problems, holding a couple of snakes in his hands to bring on the rain. The chief was successful twice, but only for a short time. Our people became angry, especially seeing their lands quickly whither away before their eyes. One morning, I went to the Cliff Palace to have an early morning meeting with him. The meeting never happened. Amozeltec and Red Deer had both been stung by scorpions. Death must have been instantaneous.

"Their burials occurred in the Canyon of the Spirits, the one that goes to the underworld. The Utes granted us permission to come onto their land and the artists inscribed on the canyon walls outside the cave, 'Here lies the last rulers of the Anasazi, Amozeltec and Red Deer.' We also inscribed where the heavens were at the time of their death just underneath." He gazed into Standing Deer's watery eyes, saying, "Our hearts are with you, friend of my people."

Standing Deer clenched his friend's shoulder and nodded his head to thank him for the truth. He turned to go back towards the plaza but couldn't get very far. Straight Heart and Little Feather had already arrived at the scene hoping to hear good news from home. His wife knew from the look on his face tragedy had struck. They embraced each other tightly while the others filed on by. As they broke their embrace, after several minutes, Little Feather walked up to them and said, "Let's go home, Father." Standing Deer took him by the hand, with Straight Heart already holding his other one, and walked back to the center of the village.

CHAPTER 2

July, 1962

Detroit, Michigan. fifth largest city in the United States with a population slightly under 2 million people. A city struggling with an increasing exodus of the white population to the suburbs as blacks and immigrants quickly replaced them as the working class of the Motor City. Southeast Michigan provides thirty-five percent of all automobiles built in America and good employment is available to anyone willing to work. But the city never achieved the political identity of New York or Chicago. Legendary Woodward Avenue, named for Judge Augustus Woodward, the man who rebuilt Detroit after a devastating fire in 1805, has been the dividing line between upper and lower classes in the city.

Detroit has a unique distinction from other cities. Being an international border city, its port handles tremendous amounts of trade from its northern neighbor, Canada, nearly five million tons yearly. The Detroit River, a major part of the area, flows past the city at about 1 mph. Carrying about 85 million tons of cargo per year, it makes Detroit a leader in Iron Ore, Coal, Cement, and non-metallic minerals. Steel and Iron, along with petroleum products, lead the way as exports from the city.

The Ambassador Bridge, the dream child of banker Joseph Bower, opened in 1929. It was developed as a symbol of international peace and brotherhood between the two nations. Recreational boats used the river's north channel, while the south channel handled the big Great Lakes freighters. Called "le detroit"or "strait" by the French, both the British and French used the river as the connecting route between the upper and lower Great Lakes.

Overshadowed by the immense superstructure of the bridge, an elegantly tailored yacht lay anchored just a few yards shy of shoreline at Riverside Park.

Three men, two dressed in deck clothes and one in a blue three-piece suit, sat on the aft deck boldly toasting themselves like they just ate a canary and got away with it. A steward emerged from below deck, carrying another bottle of bubbly for the celebration. The revelry shifted into low gear as two of the principals prepared to leave. The host rose to toast his fellow conferees while row boats were positioned to take them ashore to their awaiting limos in Riverside Park.

Antonio Joseph Marvelli raised his glass to toast his guests as they gathered on the aft deck, smiling inwardly at his accomplishment. His ultimate goal was to gain control of the city of Detroit from the current government and put everything under his thumb. That phrase struck a note with him. His guests, Darryl Carstairs, administrative assistant to Detroit's mayor, Jewel Christie and Bruce Hofen, National Security Advisor to the president, lifted their glasses in celebration. The swells of the river slowly rocked his yacht, the Silver Wind, spinning it round and round on its anchor as the party rambled on. Tony smiled boldly at his guests, knowing quite well that he was the cat who got the canary. As Mayor Christie first took office in 1961, he commissioned numerous businessmen, politicians, and professors to plan out a future for the city. Tony Marvelli, the city's most prolific employer and supporter, with underworld connections, jumped on board. He pushed for the commission to adopt a broad plan to build up industry to a level not seen anywhere. Marvelli, Inc, would oversee everything, opening the door to accomplish a dream that he had carried with him since his early days on the northeast side. To his surprise, the plan went unopposed.

As Carstairs and Hofen climbed into the boat to take them back to shore and their waiting limousines, T.J., held in his hands their agreement. Marvelli Enterprises would control all redevelopment in the city for the next ten years, with the blessing of the president. If the boys in New York could see him now, he thought gleefully. His gut told him to get this thing in his safe in his Penobscot office quickly. He ordered the captain to get under way.

"Hey, Sal, let's button this bucket up for the night." The captain just tipped his hat and started the engines for the return to the Detroit Yacht Club, on Belle Isle. Marvelli gave one last wave to his guests as they disembarked to their limos waiting in Riverside Park. Beaming regally, Tony turned and plopped into the nearest deck chair with his champagne. The crew raised the anchor and sails, cleared to enter the channel to return home.

Pushing a barge north, from Zug Island loaded with scrap iron, the tug BH Becker chugged towards the bridge with the captain and an unknown visitor, conferring privately outside the wheelhouse. The visitor was involved in intense radio communications with someone on shore about an event that would happen soon. He finally choose to enlighten the captain, Bertrand O. Masters, what his mission would be.

"Just around the bend, Captain, is a British freighter called the Montrose. At this point on the map, you will ram the Montrose broadside and push it towards the shore, till it tips over near the shore. Are we clear on the mission?" asked the visitor.

"Yes, sir," replied the captain.

The Montrose sailed gracefully down the Detroit River on its maiden Great Lakes voyage. Its captain, Ralph Eyre-Walker, read the reports from his departments, pleased with their efficiency. Confident that things would continue, the captain ordered his first officer off watch and left his second officer in charge so he could snooze. None of the forty-four crewmen knew what lay on the other side of the bridge.

The visitor, on the tug, saw the Montrose just pass under the bridge and start the turn for the bend.

"Now!"he suddenly yelled. The captain quickly changed course heading directly amidships of the Montrose. He saw the crewmen try to wave the Becker off, but it just kept chugging. The tug hit the freighter and started pushing. The Montrose pushed its screws to the max, but nothing helped.

The visitor pushed Captain Masters for more, emphasizing the importance of ramming the freighter. Captain Masters thought he was crazy, but obliged. An extra effort was given and the Montrose gave way. The four-hundred forty-four foot freighter toppled in thirty feet of water and cemented itself forever into the history books of the Great Lakes.

A gaggle of loud splashes woke Tony from his blissful daydream. Jumping out of his deck chair, he saw most of his crew swimming frantically towards shore. Suddenly, the captain shot across the deck and into the water, swimming like an olympian. A loud, churning sound reached Tony's ears that sounded like propellers. Turning, T.J. froze in his tracks. A very large freighter was heading right towards him, severely listing at a sixty-degree angle. The boat quickly toppled onto the Silver Wind and its only occupant. There was not even a second to scream, everything happened so fast. The last sound Marvelli uttered was the release of bubbles underwater when the air was pushed from his lungs and he became planted forever in the riverbed.

Detroit has always struggled to gain the upper hand over its criminal element. Since the advent of the first police force in 1865, some form of malcontent has besieged the city one way or another. Harassment and brutality have been two charges thrown at Detroit's finest since World War II. It would be a curse that would follow the department into the twenty-first century.

Lieutenant Gerald Firman stood atop the over-turned freighter, carefully watching the bubbles of his divers searching for evidence from the accident. The diving team was on its sixth dive as Harbor Division patrol boats searched the surface as well. Residents on shore reported a large boat trapped when the freighter tipped over. Coast Guard helicopters flew over the shorelines looking for any sign of the tug and its skipper that was responsible for this mess. FBI investigators felt that the perpetrators had to be nearby since they were last seen southbound in the channel.

George, the oldest of three children, was born to German parents in the summer of 1929. Speeding through school and college, Firman joined the army in 1948. His two-year stint lasted four long years with the onset of the Korean War. In January, 1936,an event happened that set the future course for Fireman. They were walking down McGraw behind Olympia Arena to watch the Red Wings fight for a spot in hockey history. From the darkness, a man jumped in front of them blocking their path. With knife drawn, the robber grabbed George by the coat, threatening harm to the boy if his demands weren't met. The parents began to empty all of their money and jewelry onto the ground as George watched, trembling violently in his attackers arms. Suddenly, the attacker suddenly collapsed onto the concrete. A man disarmed the attacker, cuffing him and told him he was going downtown. The family was stunned. An angel of the night had saved their lives. The elder Firman stared at the man in blue and said, "Who are you?"

The stranger responded, "I am Sergeant Willie Fines of the Detroit Police Department. We've been tailing this man for weeks. He's been robbing the poor people off of the Cass Corridor, but recently moved his area to cover the major arenas in the city. We expected him to make a move tonight. I'm just glad I was able to be here to protect you."

Young Gerald felt his adrenaline start pumping overtime. He berated the Sergeant with question after question about being a policeman and how to become one. Fines answered the questions willingly while keeping his newest arrest in tow to the Olympia substation. His diligence made the evening a memorable one that would forever change the future of the department.

Firman stood at the rear of the Harbor master's boat, patiently waiting for his divers to resurface after a final dive to the bottom of the river. After 29 years, this had developed into his most puzzling case ever. After three hours, there was no sign of any person or persons responsible for the incident. Firman's head turned quickly as the surface of the river broke loose with the arrival of one of the divers. In his hand was some sort of leather briefcase. He signaled for the diver to come forward, but it was never received. Shots ripped through the tranquil ambience of the river. Marvelli's organization attacked from in their defenses on the shoreline. Manny Zerilli, executive Vice-President of the organization led the raid.

"Jocko, take your two guys and take positions to keep those two bums on the boat pinned down and away from the river. Remember, do not hurt them, just restrict their movement so the second team can secure the search area."

"Right, boss. I'll spread them like peanut butter," replied Jocko.

Firman slammed his body on the hull as a volley of bullets whizzed past him and Captain Walker. One by one, the divers struggled to escape the assault, only to be picked off like ducks in a shooting gallery. Bodies floated face down in the river as a silence swept over the make-shift battle theater. Zerilli sent one of his men, in diving gear, to retrieve something of importance floating free from the skirmish. He entered the river under the scrutinizing eye of his hawkish leaders.

Firman whispered to the captain to keep his head down while he looked around. With a nod from the skipper, the detective lifted his head and saw an armed contingent on shore. Marvelli's raiders stood at the edge of the park, ardently watching their diver swim through the carnage. All eyes were diverted away from the freighter so Firman slid off the stern of the ship carefully breast stroking his way towards the location of his dead divers. Slowly, he crept foot by foot, approaching his opponent as a lion goes after his prey. The distance quickly changed from yards to inches.

Sandy Rizzo had been diving in the Great Lakes for twenty years. It seemed like a lifetime since T.J. Marvelli paid for his diving lessons so he could lead expeditions to shipwrecks throughout the seaway. His mission was clear today. Find a pouch, that might have an official mark of some kind and bring it back to shore. Floating around the surface brought nothing and his bosses were getting very unstable. Diving to the riverbed he felt would bring better results. Again, another goose egg. Circling around for one more pass by the freighter, Rizzo prayed for success rather than reap the harsh punishment from the family. Suddenly, a sliver of light sparkled through the depths, giving Rizzo a good look at the port underside of the freighter. A small reflection of something flickered in the mud, holding its light until he could reach it. Patience had persevered. Rizzo had found a pouch that fit the description the lieutenant gave him. He grabbed his treasure and carefully rose to the surface, smiling from ear to ear.

Firman could see bubbles coming up from underwater, carefully hiding behind two bodies of the diving team. When the other diver broke the surface, Fireman slid behind him as he showed off his prize. The diver twirled around, staring his enemy right in the face. Fireman reached for his air hose and sliced it right in half. He grabbed the hose and pulled the other man into a sleeper lock, while trying to remove the pouch from his other hand. With victory in hand, the detective started to let his enemy go when a bullet pierced his right shoulder, sending him sprawled and floating in the river. Two men jumped in to rescue their comrade as emergency sirens began to race down Michigan Avenue. The diver and his entourage sped south down Fort Street, well ahead of their pursuers.

Three weeks later, after a medical leave, Detective Fireman strolled into headquarters, heading straight for the captain's office. Jonas Rawlings, a thirty-year veteran of the force, was buried by a mountain of paperwork that was becoming a very regular thing for him.

"Well, Captain, what's left of the Montrose case?"

Rawlings slowly raised his head out of paperwork, locking eyes with Firman instantly.

"The case has been moth balled permanently. The decision came from upstairs. And I suppose you're going to ask me why, but save your breath. This goes higher than just this department so just leave it. Now, get out of here. And by the way, welcome back."

Stunned, Fireman walked out to his desk, unsure of why he was even there. He reached into his inbox, burying his frustrations in the mountains of paper that waited for his return.

CHAPTER 3

An azure blue sunset befell the city gracefully showcasing a sprinkling of stars in the early night sky. Commuters muddled through the leftovers of an afternoon shower as they muddled the road home to their cozy suburban homes. A large black woman struggled with her bags of groceries as she hurried home to fix supper for that herd she called her family. A young boy ran ahead of her, jumping into every puddle in his way.

"Wilbur, stay out of that water!" she hollered.

"Yes, Mama," replied the boy, stopping in his tracks so his mother could catch up with him. Retrieving one of the grocery bags, the boy led the way to his house on the 5000 block of Martin. A black 1970 Boss 350 Mustang was still at the same spot on the street as it was when they left a couple of hours ago, she mused. *Some things never change*, she thought, rushing home to fix dinner for her family.

A stranger sat inside the Mustang, munching on his dinner of a Whopper, large fries and a diet Coke, staring at a dilapidated house across from him at

5120 Martin Street. His prey awaited him inside. That person was Evert Wilsup, the last member of Dutch Mafia family that at one time rivaled the New York families as the boss of crime in the city.

Putting down the police file, he surveyed the house again. Taking note of several burned-out hulks of houses that have become fixtures in the neighborhoods since the 1970s. They would make good cover as he made his approach. He pulled his Glock out of its case and popped the clip out of its housing, It was full. *Hopefully, I won't have to use it*, he thought. Slipping on black gloves, he zipped up his jacket and opened the door. Leaving his car, he pressed the alarm button. The Mustang chirped good-bye. Tugging at his black leather jacket, the stranger started walking towards the old Wilsup house, concealing himself from any occupants inside. Abandoned houses were not only good concealment after dark, but was a persistent blister on this once "Arsenal of Democracy."

The stranger approached the back porch of Wilsup's house very cautiously, traveling through neighboring yards that were tantamount to surviving the "Junkyard Wars" The contraptions that laid out, unjointed in the back yards, would have challenged even the best inventors. Shrouds of shrubbery, thoroughly concealed his arrival at the back door unimpaired. Lifting his pant leg, he removed a lock picking kit, standard issue for all detectives, and proceeded to undo the old-fashioned security lock off the 1950's style porch door. CLICK. Just like the book said, he chuckled. Replacing the kit back on his leg, he slowly opened the backdoor, giving up the role as stranger and taking on the new role of intruder.

The kitchen was a war zone. Tiptoeing through the maze of utensils, his shoes began sticking to the floor as he struggled through the room. Flour, eggs, jellied preserves and pancake batter lay strewn across the floor, in no consistent order. Something important came up for them to leave this mess so suddenly. Slipping off his shoes, the intruder entered the foyer discreetly placing his footsteps close to the walls of the hallway. Laughter, and screams of pleasure were coming from the far end of the upstairs level of the house. He started laughing to himself, remembering his days as a teenager. Oh, the joys of youth, he recalled. Composing himself, he approached the stairway stealthily, concealing his appearance until the most favorable moment. Quietly his weight went onto the first step of the aging staircase. No sound. Moving to the second step, he repeated his process. A loud groan erupted, reverberating throughout the house. The intruder ran for cover under curtains in the living room entry way. Totally hidden from view, he observed the upstairs balcony by using a six foot tall plate glass mirror, positioned by the front door.

Wilsup's jelly-covered face suddenly jerked up from between Lisa's legs.

"What was that?" he exclaimed vociferously.

"Just one of the rats that run through these walls, lover. Just ignore them and get back to what you were doing. Ohhh, please baby, please," Lisa cried passionately.

"I'm going down anyway. It could be something. But remember, I will return," he replied.

"You had better, lover. After all, you've only reached the appetizer. The main course is yet to come," she cooed, passionately licking her luscious red lips.

Wilsup took the safety off his .45, cocked it, blew her a kiss and walked out the door. The pewter colored hallway opened before him. Awesome family icons hung from ancient wall hangers, acutely observing his trek. Grandfather Nils looked down on his grandson as he glided down the corridor. Grandpa used to tell stories about rum-running across the Detroit River during Prohibition. Detroit was the easiest port to bring illegal booze into the country overnight. He would sit in front of the fire, listening to the stories till the tales wove through his brain and he fell asleep on the living room sofa. His father Darwin, held the next hallowed position in the hall. Evert and Dad saw the family business from two different schools of thought. Darwin Wilsup took his father's prohibition business and followed the way of the New York syndicates. Prostitution, drug smuggling, protection rackets plus other Sundre operations, had changed. Millions entered the family treasury, allowing them greater influence within the city and its political bureaucracy. When Darwin died, Evert approached the Marvelli organization, and unloaded all of the family's hard work, toil and labor for the paltry sum of just ten million dollars plus ten percent yearly take from their drug trade. Marvelli jumped at the chance, eliminating his competition thus controlling the city totally. Wilsup and Lisa immediately took off on an around the world trip, scamming unsuspecting businessmen while increasing their fortunes. They were now wanted in thirty-five countries.

Wilsup pushed his body up to the balcony railing, shivering in the chilly air of the old house. Steadying himself along the railing, he cautiously peered around the corner and into the foyer. Nothing. He sauntered out along the rail and saw something move to his right. Powder burn residue settled on his hands as he fired a shot at his reflection in the plate glass mirror. The majestic work shattered into a thousand little masterpieces.

"Are you all right, Elvy?" cried Lisa, wrapped up loosely in a sheet, standing at the bedroom door.

"I just shot my reflection in the mirror, lover. I'm OK," he replied.

"Well then, come back and get your main course while it's hot," she purred. With that invitation, Wilsup slipped back to the bedroom, dropping his gun and scooping up Lisa along the way. The intruder stood quietly behind a curtain at the living room entrance. When Wilsup shot at himself in the mirror, he snickered. Biting his tongue to the point of bleeding, he kept his chuckles camouflaged, to keep his prey off guard. Keeping a watchful eye on the once grand landmark of the house, the intruder carefully watched as Wilsup gave up his search and run back to his playroom.

Slipping from his alcove, the intruder slid quickly to the stairway, succinctly crossing over that precarious second step, journeying upstairs to his ultimate goal. The intruder planted his footsteps carefully, as he reached the top, following the sounds coming from the end of the hall. The door was ajar, with a clear shot of everything. Suddenly, a blood curdling scream broke the uneasy silence. He waited until a calm quiet came over the old house before playing his trump card.

"That was quite a show, you two. Too bad it's gonna be your last." He smiled, observing their reactions.

"Just who the hell are you?" Wilsup exclaimed.

"Consider me your worst nightmare. Move to the footboard. Now!" He pulled out his Glock motioning them to move down to the end of the bed. This is going to be the easiest money I've ever made, the intruder thought evilly. His captives slid down to the end of the bed apprehensively, never taking their eyes off the visitor and his gun. They waited intently for any advantage that they could grab.

Reaching behind his back, the stranger unbuckled a pouch on his belt and removed a pair of handcuffs. Opening both ends, he handed them to Wilsup.

"Both of you put one arm through the brass footboard, then you, mister, will clip a handcuff on one of your wrists." Shaking thoroughly, Wilsup obliged, clipping the cuffs onto his wrist first, then on Lisa's, securing them both to the bed. The man flipped out his cell phone, pressed speed dial and waited. The phone started to ring.

"Nicholson here."

"Barney, this is Skip. Job complete."

"You got both of them?"

"Signed, sealed and waiting to be delivered."

"You're going to have one hell of a payday."

"I'll take it in small, unmarked bills please. Pick them up at the old Wilsup place on Martin. By the way, bring some peanut butter. It'll go well with the jelly they're covered with."

"Still a kidder. A car is on the way." The intruder hung up the phone, checked the footboard and handcuffs making sure they were secure before he left.

"You still didn't answer his question. Who are you? Jack Ryan or something?" demanded Lisa.

Looking down at his two captives, he smiled, shouldering his gun in his holster as he spoke.

"The name is Mitchell. Skip Mitchell." Their mouths dropped as he pivoted on his heel and walked out of their lives.

A single, solitary star intensely glared down onto the rugged Colorado landscape. Wave after wave of intense heat blasted this tempestuous landscape daily. For millennia, man's mission was to adapt to nature and learn to live with the land God gave them. Through nine thousand recorded years of life, man still battles that unmovable, but life giving light, looking for the day he could win the battle.

The infamous Highway 666 followed a route similar to the Great Road, built in the fifth century by the Anasazi. A conclave of archaeologists convened at its junction with Road G. Amy Renee Mitchell, Professor of Archaeology from the University of Michigan, led this team. Their goal; locate an ancient burial place, known as the Canyon of the Spirits.

Amy's interest in Indians started with tales her grandfather told her nightly as bedtime stories. Her interest blossomed, leading her to a Ph.D. in Archaeology at The University of Michigan to pursue that interest further. Being one-half Pueblo Indian, Amy found that these expeditions searching the land of her ancestors, was becoming more personal than see would admit.

The University of Colorado's Tim Moran joined the project in a flash. He met Amy while touring together on the Native American Cultures lecture tour The two became friends and developed a common interest in working jointly on further expeditions. CU was the leader in archaeological research in Colorado and Moran was the motivation to their success.

The University of New Mexico held probably the largest library on the ancient Indian cultures of the Mesa Verde area. Maria Salinas, the head of the Native Indian Cultures department, led more explorations than anyone else in the area, including Moran. Tim recommended her highly. Amy agreed. She came on board. Maria was to keep the records of every discovery they made.

Fifteen miles south of Cortez, conglomerations of specialists gathered at the intersection of 666 and Road G, leading into the Ute Mountain Indian Reservation. Several members of the Ute tribe volunteered to serve as their guides to the ancient Anasazi burial ground. John Runningfox, Tisha Yellowfeather and Drew Eaglewing, stood around the expedition leaders pointing out the expected highlights of their upcoming trip.

"We'll take the jeeps within five miles of Sand Canyon. From there, we will break out the ATVs and head south towards the mountain of the Sleeping Ute. Ancient tales lean towards this as the location you seek," Runningfox stated.

"John, take the lead vehicle with Tisha.," said Tim. "Put the ATV haulers behind you, with the rest of us in the rear car." They broke their encampment and marched west, like the pioneers of old he thought. Within minutes, their camp became a dust cloud heading westward towards the desert.

The search for the canyon encompassed most of Montezuma County and the Mesa Verde plateau. Tales put it west of Cortez and north of the Ute Indian Reservation, the major northern boundary of civilizations in the area. A giant rock was the key to point the way to the final resting place of the ancient Anasazi.

Amy sat amazed at the accomplishments the Anasazi created in the thirteen centuries of existence. Evidence of their life laid everywhere she looked. Pottery shards littered their way as they traveled to Sand Canyon. Simple gray ware, coiled and corregated gray pots lined the trails as well as beautiful black and white pieces with designs and figures. At Castle Rock, the trail head to Sand Canyon, pottery lay exposed along the trail to the Great Rock, reminding her that we are just a small piece of the puzzle.

The convoy arrived at the great rock near dusk. Moran ordered everyone to set up camp for the night. The local Ute tribesmen quickly unloaded the ATVs and popped up the nylon domed tents before the Sun settled in for the night. Dinner was quickly served and most of the group dozed off to dreams of places far away. Tisha, John, and Drew sat around the campfire, passing around an ancient peace pipe, communing with the spirit who watches over them. The peyote they smoked, from the Mescal buttons of local cacti in the area, swirled a sweet, spiritual aroma throughout the camp. The trio began their chant calling to the Great Spirit. They cleansed their minds and bodies of all physical desires, permitting total spiritual union with a higher power.

Someone was standing in the shadows, away from view. The Indians felt the nearby soul and called to it to join in communion with their ancient ones. The shadow walked closer, into the light of the fire, making itself known. It was Amy. Tisha took her hand and they all joined together. Chanting continued until she felt a presence envelop her through the bond with the others. The presence grew stronger, as the smell of peyote swirled through her head. She saw the Canyon of the Spirits clearly. It was so clear that she could feel the presence of the leaders.

"Look for a rock that should not be," the Spirit spoke to her, "and you will find your destiny. Beware of what awaits you. Much evil still flows through the land. Follow your brothers, they will protect you." Shocked awake from the trance she was in, Amy sat apprehensively by the fire. John, Drew and Tisha sat across from her, carefully questioning her with their eyes.

"I just had the most incredible vision," she said.

"We know," replied Tisha. "We will be your guides through the dangers."

"Tomorrow, you must reveal the secret of your expedition before evil sets in. Many tales are told about spirits who wander the land of the Ute. To travel on their land, one needs knowledge and purpose to achieve safety," replied John.

The trio looked wantonly at Amy, knowing that she was now forced with one of the most difficult decisions in her life. With a nod of John's head the four returned to their tents to seek a peaceful and fulfilling sleep. One member of that group would never see the next moon.

The stars twinkled brightly amidst the violet night sky. Laying there in the grass, her mind imagined that it was her own personal diamond collection. A full moon stood out so clearly that she felt it was close enough to touch. Her dad's presence was very near right now, just like when the camping trips they had when she was younger. She dearly longed for those days.

Just west of Cortez, Wanda Willington stretched out in the grass gazing at the starry blue night sky of the Rockies. Life was flowing smoothly. Tony Marvelli promised to make her rich and she was. But things were not complete. The kids were grown and had their own careers, Amy was an archaeologist and Ray was a career military man. Her manager, the owner of Renaissance Records, had also become her lover. But she always had a sense for when something major was brewing and protected the people closest to her. The alarms in her head said that time was now. She kept dreaming of her ex-husband who she divorced twelve years ago, but never got him out of her heart. A reunion three years ago at Detroit's Tri-Centennial included a replay of all the passion that they had in their marriage. But when he rescued her from kidnappers during that celebration, she told her ex, Skip Mitchell, a local weatherman for WGCB-TV30, she needed time recover from the traumatizing experience. Devastated, Skip slipped into isolation, refusing to talk to her. Wanda retreated to the Cortez ranch, only doing Vegas and LA gigs to keep her career active. With the moon's orangish glow spell-binding her mind,, her heart began talking. She bolted into the house, straight to phone. Wanda dialed Skip's number at his Riverfront Towers apartment. After three rings, the voice mail clicked on. Typical of him she thought. Anything to avoid talking.

The tone sounded and Wanda left her message. She called to Carlos the chauffeur, "Bring the car around right away. Call the airport and have the jet fueled for a trip to Detroit. I've got to leave right away." She ran to her bedroom to pack a small bag. Her blood began to burn feverishly throughout her body. Just the thought of seeing Skip again made her feel like they were on their first date. Wanda's future was about to take a serious twist.

The seventeenth floor of Tower Two of the Riverfront Condos is an unofficial landmark for this city. He stood watching the freighter, William Clay Ford, sail slowly up the river to the ore mines in Minnesota. Skip sipped a whiskey and diet Pepsi, musing silently how appropriate it was for him to have rented a condo where a famous Detroit politician passed away. Wanda's message disturbed him. His stomach churned just thinking about her. She was troubled about something. He walked back to the bedroom, scratching Maxwell's back as he went. The cat jumped off the couch, followed Mitchell to bed and curled up on the pillow by his head. Sleep came fitfully to Skip as dreams of the past recycled throughout the night.

CHAPTER 4

Detroit, 2007

A Sikorsky-C106 chopped its way through the remnants of the morning fog that laid a blanket of dampness over the city. A very confident man stared out of the left rear window at the world below that he had just created. Anthony J. Marvelli, Jr., the youngest and sharpest businessmen in the country, was surveying his newest company, a three mile long, $125 billion dollar dock and shipbuilding facility, equipped with the most modern equipment for loading and unloading Great Lakes freighters. Located near the base of the Ambassador Bridge, the shipyard was already averaging unloads of four to six freighters a day.

Mayor Kirkland Asher glanced out the other window, smiling like the wolf who just ate the three little pigs. Elected on a platform of job creation and housing renewal, Asher quickly discovered Detroit government and the fable, tortoise and the hare, were identical. No matter how fast he acted from his office, low-level civil service employees were slow in implementing them. His predecessor left office for those reasons. Promising to bridge that gap, Asher worked hard to create a more responsive administration that people would relate to. Reinventing Detroit was a major part of his plan. He looked over at Tony as they cruised over the new shipyard.

"You're an asset to the city, Tony. Everything you've done sends new life into Detroit's soul. The salt mines are active again. Tiger Stadium is now a concert/amusement park. And employment hasn't been this high since the 1920s. And all done with no taxpayer money."

"The Motown spirit was rekindled with Renaissance Records. Our kids now have a venue for their talents. Your commitment to this city is overwhelming." Tony paused a moment, soaking in the mayor's praise.

"My father told me to carry on his dream if he was unable. Marvelli Industries made it its goal to fulfill that dream."

The helicopter banked left, heading towards City Airport. Passing over Little Bloody Run, one of Detroit's early historical landmarks, it now served peaceful duties in Elmwood Cemetery below. Tony's Michigan history knowledge flashed an image of that 1763 battle between the British and the Indians. Blood shed during that battle washed vociferously into the little brook giving it its name. It passed undisturbed beneath them as the helicopter flew eastward.

Banking up Gratiot, the chopper's path exposed more of Detroit's decayed neighborhoods as they flew buy. Homeless people traversed the avenues, scraping out a meager existence from the city's refuse. Neighborhoods improved the closer they came to City Airport. Disparity was rampant, Tony thought. The time is now, he smiled.

"Father told me when I was young, that his dream could not be fulfilled until the city was revitalized. He loved this city and he died trying to build a future for it. I carry that torch now for him and the family." A lump in his throat developed at the mention of his dad.

"I praise God daily that we have people like you in this city,"said the mayor, gazing out the window towards Foxtown."

The mayor began dreaming about the successes Detroit has scored recently. Home of two new professional sports stadiums, new downtown facilities on the Campus Martius, and now a strong theater district with Renaissance Records on the Detroit scene. Housed in the old Motown building, Marvelli's record company rebuilt Detroit's image as the city of soul. Led by nightclub singer, Wanda Detroit, new groups in hip-hop, hard rock and classical came out of the woodworks to become overnight sensations. Adding the new shipyard put Marvelli Industries near the brink of becoming the single largest employer since Ford moved out of the RenCen and back to Dearborn. Asher drooled as he pondered his political futures. Abruptly, Tony's cell phone chimed its "Godfather" theme.

"Yes. OK. I understand. Thanks." Closing up his phone, Tony slipped it back into his pocket.

"Anything wrong?" asked Asher.

"Nothing I can't handle, Mr. Mayor. I'm afraid the tour is over right now. We'll have your car waiting." Tony calmly pulled out his cell phone again and pressed the number one off his speed dial menu.

"Helford, the canary has flown the coop. Find her and call me." Hanging up the phone, Tony turned to the mayor. "I'll have my office coordinate an official grand tour for the media to see Detroit's first shipbuilding facility since E.B. Ward's in the late 1880s.

Asher replied, "Sounds like a plan, Tony. I'll look forward to it."

They landed at the Marvelli pad near the corporate hangars. Shaking the mayor's hand, Tony jumped into his waiting limo, heading straight for his office in his Campus Martius building, on the site of the old Hudson's department store.

Near the McNamara Terminal at Rosa Parks International Airport, a tall man stood quietly in the shadows near the Marvelli hangar. Known as Detroit Metropolitan for over 40 years, the airport changed its name as preparation for the twenty-first century. Public acceptance was phenomenal. Named for the lady that sparked the modern civil rights movement, city and county leaders supported giving her a lasting legacy in Detroit. For nearly a century, Rosa Parks was an inspiration to all young people. The name, Parks International, became a major advertising tool for promotion of the airport and the city as a major hub for international travel.

A L4 Lear-jet, with a big "M" on the fuselage, taxied into view off runway 27L. The plane came to a stop about 200 yards from the hangar and shut down their engines. The ground crew waited thirty seconds before placing the chalks around the tires for passengers to disembark. The door opened and the passengers came down the stairway. The steward came first, followed by Wanda and the crew. Skip's heart flip-flopped a beat when he saw her. Blonde hair now adorned her head, but she still looked as delectable as when they first met. Seductively glued into a black vinyl pantsuit, she strutted towards him. Watching her carefully, his thoughts began to drift as they always did whenever they got together.

Thirty years ago at a wedding in Pontiac, Michigan, a friend fixed the two of them up so he wouldn't have to take her home when he left for his honeymoon. Her pink dress blended well with the pink walls of the church, but it was her chestnut hair, titillating eyes and a diamond necklace with matching earrings made her the spotlight of the pre-wedding festivities. Her eyes locked on him as he walked through the door to the front of the sanctuary to meet the groom. They returned to the pew where she was standing, surrounded by a dozen men. Introductions were made and she walked away from the other men. They stayed together through the ceremony, reception and a couple of parties. About 4 AM, they strolled into her place only to find her mother waiting up for her. She welcomed them with open arms, catching him off guard. After pleasantries, they shared a very passionate good-bye kiss. Skip burned with desire to pursue this woman further. He did and nine months and three days later, they were married in the same church with friends and family in attendance. Skip pursued his career in television, keeping him away many nights a week. Wanda pursued the life of a homemaker. Their first two kids, Amy and Ray, came in their first five years of marriage. Drew, who came along about a dozen years later, was their biggest challenge. Constantly searching for answers about his purpose in life, Drew ran away at age twelve to find those answers. Authorities looked nationwide for him for six years with no results.

After 10 years together, Skip got a curve thrown at him when he contracted Hodgkin's Disease. It stunned everyone. Wanda visited the hospital daily, with kids in tow. Though he came through the early treatments fine, the chemotherapy created a cornucopia of problems. His disposition changed from the strong, quiet type to one like Jekyll and Hyde. He became so abusive, physically and emotionally, that Wanda kicked him out and filed for divorce. Her decision was a knife in Skip's heart. Moving in with her mom, Wanda immediately set out after a new career. Answering an ad for auditions with Renaissance Records, Wanda scored well on the audition and with Tony,Jr. He signed her, coached her and made her his major star. Working only weekends, she rose to be a major singing star in under two years. Years after the divorce, Skip discovered that he had developed Bi-Polar disorder. After getting help, he attempted to resurrect his career with the help of his old college pal, Ron Firman. Firman lined up a weather caster job at WGCB, channel 30 in Rochester,MI, broadcasting the weather five nights a week. He quickly rose to the top of his field in Detroit. On the flip side, he graduated from the Slade private eye school as a fully licensed private eye. Hanging up a shingle downtown, in the Penobscot building, he supplemented his income on weekends with divorce cases. A few years ago, they had a reunion at the Detroit Tri-Centennial party at Hart Plaza. Skip watched from his front row seat, as Wanda bantered with Tim Allen before she graced Detroit with her angelic tones. That candy-apple red dress she wore, with the slit in the side, kept his eyes glued on her. After the show, they sped off in his 1965 Mustang GT towards her hotel. While deep in the middle of their first time together in years, two men jumped out of the closet, smothered her with chloroform, and knocked Skip out cold. When he awoke, a ransom note demanding two million dollars for the release of Wanda laid on the pillow. Two days later, Wanda reappeared at Renaissance Records explaining that she was taken to a warehouse, bound and gagged her until she just escaped two hours ago. The press accused Renaissance of pulling the stunt to sell Wanda's newest album. He didn't buy it. A fox was in the hen house and he would find it. Snapping back to reality, Wanda was running towards him. She jumped into his arms, avoiding a baggage truck that almost struck her. That jump aroused old feelings in him that he had forgotten were there. Releasing her grip on him, she carefully kept her eyes glued to his chocolate brown lenses. Smiling affectionately, her fingers caressed his hair while he stirred up the courage to speak.

"Ok, you said this was urgent," said Skip.

"Can we go someplace private?" she replied. He nodded.

Hand in hand, they walked to his Mustang, parked by the maintenance hangar. Jumping in, Skip started the trusty 350 V8 engine,with dual exhaust and exited the airport, turning north on Middlebelt Road towards I-94. Traveling the Ford freeway east, they put distance between them and the airport. Once they were a safe distance away, he touched her hand to reassure her. The floodgates poured opened.

"About two years ago, when the Cortez ranch was began making money, Tony mysteriously started expanding into other things. First, he built a long runway big enough for transport aircraft. Second was many hangar-type buildings built at the far edge of the runway.

"I became extremely suspicious when the visitors to the ranch increased, always heading towards the area of the runway buildings. Planes arrived at night flying so low, they jarred me awake.

"A month ago, young native Indian men started arriving for what looked like military exercises. With real bayonets on rifles, these men went through intensive exercises in crowd control, explosives placement and attack and containment maneuvers. I never let them out of my sight. Limos, loaded with older Indian men, consistently visited the ranch and walked with Tony while observing these recruits in action. Then, three weeks ago, out of the blue, Tony asked me to marry him. Totally stunned, my intuition smelled a rat. I know we have been a hot number over the last year, but to me, he is only a companion. Well, I started snooping around and was shocked.

"First was this floor plan of an arena. On it were marked locations for certain things to be carried out during an event. Next, many letters were addressed to different people all talking about an Operation Reclaim. Hundreds of letters dealt with this and all were addressed to different parts of the country, mostly with addresses to Indian reservations.

"The final straw was when I found out that he was building something with nerve gas in an abandoned mine, using a mining operation as cover. There was also mention of helicopters. Skip, I've got a bad feeling about this." She squeezed his hand nervously, trembling like a windblown leaves on a fall Michigan day.

"Wanda, let's get you secure and make a few calls," he replied sincerely looking into those tearfully luscious brown eyes. They floated down the freeway, turning down the Lodge towards Downtown and his riverside apartment. Four cars behind them, a black 2004 Chevy Malibu, with tinted windows and four people inside, continued to tail them all the way to his Riverfront home. Verifying that the couple had entered, they set up their observation post on the top level of the Joe Louis Arena parking garage.

The Leviathan towered over the surrounding neighborhoods with more grimace than when it entered this life. It was born just as the city caught up with the rest of the country in the Great Depression. Its arms stretched for eons connecting the city and country with the world in a time of despair. The windowless orifices of the once grand structure, now stared blankly over what was once considered the most perfect city, a "freeman's" city in an era of political machines. The homeless of Michigan Avenue called it their motel. A role that gave it purpose on this warm July night.

He pushed his shopping cart through a hole he found in the fence over a year ago. It was now a major thoroughfare for the street people daily, dangerously pushing the security fence to its structural limits, leaving the door open to endanger little children from the nearby neighborhood. He climbed up the well-worn stairwell, carefully avoiding piles of fallen history as he had done so many times before, to what he referred to as his third floor suite. Life stayed the same for the man affectionately called "The Latin Cherub".On the streets since the days of Ronald Reagan, he lost a good paying engineer's job with Chrysler and his whole family in one fell swoop. Through the help of agencies such as Salvation Army and COTS, The Latin Cherub, also known as George Perez, became the perfect example of "Surviving the Streets."

The humidity of the summer was the worst in Michigan's history. At no point in the day did it fall below 80%. The occupants in the old Michigan Central Terminal tossed and turned in the uncomfortably sticky dampness that hung over the whole river area. No one slept a wink, not even Perez. As the humid stickiness covered their bodies, the residents of Michigan Avenue were consciously contemplating their next day of survival on the city's streets,.going to the Harbor Light mission for their dinner meal would at least be a treat. Suddenly, a thud disturbed their peaceful non-slumber on this sticky night. Perez saw a dim light snake its way through frail but noisy hole in the floor. Jumping to his feet, Perez walked towards the light that was becoming increasingly brighter. Kneeling down to look at the floor below, he heard most of his bunkmates wake, coughing from the encompassing smoke. Ignoring their quandaries, Perez slid over, peeking through the hole in the floor. In its beginning throes was a fire, growing in intensity below. A semi-sweet smell passed by his nose. He had smelled this before, something from the auto plant, he thought. His brain then exploded like a cannon. It was Tefrin. A highly flammable paint thinner now fueling flames would soon envelop the small population that stayed here. Perez only had one decision to make.

Five miles away, Detroit's Emergency Response Center picked up a 911 call from a cell phone caller on the Southfield Freeway. The center immediately sprang into action, dispatching all necessary departments to the call. Tonight, though, was different for Judith Rue. She slid into her chair, fresh from a party celebrating her upcoming retirement, ready for a good shift through her usual long, restless night. Like a hoard of locusts besieging a field of wheat, her terminal began to light up like slot machines at the Greek town Casino. Judy took the tenth call.

"911 Operator."

"There's a fire at the old train station, down by Roosevelt Park."

"Are people trapped?" asked Judy.

"All I can tell you is it looks like a pretty nasty one. Get someone up their soon."

"Emergency units are on their way. Stand by for the fire department." Judy quickly switched her line so her caller could relay specifics to the fire department as she informed the fire chief.

Two blocks away, Fire Chief Joe Pilog sat at his desk in his fifth floor office in Station One, Detroit's fire headquarters at the corner of Washington and Larned. Quarterly evaluations kept him burning the midnight oil. He was wrapping up when he got the emergency call.

"Pilog."

"Chief, this is 911. There's a fire at the old Michigan Central Station near Roosevelt Park. Our report says it's a nasty one. How do you want to handle this? Two pumper companies are on their way from stations eight and sixteen off Trumbull and Grand Boulevard."

"That's good. Add two ladder companies plus lots of police support. I'm on my way." He dropped the briefcase on his desk and threw on his fireproof coat, running out the door, heading to the turbo charged GMC Suburban that came with the job. He rushed to the site with sirens blaring.

Darkness enveloped his soul as he struggled with his most fitful sleep in years. Sprawled on his tiny love seat, Skip struggled to sleep in a fetal position, fighting a losing battle of body versus mind over sleep. His two bedroom condo in the Riverfront Towers was high enough to see all of Michigan Avenue from downtown to the Ambassador Bridge. From his window, he saw a half-dozen pumper trucks travel down to the old Michigan Central Terminal, Several ladder trucks followed in their wake from downtown. Smoke rose higher and higher as firefighters rushed to contain the blaze. Flames began sparking up over the surrounding buildings, just as more sirens jarred him back to reality. A sudden movement behind the terminal building caught his eye. Grabbing his binoculars, Mitchell watched an Army Cobra helicopter taking off from the track bed. Hovering about one hundred feet above, two projectiles appeared out of no where, heading straight for the terminal. The resulting explosion shook the ground at about 4.0 on the Richter scale. The top four floors convulsed outward as if something didn't set well with its stomach. The other two, served as axes, causing the main superstructure to crumble and fall, sending tons of history crashing to the ground. A soft hand caressed his arm as he stood by the window. Her face echoed the horrors that were unfolding before them.

His heart dropped right into his stomach. George Perez immediately forced everyone on his third floor flat, as he called it, to rush down the stairwells.

"Gentlemen, I don't know why this is happening, but with all the commotion, it's apparent that somebody feels we have to start paying rent." Everyone jumped up, leaving belongings behind and running for safety. Perez stayed focused on only one goal, getting his friends out of the building.

Traversing the rubble in the stairwell, the overnight stayers felt their body heat increase as they paralleled the second floor. By now, the blaze was elevated to a major fire. The street people ignored the heat and flames, continuing down to the ground floor. Smoke perilously swirled around them as Perez and his followers stumbled they way towards safety.

On the ground floor, Jonny Boy, the lead person of the troop, hollered out, "I see the door. Hurry!" The dozen men jumped over immense chunks of concrete that had fallen from years of no maintenance. One by one they slipped through the majestically ornamented archway and out into freedom. A loud crack, like lightning striking, followed by a loud rumble almost stopped the homeless people in their tracks. Perez pushed them harder towards the front door and safety. Cries of help silenced as the building collapsed around them.

Of the dozen people The Latin Cherub led to safety, only eight survived. George Perez perished in the rubble with two of his closest friends, just inches away from freedom. Fifty-one homeless people perished with Perez in one of Detroit's worst disasters.

Sirens continued to blare as extra policemen rushed to the scene. Chief Nicholson followed closely, traveling the left turn lanes to speed up his arrival. He saw what looked like two Stinger missiles hit the rear of the building with an earth shattering explosion. It looked like they were launched from somewhere near the base of the bridge. That seemed inconsequential compared to the disaster unfolding before him.

Upon arriving, he noticed that the Feds were already there en masse. Puzzling as it was, Nicholson knew that trouble always followed when Washington was involved. Recognizing a familiar face, he approached cautiously seeking answers to his questions.

"Well, Cliff, what brings you out at this hour?" he asked.

"Oh, hello, Barney. I wasn't expecting to see you tonight," replied Cliff.

"You may as well start explaining why you're here."

Cliff Obo led the Detroit branch of the FBI. His friendship with the chief extended back to their prep school days. Barney chose the local route, wanting to serve his city, while Cliff wanted a larger challenge. He graduated in the top ten of his class, immediately assigned to the Los Angeles field office. In the last twenty years, he has climbed his way up the ladder, just two rungs away from Washington.

Barney looked intensively at his old friend, intent on finding the reason for his presence.

"You never come out for a fire any time in my city, Cliff. Why now?"

"This is a national security matter, Barney, you don't have any clearance," he retorted.

"Damn you. If you know something that involves my city, I have a right to know."

"All right. Set up a meeting tomorrow, somewhere neutral, and I'll contact my superiors about bringing you and your people into the loop. Agreed?"

"Ok, I'll agree to that, but you must be able to tell me something tonight?" asked Barney.

"Let's just say that it looks like old flames are rekindling," replied Cliff. Barney stared blankly at his friend as he absorbed the information he just received. As if already programed, Nicholson turned and walked to his car. He picked up the phone and immediately dialed the mayor.

"Kirk, history is repeating itself. We need to talk now."

CHAPTER 5

Rays of light slowly pushed the velvet night over the horizon, relinquishing its hold on the land. Many of today's Native American tribes still rose with that light to the relative obscurity granted them by the white man in the late nineteenth century. As in ancient times, the Indians still considered themselves a major part of nature's eternal equation. Though opportunities increased for Indians in today's society, bad blood still flows to this day.

The Yondotega club was created in 1891as a meeting place for Detroit's rich and famous. Named for the Algonquin word for village, the Yon, as the club became known, had a standing rule permitting no one to be able to discuss what went on in the club, thus creating a certain mystique. Women joined in the 1980s. Detroit's big money frequented the Yon; Ford, Fisher, Hudson, Fruehauf, Booth, Thurber, Stroh, and McMillan. Teddy Roosevelt called it the "Best Club in America." Tonight, though, it would lay claim to fathering the worst uprising since the "1880s."Five men met secluded from the world, to script a new course in their history. Four of the most powerful leaders in the American Indian Independence movement met to breathe life into their plan of a new Indian nation. This was to be the final planning session before the Great American Indian Pow-Wow at Joe Louis Arena later that month, the first one ever in Detroit.

Richard Night-Owl was chief of the Chippewa tribe of Michigan. Notorious for stealing identities, he used them to embezelle money from their casino operation for himself, not the tribe. Once discovered, the tribal council attempted to remove him and fell one vote short. Night Owl had called in his markers to sway the decision his way. Life went on as before, but he covered his tracks better than his ancestors. His Oglala Sioux brother was Daniel Running-Horse. Rebuilding the fighting spirit of the people who defeated General Custer, his people began midnight raids of nearby ranches, leaving officials baffled for clues to the culprits. Tribal coffers bulged at their seams as their ill-gotten loot,combined with casino revenues, made the Sioux one the richest tribes in the country.

Across the table sat the elder statesman of the Native Americans. Richard Johnson led his tribe like a Mafia Don. The Athapascan Apaches kept their land locked tight as a fortress. Johnson had braves constantly patrolling the perimeter of his land, with 95% of his casino operations loading his family's pockets more than his people. Those who spoke out usually never saw the next sunrise.

The final member of this quartet came from the land of the alligators. George Tecumseh was supreme chief of the Seminole Tribal council. Through his tutelage, his people had profited handily just from their casino revenues alone. Intrinsic planning, as well as profitable financial investments, helped cement a solid future for his people. But it was not enough. The Seminoles wanted more. These four men, all dressed in their Brooks Brothers suits, simultaneously turned as the door to their dining salon burst open. Silhouetted by the chandelier stood a very, tall man shadowed by two men of equal qualifications. The center man was of sturdy build, about 6'4", 275 pounds. He wore a dark bowler, a style that has stayed in the family since the days of his father. One of his assistants removed the full length cape from his shoulders while the other took his silver tipped cane from his hand, identical to the one Bat Masterson used on his western trips. He carefully walked across the room to the head of the table with his guards in tow. Sitting down in a chair that was waiting for him, he turned to face the quartet, moving close enough to see every detail of their proud faces. Johnson spoke first to break the tension.

"Sir, we have completed all of the tasks assigned to us. Our people grow impatient with the advent of the Great Pow-Wow. Do you have the cave prepared? Are the people aware? Will we be able to strike the people unaware of events that will soon overcome them? These are questions our people ask daily. We look to you for answers." The stranger calmly unbundled his napkin, meticulously unfolding it and placing it on his lap. The other men copied him. He brought his hands up from his lap and clasped them in front of him as he began to speak. Leaning forward, towards his dinner guests, the dim overhead light cast a ghostly shadow over his barely discernable features.

"Gentlemen, the puzzle is ready to complete. The pieces are all lined up. Once we knock the enemy off the mountain, we will absorb their system and crush the ants within it. Next week, we will go hunting on the mountain to remove the King Ram of the Bighorns. On his execution, our followers will begin to move in and herd the ants into absorption. Will you have any problems with that schedule? Speak now, for you will not receive another chance."

The four men carefully glanced at each other out of the corner of their eyes. Their job had been to mobilize their men into fighting machines with the sole purpose of furthering the Native American cause. They had joined with this man to achieve their ultimate goal, a new, more permanent home. Their day was almost near and their tensions were rising like volcanoes. One mistake, one wrong comment could destroy years of painstakingly detailed work to achieve it. The four turned and looked at the mysterious man at the head of their table. Night-Owl spoke for the other participants.

"Our men are ready. They will arrive at prearranged locations as the sun rises. Supplies and instructions are in place as to their assignments. The rest will be as scripted."

"Our preparations are in place. No one, not even the president, can stop us now. Let us conclude this meeting of the revolutionary council with this thought; revenge is said to be sweeter than honey. Let us use that principle as our banner to maximize the full benefits of this endeavor. We will be victorious and our people will be able to live on ancient lands once more. The four of you will wait fifteen minutes after my departure. After that, leave at five minute intervals. You will be notified of the next meeting if it is deemed necessary. Otherwise, may the Great Spirit shower glory on us through the coming days."

Finished, the stranger rose from the table. His two bodyguards, with their slicked-back hair and bodies built like football players, stepped forward without command. The one on the left place the cape back on his shoulders. The one on the right handed the silver-tipped cane back to the stranger's right hand. The trio turned and strolled through the club to their waiting limo, outside the front entrance. They sped off indiscretely down Jefferson towards Belle Isle, absorbed quickly by the afternoon rush hour traffic.

The camp at Sand Canyon was a bustle of activity just as the sun began to show its head just over the horizon. A definite sense of urgency swept the site as they prepared it for, what they hoped would be, the final day of their search. For three weeks, this expedition had traveled more miles in the Four Corners alone than in the whole state of New Mexico. The last leg would be the most treacherous of all. Still dazed after her night at the peyote campfire, Amy Mitchell gathered her morning cup of coffee and went straight to one of the lead vehicles where Moran had maps spread out all over the hood. Their three Ute guides were there as well. Questions started to fly as they thought of rewards promised them when they completed this project.

Tim pointed out their route to John as Amy walked up to the Land Rover and into the conversation.

"From what we have gathered through old Indian tales and archaeological theories is that by taking the Sand Canyon road into the reservation, we will travel about five miles before..."

Abruptly, Amy chimed in, "Before we come across a large flat rock raised off the ground with smaller amounts of marl. When find this landmark, our journey's end is near." Amy immediately felt Trisha send her a telepathic message of approval.

"Don't forget." Their eyes met in a momentary glance of compassion. Everyone's eyes remained glued to Amy as she continued.

"All of you have been diligent in our efforts to find the burial site. But I must confess a secret behind my motives. In one of the burial caves lies the body of an ancient Mayan priest who was crowned the last chief of the Anasazi. It was this chief who commissioned a relative of my mother's by way of my maternal grandmother, to create a regal headdress, showcasing his leadership of the tribe. That person was his squaw and my great-great-great-great-great grandmother, Red Deer. This headdress is said to hold two turquoise stones that supposedly gave him supernatural abilities. To recover this would be not only an archaeological coup, but a personal coup for my family that could well use a good shot in the arm now. Any questions?"

Everyone still gazed at her very intently.

"Alright then, let's get going." On that command, camp was broken and everyone loaded up the Land Rovers to move to the reservation.

Within thirty minutes, Tim got up on the lead Rover and hollered, "Move 'em out!"

Off they went down the canyon road towards destiny. Four hours passed as the wagon train of Land Rovers laid claim to nothing but a colossal dust bowl. Layers and layers of the gritty substance collected all over their vehicles. Strangely high winds created an extremely thick, swirling cloud totally blocking the sunlight and the other cars around them.

"STOP!" blared out the two-way radio hanging from under the dash of the truck. It was Amy.

Tim answered, "What's wrong?"

"If I am correct, you will find an extremely large boulder blocking our path, that could have killed you. Have John put on the dust storm gear to confirm this and radio back." Quickly, John grabbed the glasses and pulled up his hood for protection as he journeyed into the malaise around them. The wind howled about his body as he ventured into the unknown, away from his safe haven. Tim watched as John quickly disappeared into the swirling grit. He kept radioing updates about John's status. Minutes stretched into hours. Amy grew irritatingly restless with the lack of any word. She reached for the radio one more time when a voice blared from the tiny speaker.

"All right, everybody. I'm back." It was John's voice she heard, breathing a sigh of relief from her tension.

"Amy, it was a good thing you had us stop because about 500 yards ahead of us was a twenty-ton boulder that stretched from one side of the road to the other. Good news is I think I located the flat rock you talked about earlier. It lies one-half mile on the other side of the boulder. But the only way to get their will take another hour following a detour. That's what took me so long, confirming the alternate route for you. If you want, I can lead you there now."

"Go for it," Amy ordered. She felt relieved that she had saved the lives of her expedition. The lead Rover, containing Tim and John, were swallowed quickly by the ensuing cloud. A different world awaited them as they drove towards their moment of glory.

The Midwestern sun began to beat down ferociously on the units mopping up last night's big fire. Arson investigators now combed the burned out sarcophagus of the old train station as the sun broke above the horizon. That inferno had reduced one of Detroit's great landmarks to a three-story piece of rubble. Several of the bodies discovered were found to be frequent nightly visitors to this antiquated motel. Fire Chief Joe Pilog stood in the circle entrance drive near Michigan with Police Chief Barney Nicholson carefully observing arson and homicide investigators looking for evidence as the coroner removed the corpses. Rows and rows of emergency vehicles continued to cause a major traffic jam keeping Michigan Avenue blocked. Only necessary personnel were permitted past the outer perimeter. A tall, muscular man, dressed totally in black, walked through the maze towards the central hub of the relief operation.

"Well, I gave you a few hours. So tell me what you've found."

Nicholson remarked, "Skip, where the hell did you come from?"

"Just went out for a leisurely stroll and found another mess the city has itself in," answered Mitchell.

"The scoop on this one is it look likes a torch job. There is a large residue of Tefrin over a lot of the rubble that has been gone through. It also appeared on the clothing of some of the victims. Overall, I would call this an insurance job. There is no other way to look at it."

"So your people found no evidence of two stinger missiles fired at the back of the building."

Nicholson and Pilog both looked at each other and exclaimed, "WHAT!"

Mitchell replied quietly, "While trying to get to sleep, I was looking out my balcony window and saw what looked like a Cobra helicopter lifting off from the track bed at the rear of the building. As he rose towards the top, two bright orange streaks preceded a very loud explosion that everyone probably heard before you arrived on scene. The Cobra then turned and headed down river. That's the last thing I saw."

"One other thing, Barney, I saw two rockets fired but only one small explosion. You could have some unexploded munitions on site." Barney went into action immediately, with the Fire Chief right behind. They cordoned off the area while the bomb squad arrived on the scene.

Less than a mile away, a groggy Wanda woke to four paramedics and a Gurney, flittering around her like she had died. As her eyes focused, her mind recognized a couple of faces. She immediately screamed, "Skip!" but Helford, an aide to her mentor T.J. Marvelli, squirted chloroform over her mouth and nose knocking her unconscious. Helford directed his henchmen to load her onto the Gurney and transport her down to a waiting ambulance for delivery at a pre-arraigned location. Their operation ran so smoothly, nothing stood in their way. The boss will be pleased.

Back at the mop-up, Skip was talking to Barney when he turned his head quickly back towards his apartment where he had left a sleeping Wanda.

"Oh My God!" went the lights in his head as he realized he left her vulnerable.

"Barney, I need to borrow a car for twenty minutes. I'll take this one. Thanks." As a dumbfounded police chief looked on, Mitchell commandeered a squad car, whipped it 180 and went barreling down Michigan Avenue with sirens blaring.

"That's my Skip," were the only words that were heard coming out of his mouth as the cruiser sped out of view. The elevator doors opened wide as the ground floor lobby came into view to the four paramedics. Helford led the way as they took their quarry to their awaiting ambulance. An IV was taped to her arm for added effect. Helford knew he was working with rookies and wanted to make it as real as possible. The front door and the awaiting ambulance were just seconds away. He ordered two of his men to go out and prepare the vehicle, while he waited just inside until they were ready. Like a well oiled machine, they handled it like clockwork. The ambulance opened and one of the other technicians jumped to get the lobby door. Wanda's Gurney was pushed out and turned towards the rear door. Helford noticed a siren that kept sounding louder and louder. As he turned around, fear shot all through him because Skip Mitchell, Detroit's best private eye had screeched to a stop in a police squad car, of all things.

"Get in and go now!" exclaimed Helford as Mitchell was exiting the squad car. The chase was on. With sirens wailing, Mitchell and Helford played a continuous game of cat and mouse under Cobo Center and down Jefferson. Mitchell went on the air with an APB on the streaking ambulance.

"Calling all cars. We have a stolen AMR ambulance blazing down Jefferson with a possible kidnap victim inside. Advise if you can assist." Two cars responded immediately and put up a roadblock at Jefferson and Mt. Elliott, turning the kidnappers north into a residential area. Mitchell did not lose an inch in his pursuit.

"Mitchell," cried the mysterious voice in his car, that he could not pinpoint.

"Why don't you pick up your radio, dummy. We need to have a little talk."

"Better make this good," Skip retorted.

"Oh, you can count on it. Have you forgotten that we have another passenger in here? Well, she wants to talk to you," said the voice. For the next few minutes, his heart slowly sank as he drove.

"Skip, it's Wanda. They told me I had better talk or they'd kill me. Call off the chase or they will do that." The voice abruptly changed octaves as the next words were spoke.

"That's right. Your gorgeous ex-wife will be history. Now back off!" Stunned, Mitchell and the other squad cars slowed as the ambulance sped away with Wanda inside. As if programmed, Mitchell asked for a private line to Chief Nicholson.

"Barney, old friend, I think we better have a heart to heart talk right away."

He floored the accelerator, speeding down Gratiot towards Beaubien. The car pulled up in front of police headquarters, like it had a mind of its own. Mitchell jumped out of the moving car, ran halfway up the steps before the car fully stopped. Two other cars, a 2003 Lexus and a 2002 BMW, were slightly damaged by the free-wheeling car. Barney will not be pleased.

The Great American Indian Pow-Wow got its roots in the western city of Denver. In the early twentieth century, local promoters organized it into a showcase of goods that each tribe created for use and be able to sell the items for their own personal gain annually. This year. an anonymous sponsor invited the Pow-Wow to come to the Motor City. It would be a colossal event, full of booths showcasing their wares, a carnival nightly for the kids and a forum for all tribes nationwide to discuss issues affecting each tribe. Four very powerful men from different tribes led the organization of the event. Their efforts though were cloaked in tightest secrecy permitted. Tuesday, July 21st was to be a date to be remembered in Detroit. Over four hundred buses swarmed throughout the morning rush. Things got even more complicated when an aerial distraction of sixty Cobra AZK attack helicopters flying low over the city. Captain Ron Brewer (an honorary title given by the group flying with him) radioed ahead to the City Airport tower for clearance to land.

"City Tower, this is 3576 Delta Vega requesting clearance for my squad of Cobras to land at the south end of the runway."

"Sixty helicopters! Just what do you have going?"

"There is some exhibition during the upcoming event. We were told to park in the Marvelli hangars and we'll be met by someone from the exhibition."

"Ahh roger that. You are clear to land on runway 27Left. Welcome to Detroit."

"Thanks." The captain switched frequencies to talk to the rest of his squad undetected.

"Gentleman, we have crossed the first stone on our path. Follow my lead." With that command, Brewer led his squadron down to a pinpoint landing on the tarmac. The choppers were then wheeled into an open hangar till the day they would be needed.

Nearly three hundred buses also arrived bursting with young men dressed in fatigues. Traffic was snarled throughout the city as the buses pushed through to their final destinations. Police closed down specific lanes to accommodate the buses. The first group exited off I-94 into Melvindale with their destination the newly restored Salt Mine facility, now owned by Marvelli Enterprises. The second group broke from the M10 freeway traffic at 8 Mile Road. They eventually turned east, stopping at the abandoned 8 Mile Armory. The last group left the Ford Freeway at Moross and turned into a large warehouse complex, across the street from St. John's Hospital.

Commuters were irate, calling every radio talk show they could to complain. It made for good ratings, even though it fell on deaf ears.

The men were immediately sequestered inside each facility to keep them focused on their purpose. Skip passed by the armory, on his way to a meeting with Police Chief Nicholson, listening to all the complaints on one of the local morning shows. One caller piqued his interest. This one told of how this one passenger stuck his head out the window of the bus and said "We've come to make Detroit a better place. He was immediately pulled back in and the window slammed shut."

"And where did his bus go may I ask?" replied the host.

"Why the 8Mile Armory!" the caller said.

Mitchell immediately did a Michigan left and headed back west. A half-mile east of the freeway, he pulled up to the curb, locked his doors and walked the extra half block to the fence surrounding the armory grounds. An abandoned gas station left him with easy access to the fence without violating someone's property. Hearing what sounded like a punishment activity beyond the fence, Skip stealthily jumped onto two abandoned cars left beside the old gas station, affording him a nearly perfect view of the complex. He saw nothing in the front of the grounds. But activity towards the back piqued his interest.

A garage door had been left open, showing a few of the buses and some activity inside. Right at the doorway, three men in fatigues stood smoking cigarettes. Their conversation was becoming very interesting. The first man said, "In a few days, this will be all over and I can move my family here permanently."

The second one replied, "Yeah, all we have to do is to get rid of two roadblocks and we're free."

A third one shared, "Just remember, you cannot say anything to anyone about this. It will be your life, just like that fool did earlier."

A rifle shot echoed through the complex, startling Mitchell. He jumped up from his perch, high enough where he was spotted by the three men in the doorway. They sounded the alarm, taking off to try and catch him or at least a description of him. Skip's luck was with him today. He got to his car, his Boss Mustang with the tinted windows, flying with both sides of his 350 V8 pumping away fiercely. He left a trail of rubber as he raced toward the freeway.

The upper echelon of Detroit's Police Department lives on the 14th floor of 1300 Beaubein. Members of the Police Commission shared temporary offices while almost half of the floor was allotted to the police chief. It held a large auditorium for news conferences, two smaller venues for classroom instruction, a large conference room for the chief's private meetings and a well-equipped office suite. Mitchell arrived with all of the materials Wanda had brought with her. Close behind was Roy Maxim, his partner of ten years. A very slender man, Maxim joined the firm fresh from the Marine Corps. He earned Skip's trust immediately by cracking a robbery case that the police were stymied on. It was then that he learned about his experience as an investigator for the Defense Intelligence Agency. Skip smiled as they sat down in the two seats to the left of the head of the table. Across the table sat two other participants. One was Bruce Watson of the FBI. A slightly pudgy man of average height, Watson stayed physically fit for any case that he handled personally. The other was Randy Meashon, vice mayor of the city. Meashon was an enigma to Mitchell. Though he appeared loyal to the mayor, he just didn't trust him.

Back at the fire site, members of the police bomb squad, joined by munitions specialists from Selfridge Air National Guard base in Mt. Clemens, worked tirelessly to disarm an unexploded Stinger missile hidden under the rubble near the back of the building. Staff Sergeant Raymond Mitchell controlled the procedures right down to the minutest detail. Any wrong move by any member of his team would be disastrous for anyone within a ten block area of the missile. The team of experts from Selfridge immediately went to work to disarm the missile while the police bomb squad stood back to create a perimeter for the other workers to stay behind. Assistant Police Chief Roland Ossey stepped in for Chief Nicholson after an emergency meeting was called downtown. He watched safely from the police helicopter as the men went through their motions. He was to report to the chief the minute the missile was neutralized.

Specialist First Class Tania DeSoto carefully unscrewed the panel on the side of the missile to gain access to timing and detonation mechanisms. She took each quarter inch screw and carefully turned it so that nothing could possibly trigger detonation. One, then two were out, followed by numbers three and four. About twenty sighs of relief were heard as she slowly removed the panel from the fuselage and set it on the ground. Now came the hardest part. There were three wires leading to the trigger box in the missile, one black, one green and one white that was the main wire. But she noticed something different with this one right away. A very thick red wire was spliced into the white wire. DeSoto followed it with hand until it stopped near the nose of the Stinger.

"Give me a flashlight," she ordered. One was given to her almost immediately. She shined the light onto the wire and followed it. Two-thirds of the way up the wire, she noticed a very large bare spot in the wire, with black soot all around it. She ascertained that a short must have occurred. She tilted the wire more towards the nose and gasped. The end was terminated in about two pounds of C4 explosive, enough to take out twenty city blocks or level a building.

"Quiet," she hollered, "get the sergeant." Ray Mitchell cautiously hurried towards his team. Tania showed him what she found. His reaction was immediate.

"Get on the horn. I want a Huey down here stat. Tell them they have a sensitive transport back to the base immediately. Now clear the area." The squad dispersed to alert the police and set the new parameters of the safe area.

"DeSoto, you stay here with me," Mitchell ordered. She stopped in her tracks and returned to await the arrival of the transport helicopter.

Tuesday July 21st will go down in history as the "Day the Freeways failed." Hundreds of buses from all over the country besieged Detroit at the worst time of the day, the morning rush. Most of the buses carried participants for the Pow-Wow this Saturday and Sunday. But a select few carried a specially trained group of men sent here to change the history of this country. The first group of buses pulled into the old salt mine facility, now run by Marvelli Enterprises, Inc., and went straight underground. The second group pulled into the old 8Mile Armory facility in Southfield. The final group entered a warehouse district near St. John's Hospital at Moross and Jefferson. These were picked as strategic deployment locations for events scheduled to happen this weekend.

Lieutenant George Red Feather reviewed his motley crew as they exited their chariots at the salt mine. Though all had come through training at the camp in Cortez, his company looked like they were all pulled off the streets. The men were unshaven, some even with long scars that they picked up at protest rallies against the United States Government. Their eyes showed a ferocity in them that he had not seen since his days in the Gulf War. There he led a squad that became known as "the Dirty Dozen II." They went on suicide missions, performing impossible feats. That is why Richard Johnson recruited him to lead this mission. Its true purpose, though, still eluded him and his group. Once everyone disembarked from their buses, they were ordered to stay sequestered until the Thursday before the Pow-Wow. At that time, they will receive their final instructions.

Forests have always been part of the Michigan landscape. The birches, oaks, evergreens and other varieties of deciduous trees still cover over three quarters of the state. That was one reason for the continuing exodus of people from Detroit. Oakland County, just north of the city, was a major player in this game of the flight to suburbia. It now ranks as the third richest county in the nation. It was named for the number of oak trees that resided within its boundaries. Today, many of Oakland's northern townships still have the thick forests that the state is known for. Though Oxford township is growing in development, the others (Holly, Brandon, Groveland, Addison) are still like step back into the past.

About five miles north of Ortonville, a northern suburb of Detroit in Oakland County, an ambulance slid quietly onto a roadway that led to a cabin hidden from the road by twenty feet of brush on all sides. The attendants opened the door and took the unconscious passenger out of the vehicle, swiftly entering the awaiting homestead. An older man stood back, watching the whole event and following everyone inside. The man removed a vial from his pocket and reached for a hypo to prepare an injection for their patient. One of the attendants grabbed a tourniquet and wrapped it around the arm. The first man administered the injection and stood back while his patient slowly stirred. The patient started to moan, eventually opening her eyes to realize she wasn't in Vegas, like her dreams portrayed her as. A familiar face crossed the path of her eyes. She recognized him as someone who was very close to her.

"Helford, is that you? What is the meaning of this? What's going on? I want an explanation now!" She was never one to mince words or hold back her feelings. Helford responded very off the cuff.

"Now, Miss Wanda, Master Tony wanted me to find out why you left the ranch so quickly, eventually spending the night in Mr. Mitchell's condo. So would you like to tell me now or wait till HE gets here."

She looked at him dead center into the pupils of his eyes, hoping to gain an edge over him. She had a reputation for staying one step ahead of potential suitors or enemies that way. After all, Wanda Willington, the nation's hottest nightclub singer and the bread and butter of Renaissance Records, was a hot commodity. Anyone just knowing her could name his own meal ticket. Right now, she was ready to sell her soul just to see the kids one more time, especially Drew, her youngest, who left her some twelve years ago. Fear flowed from one nerve ending to the another almost continuously. Her demise was imminent. Tony would find out what she knew and then be done with her. She started speculating what he could do to her when Helford returned to the room with a cell phone in hand.

"You can relax and rest, Miss Wanda. Master Tony has ordered us to treat you like a queen, but put you under twenty-four guard until your ceremony on Sunday."

"Ceremony! What ceremony?" she asked, puzzled.

"Why your wedding of course. It is to be the highlight of the big Indian meeting this weekend. You are to be married on Sunday." An alarm went off in her head. Suddenly, she knew what was going on. Skip needed to know right away. She needed a plan. What would Skip do?

Watson continued his assessment of the situation as the others listened intently, some internally appalled by what they were hearing.

"So, what the FBI has determined is that the American Indian Independence Movement, in consort with certain mafia sects in the country, are going to attempt to take over a large metropolitan area to create a new country for the tribes to move to, thus eliminating the need for their adherence to the treaties. Any questions?"

Chief Nicholson cautiously rubbed his chin, glancing at Skip before he spoke.

"So summing up, you're saying that Indians, with help, are planning to take over my city and remove the people from homes they were worked hard for. It just seems totally outrageous!"

"The problem, Barney, is that it is very possibly true," Skip added. "Wanda flew in two days ago to see me, she said that Marvelli was up to something. We never had a chance to talk since he apparently had her kidnaped yesterday."

Watson jumped back in. "So that's where you come in, Mitchell. Nicholson says you are the best undercover man in the city. We can outfit you with equipment that could make your job easier, but we need you on board since all of my men are tied up watching all Marvelli's operations."

Roy Maxim could not resist the opportunity to put in his two cents.

"You mean to tell me that our omniscient government has stretched itself so thin that it is begging for help?"

The Vice Mayor, Mr. Meashon, finally ended his silence. "On behalf of Mayor Asher and the Great City of Detroit, I must say that we will not condone any action taken that could blemish this city during this important event. Any plans you make will be considered against the mayor's wishes and could cost anyone their livelihood." With that outburst complete, the Vice Mayor stormed out of the chief's 13th floor conference room. Mitchell and Maxim looked at each other and nodded. They both suspected that he had ulterior motives. Question was: WHAT. This topic would be picked apart later. Back to the meeting they both thought.

Special Agent Watson spoke morbidly, "Gentlemen, it is the FBI's assumption that some of the tribes and the Marvelli family are up to something. My agents report that approximately fifteen buses arrived at three different locations around the city. At each location, there has been a lot of activity in the form of deliveries to each location, each one shrouded in secrecy. Chief, the FBI would appreciate the help of your department in this matter. Something dreadful is going to happen and everyman that can be available could make a significant difference. I throw the gauntlet to you, Barney."

Barney sat there and stared at Agent Watson. He had the ultimatum from the Vice Mayor, but he also had his gut telling that something was going to happen and he was determined to stop it.

"All right, Brian, here's what I'm gonna do. I have two SWAT teams and two Bomb disposal squads in the department. As of now, they are on temporary loan to you for 2 weeks. That should at least give you some help, though I know it's not much." Nicholson leaned back in his chair, awaiting his reply.

"That's a start. Let me know if you can get things cleared up with the mayor." Watson smiled at the chief, knowing he had a hard job ahead of him.

Nicholson suddenly perked up and added, "I also recommend the services of the Mitchell and Maxim Detective Agency. They have been of great assistance to us in the past in tracking down elusive criminals. They could be your ace in the hole."

Watson looked at both detectives. "Well, guys, what will it be?"

Skip nervously looked at his watch and said, "Well, it's time for me to go do my weather job. Roy can do the negotiating."

Maxim stared right at him, wondering what had come over him. Mitchell never gave him time to ask. He shot out of his chair and flew up the Chrysler freeway towards his destiny.

CHAPTER 6

The afternoon sun broke through the ensuing dust storm as the caravan left the canyon past the great boulder. As the landscape began to reappear, Moran found their location on the map, folding it neatly as he picked up the radio.

"Alright, people, stay right behind us. We're almost there," was the cry from the leaders. The trailing Land Rovers followed the lead vehicle down the desolate main thoroughfare of the Ute Reservation. Mile after mile passed despairingly by. Rattlesnakes poked out their heads to see what the commotion was. Scorpions scurried through the heat drenched landscape, keeping a constant defense with its poisonous stinger at readiness.

Fifteen miles south of the Great Boulder, Moran and Runningfox slowed to a steady march. Amy Mitchell, impatiently jumped on the radio for an update on their progress. She was unprepared for what she was about to here.

"Tim. John. What's going on?"

"Amy," Tim replied in his Colorado drawl, "we're here." Amy screeched to an abrupt halt while she absorbed the news. Lights and bells went off in her head making her smile. She floored her Rover, passing the other vehicles to the head of the line. Blasting out of her vehicle like an Olympic sprinter, she ran to where Tim and John stood. There before her on the desert floor, dusted with sand, was the flat rock she saw in her vision. The lead team had already opened it, revealing a very large canyon-like edifice below. As the skies above showed the orange and purple hues of sunset, Amy ordered everyone to set up camp for the night and make plans for an exhausting day tomorrow before dawn.

The nighttime sky quickly retreated as the morning sun returned for a new day. The Anasazi Expeditionary Force, as they now called themselves, rose before the sun. With the aid of homemade torches, teams already started descending into the ancient cave of the Anasazi. Each group took sections and began deciphering inscriptions found along the narrow path leading into the hallows of the eerie grotto. The walls were made of a sheer, dark granite that had been polished to its most ultimate shine. The air was damp and cool, buoying hopes that the ancient artifacts would still be intact. The cavern itself extended well down into the belly of the earth. As they entered, Amy and Tim could see dozens of torches at least four hundred feet down, checking inscriptions by each sealed cave to find the one they were looking for. People worked timelessly with torches, notepads and a workspace that amounted to just shy of one meter wide. On the other side of the pass lay a great abyss. Someone had shone a lamp towards the engulfing cavern, to everyone's disgust. All that was visible was nothing but bones. Human bones. When the question of whose bones they were, Amy and Tim both agreed to catalog that for future expeditions.

According to her research, Amy had put together a theory as to how the Anasazi marked their graves. Unlike the later plains Indians that either used the burial mound method or burned their dead on a raised platform to permit a quicker ascension to the Great Spirit. The Anasazi, though, were ones that believed in an in ground burial method utilizing caves the way cultures in the Middle East did. For many years, anthropologists have speculated that the two major oriental societies in the Far East, Japan and China, had incorporated such a ritual within their structures. The Anasazi believed that by entombing their leaders near their tribal villages on the Mesa Verde, the Great Spirit would be able to collect their souls and utilize them as conduits of information to future leaders like the Kachinas, spirits who traveled through Sipapus from the other world. So by using this cave as a burial place, the tribe was keeping everyone close to home. Hours passed with no success. All of the inscriptions showed a circular drawing, another looked like a star field, showing the apparent stars in the sky on the day of burial. The one that the explorers were looking for would contain that too. But it would also contain one significant difference from all the rest. While most of them contained a sideways circular symbol topped with something identifiable with the tribal era, this particular one would have a straight up and down circular symbol, topped with what looked like a snake's head with the chief's special headdress on top of that. That was proving to be as elusive to Dr. Mitchell as this canyon.

The Michigan Central Depot opened in 1913 at a cost of two and a half million dollars. It was designed by two architectural firms, one being Warren & Wetmore, who also designed New York's Grand Central terminal. It was given a main waiting area that was four stories high. Elements of marble, brick and plaster in some parts created the character that welcomed visitors to the city. Engagements were started between lovers in its lobby. Soldiers left for war in the 1940s. And thousands arrived to work in the auto factories. It was built in southwest Detroit, about two miles from downtown, to be near the mouth of the rail tunnel beneath the Detroit River. The most notable features were public and private bathing and changing rooms, where it was said a lady could freshen up before her carriage ride to her hotel downtown. Barbershops, flower shops and conference rooms added to the establishment of the terminal as an anchor for city life. Eight million bricks, seven thousand tons of structural steel, one hundred twenty-five thousand cubic feet of stone and twenty thousand cubic yards of concrete went into constructing such a landmark for the city. Now it lay in ruin at the site that was home for almost a century.

The dust from the destruction of the terminal traveled for miles in every direction. Homes were covered inside and out with a gray, gritty soot from the concrete collapsing. In Corktown, business owners and home owners worked side by side in their efforts to hasten the cleanup. Seniors from Detroit's Cass Tech High School gave Tiger Stadium a good once over while regular employees at the park brought everything back to normal. Across I-75 though was another story. In nearby Mexican Village, shards of steel and concrete littered the streets, hindering traffic as far south as Porter and the Ambassador Bridge. The freeway itself, aside from the cars that were crushed from flying debris, suffered minor damage. Police rerouted traffic quickly to avoid any further hazards.

A band of ladies clustered in the front of the small crowd that was left watching the demise of the grand depot. A tall, sinewy built young lady with the skin color of an Hispanic, pushed herself through the group to the front of the police line. Her only brother had used the depot for years as his evening motel. George often said to her that helping the homeless who stayed with him was more important than anything else he had ever done. Hours earlier, they had argued about him staying at her apartment near the bridge over staying at the unsafe depot. She lost again to his reasoning not knowing that would be the last time they would see each other. Seria Perez stood there like a beacon in her fluorescent outfit and shed a single tear for the last and dearest member of her family.

Suddenly, a black Hummer limo stopped right in front of her. Two men jumped out and swooped her into the rear compartment. Her body felt severely jarred from the way the two, burly henchmen, both built like Mr. Universe, threw her into the car. She sat there, surveying her surroundings, attempting to find out why she was pushed into this car. If it was sex they wanted, she would have gladly jumped in on her own, no questions asked. But this car was so dark and quiet, a dreadful fear enveloped her. The young brute who tossed her in the car, sat in front of a very well stocked bar. Her throat started craving a good stiff drink. She broke the silence and asked the young bodyguard, "Get me a good stiff drink, man. I've had a hell of a day." The bodyguard looked to the other side of the compartment, looking for some sort of acknowledgment, finally mixing her a good stiff glass of gin. Seria turned towards the area where the bodyguard looked before he made her drink. The far end of the compartment was very dark. As they traveled through the city, the darkness of the night was occasionally broken by the periodic street light breaking through the heavily tinted windows. There, her brain abruptly shouted. She saw movement in the left corner of her vision near the side window behind the driver's seat. She spoke first before thinking of the consequences.

"I don't know who you are or what you want of me, but if I don't get some damn answers soon, I'll will jump out of this car."

A shadowy figure stirred. She heard a muffled cough as the apparition fidgeted from her statement. A muffled voice filtered through the temporary abyss.

"You are a very special person, my dear. We can give you a chance for eternal freedom from prosecution. Your stellar career on the streets has led you to a greater opportunity to serve for your city."

"What the hell are you talking about! I don't give a damn about this town. My brother just got murdered."

The atmosphere in the limo became so quiet you could here a pin drop. Seria looked at the apparition sitting across from her for the longest time. Her heartbeat increased with every passing second. Finally, a voice spoke from out of the shadows.

"If you agree to do this for us, you will be rewarded handsomely. Enough to reimburse you for the loss of your relative. Would the sum of two million dollars be sufficient?"

Seria sat in the back of the limo frozen in disbelief. That was more money than she could ever hope to make in a lifetime.

The torches in the cave were beginning to burn out as twilight approached the reservation. All of the archaeological teams carefully scrutinized the inscriptions by the cave tombs, searching for the remains of her ancestor. Hour after hour, the dampness of the cavern crept into the bones of the explorers. The younger ones felt chilled while the older members felt their arthritis problems flare up. No one admitted to any problems since they were so close to the end of their journey. A few hundred feet below the entrance, Tisha and Drew shone their dwindling torch on what was their last tomb of the day. As Tisha raised her torch to read the carvings, she could not contain the excitement in her voice.

"Amy! Tim! Come down here! I think we've found it! Hurry!" The careful rush of the other teams towards the cave was felt by Tisha and Drew as they made their way down the path towards their cave.

Amy and Tim were the first to arrive. She grabbed the torch from Drew's hand and held it high over the ancient writings. There it was, a straight up and down design capped with the head of a snake. Her vision was now fulfilled. The excitement was ready to explode.

"Get fresh torches down here right away. And tell the crew upstairs to crank up the battery power. We're going to have a long night with this cave."

Long stretches of power cables laid haphazardly across the narrow path of the cavern. Several pairs of powerful Klieg lights laid in their case by Red Deer's tomb. John and Tim brought down all the archaeological tools they would need, including the portable carbon-14 dater to verify its authenticity.

"All right, let's do this," Amy said to the burly crew that stood besides the large slab of granite guarding the cave's entrance. The group split up, two on the left side and two on the right, and began to lift the slab away from the entrance. Sweat poured from their brows as their muscles quivered from the weight of the perfectly symmetrical slab. They grunted in unison as the slab lifted away from the entrance to the cave.

Drew Eaglewing and two assistants soon arrived from the surface with the needed equipment to complete their search. A humidifier was brought down to maintain a constant atmosphere within the tomb. A Carbon-14 dating system that Dr. Moran used extensively at the Denver Museum of Natural History in cataloging dinosaur excavations that were constant discoveries in Colorado was brought down for verification purposes. Numerous plastic, air-tight containers were there to place their discoveries in as they were found Drew and his crew sat everything on the path while John and Tim led the other crew in removing the granite door.

Minutes flew by as they continued working on entry to the tomb. One member of the expedition grabbed a metal bar and began to use it as a lever. Amy, Tisha and Maria stood back and watched as the circus continued. Suddenly, a rush of stale air swept through the cavern, knocking almost everyone including the crew that was working on the door. Drew went flush with the wall while the air began to escape from the cave. Several minutes passed as the escaping breeze subsided. Drew was the first one to poke his head into the dark, windowless room. Dr. Moran and John Runningfox grabbed a couple of large oil lanterns, lit them and held them high above the entrance to the cave. Before them lay a veritable art museum of ancient Indian wall sketching, encompassing every wall of the cave. In the center of the cave rose a dual rock sarcophagus with a three-inch thick granite slab on top. Near the top of the granite slab, Drew again noticed the vertical curly-cue design on the left hand sign. A smile rose on his face.

"Our journey has ended," he reiterated as he looked at Dr. Mitchell.

"Let us give the Anasazi its due glory."

Amy and Tim stepped cautiously into the cave, walking around debris from the centuries of age that lay scattered on the floor of the cave. She looked at Tim with pride before giving him an order for the night.

"Set up rotating watches of two people per shift. I want 'round the clock guards till morning. When the sun rises, we will open the sarcophagus and examine the remains of the last royal couple of the Anasazi."

Moran left Amy alone in the cave as he carried out her orders for the guard watches for the night. She walked up to the right side of the stone coffin, running her hand across the crumbly top. Tears began to well up in her eyes.

"I will help them remember, Grandpa," she said quietly to herself when no one else could here.

The whole camp rose before the sun broke over the horizon. Amy and Tim led the rush down the path to the tomb of what was Amozeltec and Red Deer, the last ruling couple of the Anasazi on the Mesa Verde.

When the three-hundred foot level was passed and the entrance to the cave was just a few feet away, a sinking feeling hit her in the gut. Something was wrong and it spelled disaster. She increased her pace as she ran down the path.

Tim and John arrived first, repositioning the lights that had fallen sometime overnight. Once they turned on the lights, It was obvious what had happened. Someone had overpowered one shift of guards during the night, cracked open the coffin and took the turquoise headdress that was the centerpiece of this expedition.

Tim saw Amy arrive at the scene with the look of utter shock sweep across her face. He quickly removed from the cave as Drew and a few others secured the cave from further disturbances.

"Tim, I want you to call every member of our expedition together. I want to question them one by one until I find the culprit who did this. I have had it with people pulling this stuff for their own personal gain."

"All right, Amy. But just remember, stay fair. The government will penalize us severely if that is not done." He took her in his arms and let her break down as the events of the night finally caught up with her.

The bowels of a television station contain many different vessels to keep the organization moving. The sales department consistently deals with encouraging people to buy commercial time with them, whether they be local or national clients. Administration consists of the cogs that keeps the wheel moving. Engineering keeps the station on the air twenty-four hours a day, seven days a week. And to keep its soul in tune with the constituency it serves, most good stations employed a thorough news department to gather and report about issues and happenings within the city it served. The constant greasing of the wheel of operation was never ending at WGCB-30 in Rochester.

Ron Firman sat at his desk in the newsroom, carefully reviewing the scripts for that night's newscast. Firman was one of those local boy makes good stories cropping up all over the city. The son of a Detroit police officer, Ron pursued his college career at Wayne State University majoring in radio-TV journalism with a a concentration in municipal government. He went up to Marquette for his first job right out of college as a reporter. For the next six years, he worked his way down the state; from Cadillac to Mt. Pleasant, to Saginaw, Lansing and finally the job as chief news anchor at Channel 30 in Rochester. Along the way, he achieved numerous Associated Press awards for his investigative reporting and feature writing. He blazed a solid path for himself, achieving the lofty position of number one news anchor. Today, things did not seem to be worth the hassle.

"Off in your dreamworld again, pal? I wonder what Kitty would say if she caught you slacking off."

Skip Mitchell, a long-time friend and member of his awarding news team, always poked his head in at four p.m. to announce his arrival with ruffles and flourishes. Ron and Skip had been inseparable since college.

Through all night study sessions for exams to helping Skip get through his divorce from America's Sweetheart, Wanda Willington. It proved to be a very strong test of their friendship. With Ron's help, Skip began to channel his anger from the divorce into other avenues, in particular his private eye business.

It got his mind off Skip and put Skip's mind back on his work. What a relief! he thought looking at the cherubic face in his doorway. Friendship does have its benefits.

"So what's new on the P.I. front, pal? I've been trying to get you all weekend with no luck."

"Are you sure you want to know?"

"Nothing you've done can ever phase me!" Ron stated emphatically.

"Well, you asked for it." Skip closed the door before he continued, always maintaining that level of privacy in his life.

"It started with the capture of that guy, Wilsup was his name I think. I caught him and his girlfriend in a very sticky situation. Then I get a call from Wanda saying to meet her at Parks International Saturday night."

She had something important to tell me that we never got around to thoroughly discussing. Then there was the destruction of the Michigan Central Depot. I think that was meant to be a distraction so that Tony could whisk Wanda out of my condo because she was kidnaped right after that happened."

"Oh God!" Ron said, "not again."

"That's just the icing on the cake. On the record, what information do you have about the explosion?"

"A set of bags filled with Tefrin were ignited when a fuse went down into a gas can. Approximately, fifty homeless people perished, including that one everyone called "The Latin Cherub. Other than that, it's an open and shut case of arson."

"Off the record here are the facts the government doesn't want you to know. About ten p.m., I noticed Cobra AZK rise from the track bed and fire two stinger missiles into the rear wall of the depot totally demolishing the structure. When I saw the command posts get set up, I walked down Michigan to tell them what I saw. It was then that I remembered that Wanda was vulnerable and asleep back at my place. I borrowed a police car from Barney, hoping to get back in time to save her. I wound up giving chase up Mack to Moross when Wanda came on the police radio to say let her go or they will kill her on the spot. I did as she asked, but I have a strong feeling that Marvelli is behind this. It sounded like his henchman, Helford, was in the background when she was talking."

"Is that all?" Ron asked.

"Not quite. Wanda was able to tell me that Marvelli was up to something but she couldn't tell what. She noticed plans for an arena with locations for snipers. There has been a major buildup of equipment at their ranch in Cortez, Co.,along with training many young men she believed to be of Native American descent. All of their training seemed to emphasize military maneuvers. She left and came to Detroit right after that discovery.

"Chief Nicholson called a meeting of all federal agencies at his office, as well as the vice mayor, my partner and me. It was learned that the feds have known about Marvelli's plans for months, but could not pinpoint where. Meashon, the vice mayor, stormed out of the meeting saying that the city would not condone any action by the police against Detroit's most prominent citizen. Barney went ahead and loaned one of his two SWAT teams to the FBI until this is over. My partner and I have to corral Tony, Jr. And find out what he's up to. So that means a seven day leave of absence to be able to concentrate on this mess."

A dumbfounded Ron looked at Skip and said, "OK, now tell me what really went on!" They looked at each other and laughed, knowing that Skip had thrown out a hook and he had to reel the fish in himself.

The view from the top floor of the Marvelli Tower gave everyone who had ever been up there a sense of power. Every crevice of this city, every spec of dust, could be viewed in intricate detail. People walked the sidewalks on Woodward like ants scurrying to their anthill. And every direction offered a view of an empire; from the salt mines to the south to the newly opened shipyard near the bridge. The man at the top surveyed his empire with glee, dreaming of the glory he was planning.Father's death would be vindicated, he thought, and can continue to build his empire. Tony Marvelli wore a grin of sadistic glee while he admired his handiwork. When his father died during the yacht accident in'62, TJ felt the thrust of the family mantel fall on his very young shoulders. With his father's bodyguard, Helford, at his side, TJ carefully learned the family business. Frequent trips to the Big Apple aided his education in the ways of the Family. Marvelli not only built up his father's enterprises, but established numerous aides that came from Special Services-US Army. Together, he stayed ahead of the competition and built a solid foundation for the family's Mafia enterprises.

Vice Mayor Randy Meashon paced hurriedly at the other end of the room. He quickly read through a folder as he turned to face Marvelli.

"Are you sure this plan will work, T.J.? I think you've got too many variables that could go awry."

Marvelli cautiously turned and faced his protégé. He first noticed Meashon as he was leading a gang on the city's east side. Randy led a crime spree of epic proportions for a teenager. At nineteen, he had a flourishing drug smuggling racket, mixed with gambling and under age Blind Pigs, rich with booze. T.J. pulled him off the streets and began educating him in the ways of city government. He now owned the second most powerful man in the city.

"I have always told you to trust in this organization. We have covered every contingency for the upcoming Pow-Wow. The air support has already arrived and in position at City Airport. Our land troops are at the staging areas doing final preparations for Operation Deep Sleep. The salt mines have been refitted with a new system to efficiently circulate the air and anything else we might put in it. Randy, by this time next week, you will be installed as the new leader of a new Indian nation. Did you line up someone to take care of the mayor as you committed to?"

"That was easy. Seria Perez, who is the sister of that homeless guy who died when the depot was blown up, has agreed to exact her revenge against the city by doing whatever I say. I will pick her up tomorrow night and give her the assignment with the possible consequences if not carried out."

"See that it is done." His top aide, Helford, walked in at that moment.

"That will be all, Randy. Keep me posted." Meashon stormed out of the office like a kid without his supper.

"OK, Helford, how is my canary?"

"She is doing fine, boss. But restlessness is setting in and I'm concerned that we may develop a situation that will jeopardize the organization. The boys keep wanting to get a piece of her."

Well, just go back to the cabin and say, 'Anyone touching any part of my future wife's body will be dropped in Lake Erie.' Do I make myself clear?"

Helford clicked his heels and saluted his boss and long time friend. With a quick pivot, he made a quick exit to his waiting car. He hoped he could get back in time.

The two guards at the cabin looked at each other with the same resolved look. They opened the door to the bedroom to find their package still wrapped up tight as a drum. Her luscious brown eyes stared sternly at them as they drooled over her as they watched her. One guard began to move closer to her.

She tried to back away, but couldn't get past the wall. Fear heightened in her eyes as lust began to take over her watchdogs.

"Come on, Miss Wanda, let's have some fun." The first guard bent down to undo her pants; she put him on the floor unconscious. The second guard took a little more effort. Now reeling with a migraine, she slipped her hands from behind her back to where she could untie her feet. The second guard started towards her, trying to stop her escape. She took her still restrained hands and wrapped them around his neck, holding firmly until he stopped moving. After a few minutes, she laid him down on the floor next to his partner. A knife was sheathed on the second guard's belt. Wanda grabbed it, cut her bindings and used them along with plenty of duct tape and secured her two guards. Disarming them totally, she ran out the door towards the nearest highway, knowing only that she was somewhere in the country. Anticipating someone might search for her, she stayed off State Park Road and Oakwood Road, slipping through woods and backyards to get to a phone and call Skip. He was the only person she could trust.

The marshy brush throughout Ortonville State Park proved to more of a hindrance to her quest. The constant prickly bushes and tangled vines spread out under a canopy of small trees causing her to sprain her ankle time and again. Eventually, she stumbled into a campground that still had a burning fire. Sounds of activity came from the tent as Wanda gathered her strength standing behind their Jeep Liberty. The sound of a zipper startled Wanda. Two occupants returned to their fire, the woman poured two mugs of coffee and gave the other one to the man. Wanda listened and learned that their names were Bruce and Cindy Shavous,, recently married in Minnesota and on their honeymoon. Still weak, she stumbled from behind the Jeep and walked towards them.

"Who's out there?" cried Bruce, grabbing his gun as he rose.

Wanda could only say two words as she faced the fire.

"Help me." She collapsed on the ground slipping quickly into unconsciousness. She drifted off, not knowing if she would ever she the end of her journey.

CHAPTER 7

City Airport was an island in the center of the city for nearly forty years. Sitting on an old swampy riverbed and shadowed by the bloodiest battlefield of the French and Indian war just across the street, now keen competition was thrown at it. Once the hub of Detroit's air traffic, the onset of World War II and the creation of two new airports, Willow Run in 1939 and Detroit Metro-Rosa Parks International in the late 1950s, most air travelers never experienced the Motor City at its finest.

Surviving as the major freight hub for the inner city, the airport periodically showcased air shows for the general public. Today's show drew the largest crowd in its history, since it was the first helicopter aerial show City Airport ever showcased. Captain Ron Brewer led his troop through their acrobatic maneuvers, thrilling the crowd with every new antic the helicopters were put through. A flashing light appeared on his intercom. He flipped the switch and clicked on his microphone.

"This is Brewer."

"Captain, this is the tower. We have someone on his way to your hangar to see you. A Mr. Johnson, I believe. Does that ring a bell?"

"Yeah, a very loud bell. I'm on my way." Brewer switched his frequency back to the other members of his corps.

"Vector two, this is Vector one. Big pow-wow for me. You carry the lance."

"Yes, Chief." Brewer slid out of the sky towards the southern end of the runway and the Marvelli hangars. A long white limo stretched out in front of the runway hangar with two of the rear occupants visible from the air. A woman poked her head through the sunroof. She had blonde hair cascading down over her shoulders, a mink stole and what looked like the shortest mini dress the captain had ever seen. Straining his eyes, since he adored women's legs, Brewer almost collided with the roof of his hangar just to get a glimpse. The man, somewhat older and graying around the temples, stood there and laughed. He knew Brewer and his weaknesses with women. All of this made leverage to utilize him to the nations' advantage. He settled his bird onto the tarmac like he was landing on air. As the rotors twirled to a complete stop, Brewer saw that the gorgeous blonde had now gotten out of the car, walking arm in arm with Johnson to meet at the helicopter.

As Brewer stepped out of the cockpit, Chief Johnson placed his outstretched hand in his, pumping furiously as they walked.

"Ron, it's always good to see you. How was your flight out? Is the hotel OK?" Johnson repeated hyperactively.

"Well, Richard, I've got no complaints so far. But then, I still don't know why my helicopter brigade has flown over fifteen hundred miles to this god forsaken place."

"You will be instrumental in our plans for this city," answered the Apache chief. " First, have you received the spraying equipment I ordered for you."

"Yes, sir," replied Ron.

"Good. Install it on all of your birds tomorrow. I will send your orders over by eighteen hundred hours. Then all of your questions can be answered." Johnson went to shake his captain's hand only to be rebuffed abruptly.

"I'll wait for your answers tomorrow." Johnson packed himself and his girl in the limo, speeding off into traffic and the Marriott Hotel at the Renaissance Center. Brewer watched puzzled, wondering what the leader of his nation was up to now.

A new day dawned at the Canyon of the Spirits. A sense of relief and anticipated accomplishment was sweeping through the base camp as everyone took care of breakfast dishes. Amy Mitchell sat in engrossed in a meeting with Tim, Maria and her Ute Indian guides about their next step.

"Tim, I think you should head up the party to enter the tomb of Amozeltec. With John, Tisha and Drew standing nearby, you will instruct the others to crack open the seal on the sarcophagus. When that is done, you will remove the headdress from the chief's head and place it into the airtight container to be brought back up to the surface for examination and validation before it is returned to Detroit."

"Shouldn't we take it back to Denver first, Amy? After all, we can expedite the validation process quite efficiently." Tim looked at her quizzically while she pondered his statement. Minutes passed slowly by before Amy finally spoke.

"Nice thought, Tim, but the headdress has to go back to the Detroit Institute of Arts immediately per agreement with the university." She paused. "You have your assignments, so let's get to work."

The archaeologists slowly walked down the narrow path of the cavern, winding their way towards the tomb of the last rulers of the Anasazi people. Anticipation of the history that would be made today stayed foremost on their minds. The path began winding down at the top of the cavern, straightening out as they neared the tomb. Turning the last corner, Tim was the first to notice that the tomb appeared to have been ransacked. The medical team hurried to Drew and the other guards as they lay unconscious on the narrow path. Dr. Mitchell arrived at the cave just as the guards were found fit by the doctors. She stood over Tim's shoulder and listened as he questioned Drew.

Their overnight duty started quietly, mostly keeping their torches lit as the night waned on. About an hour before dawn, someone dressed in a uniform from the expedition, approached them with a story that he was to relieve them one at a time, for a quick bathroom break. Well, when Drew turned around to spread the word, a sudden sharp pain to the back of his head sent stars twirling before his eyes as he slipped into blackness.

"When I awoke, that's when I realized disaster had struck. It was apparent that there was something in here that the mugger wanted. But I don't know what. Amy, please forgive me. We are all very sorry."

"Drew, it will be fine. The coffins do not appear to have been violated. We will go ahead and accomplish what we came out here for." Amy stole a glance at Tim, hoping that the ancient spirits still protected them from the curses known to the nations of the Rockies. Tim rose from his knees, pecking Amy's cheek with a kiss and strode quickly into the tomb followed by several assistants.

Each assistant took his place around the sarcophagus preparing to lift the lid off of the ancient vault. Drew and John secured the pulley stand over the coffin and fed lines down to the four strategic points. Tim paced frantically as the Indians worked to free the lid from centuries of age encrusted over the tomb. Drew passed around crowbars to his fellow tribesmen to use as levers to pry up the ancient lid from the tomb. Tim looked around, checking that every position was filled and ready for the removal of the lid. Satisfied, he barked out his command, "On my mark, you will begin. Three, two, one, mark!" The four ropes went taught as the force of the four two-hundred fifty pound men exerting their total energies to open the coffin. The minutes flew by and nothing seemed to happen. Suddenly, a load moan broke the silence and a gap appeared around the rim of the sarcophagus. The crowbar team went into immediate action, lifting in sync as the pulley team added four more members to increase the lift of the coffin's lid.

"Keep going, men. You're almost there. Our trip may soon be over." Tim's comment echoed the sentiments of everybody in the expedition. The lid finally reached a level that would permit it to be swung out of the way. Drew and his crew joined the others and helped steer the lid to the side of the tomb. They tilted it towards the side of the cave and everyone caught their breath before continuing.

Amy was the first one to look at the mummified remains of her great-great-great-great-grandmother. Tim came over to stand beside Amy as she prepared for the crowning achievement of her expedition. As Drew grabbed an airtight container to hold the ceremonial headdress, other members of his tribe removed a blanket covering the body of Amozeltec. A gasp filled the entire tomb. Every eye turned and stared at the ceremonial headdress that was rumored the most powerful element of the Anasazi world. The headdress was made of several yucca leaves woven together with the feathers of a young bald eagle, to secure a snug fit on the little chief's head. Covering the eyes, were two bright blue stones, the purest turquoise stones she had ever seen. It was said, in legends, that the stones held great psychic powers for the wearer. This will be a great exhibit for the Institute, she thought.

"Secure the area as soon as possible, Tim. I want a 24-hour guard in four shifts to guard this area until Maria gets everything catalogued." Amy carried the headdress up the path to her tent. It was placed in her safe for testing and documentation the next day.

As Amy awoke, relief swept over her exhausted body now that her goal had been finally accomplished. Grabbing her morning coffee, she walked into the office area of her tent where the safe was located. A blood-curdling scream escaped her throat. There before her was the safe, totally open, and the headdress was gone. She collapsed on the desert floor from the shock.

The expedition packed up their discoveries and left for Denver a few days later. While Maria separated the items that would stay at The Museum of Natural History, Tim stayed with Amy at the Best Western on Colorado Boulevard, desperately hoping to bring her out of the despair that befell her after the theft. Tim had struck out for the third time and was leaving the room when he ran into Drew and a few of the Ute Indian tribe he associated with. Drew raised his hands to quiet the room before he spoke.

"I stand before you today with these brothers to promise that we will find the scum who stole your discovery. The four behind me will comb the Mesa Verde area, along with the other reservations in the Four Corners until we succeed in our quest. I, though, have chosen to return with you to expand the search in Detroit. It is my belief that the thief is already in hiding there. The time has come for me to you the truth and bring my sister up to speed with what's been happening with me lately." Stunned by Drew's last comment, Amy slowly turned around and connected with Drew's eyes. That twinkle in the eyes was there. Plus he had always shown a bubbly personality and enough energy as a whole pack of mules. But there was one thing that would tell the truth about him.

"Alright, drop your pants," she ordered.

Quickly, and in front of everyone, he untied his belt and let his pants fall to the floor. She walked over to his tush and pulled down his boxers. There it was, still standing out like a sore thumb, a one-inch diameter mole that Drew had inherited from his grandfather in the same spot she last saw it twelve years ago. Grabbing his shoulder, Amy twirled Drew around and locked him in a strong embrace. It was so strong that he had to tap her shoulder for her to release him so he could get some air.

"So why did you wait so long?"

"I was waiting for the proper time. For so long, I have wanted to notify you and the rest of the family but I had to be sure that the timing was just right to reconcile the past. Now, if you don't hurry, we'll miss our plane home, sis."

Amy looked at him and smiled. Moments later, they walked out of their hotel, with Tim and the others, boarding the airport bus for Denver International Airport. She kissed Tim and whispered, "I'll call you when I land, lover."

"Amy, I want you marry me. Please call me as soon as possible." She turned quickly and boarded her plane with her new found brother, devastated from the loss of artifacts on this trip. The college board will be very tough on her when she returns.

The Coleman A. Young municipal building stands at the corner of Jefferson and Woodward. Built in the early sixties, it has seen the transition from a vibrant, bustling city to a city hanging by a thread, struggling to hold those threads together. Kirkland Asher became mayor in 2002 on a platform of encouraging businesses to return to Detroit and be a part of his redefining the city. Big Money created major roadblocks for his program. The Big Three auto companies committed money to demolition efforts, clearing nearly half of the 20,000 abandoned houses and buildings that littered the city. But new development like housing and businesses had not moved as quickly as he had hoped. As he looked out his window south towards the bridge and Mexican town. Strategies needed to be changed to accomplish his goal .The key would be hard if he couldn't find a breakthrough in his negotiations with area businessmen. A voice chimed in returning him back to reality.

"Mr. Mayor, the city is turning in disarray with the approach of this Great American Pow-Wow."

Vice-Mayor Meashon continued, "People are complaining daily about traffic jams and other events disrupting their lives. Kirk, we need to ask the governor to send in the National Guard to help." Meashon gave Asher a glaring stare, hoping to make him very irritated. Asher slowly turned from the window and walked right back to the conference table, where the vice-mayor and the city council sat discussing the pros and cons of the daily sports page.

"Ladies and gentleman, I appreciate your input in this situation. The governor informed me last week that the guard would not be available. His answer was to call up all reserves from the police departments of the border cities because of the cost to the city. Chief Nicholson has already been directed to call up his reserves for this weekend. That is the way we will go."

The vice-mayor chirped in, "Mr. Mayor, what if I can whip together some volunteers, people with military or police experience, and enlist them to help out our crisis."

Asher replied, "And the cost to the city?"

Meashon answered, "It would be minimal. I believe I can get some businessmen to help."

Asher looked at the council for their response. All eight of them gave their usual nod of approval.

"All right, Randy, make it happen." The vice-mayor strutted quickly out of the room to a date with destiny.

High over the plains of Kansas, a cold front collected from the Rocky Mountains heading east. Shapeless nimbus clouds floated ceaselessly by to a date with destiny. The Gulf of Mexico slid a massive warm front over Texas towards its destined meeting over Kansas. The cold front pushed under the warm air mass and lifted it up. Water began to crystallize as the below zero temperatures performed their handiwork. A second warm front Canada creating a weather front so massive, the thunder heads extended nearly fifty miles into the atmosphere. Inside the thunder heads, electricity sparked the water molecules to grow into baseball size hail to be dumped on unsuspecting people. The winds churned like a witches cauldron increasing in intensity as they spun faster and faster towards its highest level ever. The front cautiously moved eastward towards the Midwest and the Great Lakes.

In Norman, Oklahoma lives the National Severe Storms Lab. These dedicated people work diligently towards keeping people safe during severe storms such as tornados, floods, heavy rain and large hail of an inch or more causing a major loss of life. Their summers are always active with their coverage of all severe storms that occur in the Midwest. Tracking a bad storm was nothing new to them. They were about to get their biggest challenge ever.

WGCB was hard at work preparing for their eleven o'clock newscast. Reporters were covering major stories in the area from Detroit to as far north as Flint. Writers were grabbing stories from the networks, writing new scripts for the anchors to help keep the national angle in the newscast. Off the main room sat a smaller room with a man working diligently at his computer. Ron Firman considered himself a servant of the people. His nightly editorials on the ten o'clock newscast reinforced the desires of the every day working men of the Motor City. With a nose for news that could sniff out a story two days away, Firman gained the confidence of his viewers, leading his station to the number one ranking in the city. Something was gnawing at him today, so strong that he felt another ulcer developing. He popped two Rolaids into his mouth and went back to the daily CNN feed.

Skip Mitchell had anchored the weather at the station for ten years now. Since his divorce, concentration on his work was his main focus. Skip developed into the most accurate forecaster Detroit had ever seen. Just last year though, was definitely stressful for both himself and management.

The rumors about Wanda's possible marriage and the never ending paparazzi catching shots of him for the tabloid stories of Wanda having one last fling with her ex before she married Detroit's mafia king bothered him and his fellow employees. They followed him everywhere, even his weather office in the studio, hanging from the lighting grid. The station finally hired a security guard for protection just to keep the station running smoothly. The melee' finally ended with the arrest of a photographer posing as a UPS delivery man. After getting access to the station, the man walked into the hallway, heading to the studio. When approached by two employees as to his identity, the photog immediately assaulted them and ran to the studio to get his pictures. He was stopped before he got two feet. Eventually, he was taken to jail and sentenced to ninety days for trespassing. Normalcy returned to the station very quickly.

Skip walked across the studio to his weather station on the far wall next to the chroma-key set. He went through the motions turning on his computers to begin his preparations for tonight's newscast. The warning lights on his NOAA computer lit up like the Fourth of July. He rushed to the printer as the alerts pushed right out into Mitchell's waiting hands. His excitement rose to astonishment quickly. The reports told the story of a massive weather front, moving across the Midwest, leaving massive paths of death and destruction in its wake. Whole towns were being destroyed, leaving no known survivors. Vicious lightning destroyed acres of crops as well as trees, houses, leaving raging fires. Tornados as powerful as F-6, considered the most dangerous of all tornadoes, swept through cities and towns like they were mere toothpicks for dinner. Skip grabbed his remote and turned on his tv's, looking for some visual evidence of the atrocities being committed on people. CNN came up first, flashing a Breaking News Alert. There it was. Acres and acres of destruction ran rampant over the countryside. He saw the same on the Fox News Channel and The Weather Channel. He picked up his phone and dialed Ron's extension.

"Ron, you had better get down here. We've got a whole new lead story." He hung up and called his old college chum, Lucy Gillian of WAG-TV in Chicago.

Lucy began at the National Weather Service, compiling local forecasts for the Mississippi Valley. She became a Tornado Chaser and developed a system to covering Tornado Alley better than anyone. She dated Skip during a 1990 internship at WPZZ. It was a hot start with a cold finish. They stayed good friends over the years. She answered as cheerful as always, "WAG weather. This is Lucy."

"Hi, Lucy, it's Skip. Sounds like nature's sending you a party with a big brass band to boot."

"Have you seen the pictures? If this continues, we could see the worst path of destruction in this country's history."

"Do you have any video you could send me? I want to give Detroit and Michigan the best chance at fighting this front."

"That's no problem. I'll get a window and call you."

Ron walked through the door just as Skip hung up with Lucy. He walked briskly over to Skip's desk.

"OK, what's so important?"

"Take a look at the tubes. We've got a hell of a storm coming our way."

Ron looked in surprise.

"Oh my God. When did this start?"

"Apparently over the last 36 hours. A cold front from the Rockies and a vicious one from Canada, combined with a warm front from the Gulf, it's already taken out four towns and thousands of acres of crops ready for harvest. I've got some footage coming from Chicago. It should be here by air time."

"All right. I rearrange the rundown to put that right off the top." He left, heading immediately back to the newsroom.

Ten o'clock swung around. The theme rolled and the announcer's voice echoed, "This is the UPN30 ten o' clock report. Now here's Ron Firman and Adrian Markell."

"Good evening. Boy, have we got a story for you. Adrian, Mother Nature is tearing apart the plains like a chain saw. Let's go to Skip Mitchell who has more details."

The red light went on and Skip began his depiction of the slaughter this storm was reaping on the land. It was the worst storm ever seen. His major focus was safety procedures for when the storm hit Michigan.

"With a storm of this magnitude, do not follow the old rules of going into the basement. Local governments will be reopening the old civil defense shelters. The need for as many of these shelters will be of the utmost priority. Back to you, Adrian."

The newscast moved on as Skip walked back to his desk. The red light on his phone was blinking. It was his private line.

"Hello."

"Skip, it's Barney. Can we talk?"

"We're on the air. I'll just listen."

"I've already called Roy. I need to see you both tonight. We have a lead on

Wanda's whereabouts. Just cough once if you'll be there." He heard the muffled cough and the abrupt disconnect to know that his friend would be there. Forty-five minutes later, Mitchell was on his way down the Lodge to Downtown Police Headquarters.

The elevator door opened for him on a thirteenth floor that was dark and desolate with a dim light shining in an office at the end of the hallway. He walked and joined his partner, Roy Maxim and his friend, Barney Nicholson. They gave him a nod of acknowledgment before he sat down in one of the cushy chairs of the office.

I'll get right to the point. Two of my undercover operatives followed the ambulance that took Wanda from the apartment to somewhere in northern Oakland County. After losing them for a while, my officers were able to locate them once again, at a cabin in the Ortonville Recreation Area. Somehow though, she got away again. Right into the hands of two federal operatives. They had set up a campsite near the cabin and wound up catching their quarry. She should be arriving here any second now." The door burst open as he spoke. Wanda started to breathe a sigh of relief.

"Barney, you don't know how happy I am to see…" She stared at the back of a physique she thought she thought she recognized. When he turned around, she threw her arms around him, planting a long, passionate kiss on his lips. Undercover officers Bruce and Cindy Shavous followed her into the office, getting the nod from Barney to end the reunion.

Cindy spoke first. "Alright, Wanda, let's calm down. You're still not out of danger."

She reluctantly released her grip and sat down in the semi-circle of chairs in front of the chief's desk.

"OK, let's get down to business. Someone is up to something in my city and I plan on putting a cork in it. The Feds say TJ Marvelli is behind this and they have two of my best SWAT teams to enforce that notion. Do we have any evidence to verify their claim?"

"Ok, here's what I have. Two days ago, a very agitated woman called me from Cortez, Colorado, telling me that she was on her way to see me. She had something important to talk to me about. I picked her up at the Marvelli hangar at Parks International and immediately drove her back to my river front apartment. We were tailed by three of Marvelli's stooges, who camped outside my building and took her at the first available moment. One of them was his trusted aide, Helford, the man who was there when his father was killed in 1962. Anyway, the information that Wanda had proved invaluable.

First, TJ has been massing a cache of arms that could equip any army in the world. Cannons, half-tracks, jeeps, AK-47s, M-19s, Glock 9mm, and M-16's just to name a few. The big item here is Varan nerve gas. I discovered this when I checked out the armory on 8 Mile. His purpose with Varan is unclear. But I smell shades of WWII returning. I'll bet it has something to do with the arrival of those unexplained military vehicles yesterday."

Barney replied, " I concur with everything you said, Skip. Marvelli is making a move and I want to know how."

Roy added, " I think you should go toe to toe with the Feds. It seems like your best bet."

"He may be right," replied Skip "We should work with the Feds, but only the ones you trust."

"Let it fall on me," replied Barney. " All right. Tomorrow, ten a.m. we will meet again with the Feds in attendance. Until then, get some sleep."

Gordon Berkowitz was elected the first Jewish president in 2000. He had grown up in Oak Park, a Jewish suburb of Detroit. His father was a major car dealer and literally provided him with anything he wanted except his own attention. Gordy substituted his older brother as his father, drifting apart from his father as he matured. Politics called the young, Jewish candidate to a bright and glorious future. He became mayor of Oak Park at twenty-one. It was quickly followed by a long stint in Lansing. After twelve years, he moved to the governor's office by a landslide. So wide that a national party noticed him and convinced "Berky" to run for the Presidency. Tonight would be the worst night of his second term as president.

"Ladies and Gentleman, we have a potential crisis situation that I still cannot fathom how someone could plot to takeover a major metropolitan area, namely Detroit. I want some scenarios as to how we can stop this."

Rose Hooper of the NSA spoke first. A veteran of the Harvard JFK school of Politics, she was considered the most knowledgeable of political situations. She always began NSC meetings.

"Mr. President, we have determined that an all-out offensive is planned against Detroit. Some sixty Huey and Cobra helicopters are currently housed at Detroit City Airport. There have also been reports of illegally-procured military equipment has surfaced at three locations in Detroit. Included in this cache is one thousand canisters of the nerve gas, Varan. The purpose has yet to be determined."

Steve Marx of the FBI concurred.

"The best I can add is that Detroit PD is on the same trail as us and I recommend we pool our resources. The date of implementation is set to occur this weekend when Marvelli gets married during this Indian meeting."

"Can the CIA outfit them with special equipment, enough to thwart this effort," asked the President.

"Yes, sir, I'll send someone to Detroit tonight," added Louis Mullen of the CIA.

"And, Louise, elevate the warning level to orange. I want everyone to be prepared."

"Yes, sir," replied Louise Crelley, Homeland Security Secretary.

"This meeting is now over. Stop this madman and spare no cost. I have to give a speech there on Sunday and I want everything buttoned up by then." The Situation Room quickly emptied.

Hundreds of military units were traveling Detroit's streets. In an agreement with the vice-mayor, Marvelli Enterprises provided uniformed sentries, as they were called. They were to patrol the streets and remove any one or group from the streets and hold them till the weekend was over. The city was now losing people at the rate of twenty-thousand per day. The number was growing larger by the hour. And the populations in the salt mine, armory and the St. John warehouse grew as well. The vice-mayor had done what was expected of him. His next job was to eliminate Kirkland Asher. He drooled as he thought of the prospect of leading the tenth largest city in the country.

He walked into his apartment, being met by Maxwell, his cat. Not having seen anyone for a few days, he was very hungry and left the apartment with a very aromatic order. Skip fed his cat, refreshed his apartment and gave his cat his usual scratching on his back. As Skip turned out the lights, Maxwell cuddled with him. He thought quizzically to himself, *Is this ever going to end for us, Wanda?* With little effort, he and Max drifted off to sleep.

CHAPTER 8

The Marvelli Tower. Detroit's tallest skyscraper, was a seventy-five story icon to one man's power over the masses. The sun never set on the hub of Marvelli Enterprises as their was always a meeting going on any hour of the day. Marvelli reveled in the power and control he had over his empire. His operation was created by his father, Antonio Marvelli, Sr., the most prolific mafia kingpin in Detroit's history. In the forty plus years since his death, Tony, Jr. now controlled of ninety per cent of the businesses within the city. With an agreement his father brokered before his death, young Tony consolidated his power base, making it stronger than any other mafia family in the country. He stood at the window of the conference room on the 75th floor with a determined group of men here to discuss their future in a treacherous world. Marvelli looked at the conference table assessing every one of the participants, each an Tribal Chief of renowned distinction. His trusted four sat to either side of him; Richard Night-Owl and George Tecumseh to his left representing the eastern tribes and Daniel Running-Horse and Richard

Johnson to his right representing the western tribes. The rest sat with a sharpened intensity that reverberated throughout the room. Running Horse had just finished informing the other chiefs of the agenda. All that was left was their reply.

"So, Gentlemen, getting the people of Detroit to leave this fair city will be nothing. Our plans are bearing fruit. By Friday, this city will be ours for the taking. The land is large enough for our nations to relocate within its boundaries. By having the biggest Indian meeting here, the stage will be set for total domination of the area. Any questions?"

Marvelli spoke first.

"My brothers, this is a time that we can count many coup against our enemy. The future is in our hands to mold, my brothers. Let us join with our glorious leader to reach that goal."

Michael Gibson spoke for the Choctaw tribe.

"What guarantees can you give us that there will not be any retaliation by Washington over this."

Marvelli spoke firmly, "With our men planted firmly around the city, residents will not attempt to fight what the gods have deemed their inevitable fate. And Washington would not dare to attack with our supply of nerve gas set to explode in the most populous areas of the city."

The remaining Indian chiefs from the many nations in the United States sat spellbound with indecision as Marvelli looked on. Centuries of fear and complacency churned in their guts. The tribes of today had a good source of income with the casinos that they were permitted to run. Steady resources provided some security for each tribal member. But for some, it was just not enough. Daniel Running-Horse broke the silence and rose to speak before the meeting.

"Mr. Marvelli, your efforts to gain parity between our tribes and Washington has been commendable. I speak for the council in saying that we join you in the chance to create a new nation for our people. Your mission will reestablish our dignity. Our full support is with you."

All eyes turned to the tall, bronze muscular man who stood looking out the massive window wall onto Comerica Park. No one could see the sinister smile that appeared across his face. A glow of achievement grew within his bosom. His day had arrived.

"Alright, gentlemen. I am glad to finally have everyone on board. My father would be proud of our efforts. A toast to his memory." Everyone raised their champagne glasses as Marvelli led the toast.

"May the gods provide us with the guidance necessary to complete our task in the memory of my father. Let us bring glory to everyone involved." Glasses were raised and the toast completed.

"The Pow-Wow will start at Joe Louis Arena in two days. As your people arrive, please instruct them as to their duties during Operation Move Out. That will be all." Everyone rose silently and filed out of the conference room. Marvelli looked at Running Horse and Johnson, issuing final commands.

"Saturday, we will start our air attack at 1600 hours. Make sure your captain is prepared. Dan, speed up the forces that will round citizens this week. I want elimination to start immediately."

"Yes, sir." Their unified response echoed as they turned and left the room.

The Penobscot Building ranks as one of the city's prominent structures of the 20th century. For years, it stood alone as the premier skyscraper of Detroit's skyline. It has been the home of many prominent attorneys, local corporations and at one time, the main stock exchange for the Midwest which refused to acknowledge that the country was in a depression until January,1930, when it was forced to fold. The city and state then joined the country in their woeful predicament. Today, the skyscraper boasts almost total occupancy, everything from radio stations to a few local detective agencies.

Sally Conaway sat working at her desk in the corner office of the M and M Detective Agency. It faced Griswold Boulevard, an avenue flowing with the activity from a newly revitalized downtown. She was putting the finishing touches on the Wilsup file, laughing hysterically as she transcribed Skip's notes. Her bosses, Skip Mitchell and Roy Maxim, were good at their job, but they were not the neatest.Transcribing Skip's notes was always a challenge for her. Their reputation as bounty hunters was well known. Detroit Police always counted on them to find felons known to stay underground. The police files were overwhelming the agency and Sally had already made inquiries as to larger space. As she entered Mitchell's office, Sally turned on the light to make one final check. She looked around carefully, turning off the lights and went to Maxim's office. A thud came from behind the door. Sally stopped in her tracks. Something moved and then suddenly disappeared. She opened the door, finding Maxim's office totally in disarray. Every file cabinet was rummaged through as was his desk and safe. Laying on the floor with a major gash to his head was Maxim She screamed and ran to her desk to call 911.

Skip walked in to a sea of investigators examining Maxim's office. Detroit's crime lab dusted the place for prints while detectives interrogated Sally. Skip saw Lt. Max Lindstrom coordinating the investigation and walked across the anteroom towards him.

"Well, Max, what's the word."

"This was a professional job, Skip. Somebody came in here looking for something specific but got spooked when Sally screamed. They left out the window before being spotted. But they left this." He handed Mitchell something that looked like an ID wallet. He opened it up a and looked at the picture and recognized it right away. It was his old buddy, Stu Wilson of the CIA. He looked at Max and asked, "Does Barney know?"

"Yeah. And he is steaming mad. When I last talked to him, he was deep in discussions with Washington about what's going on here. Oh, by the way. You're due at a meeting in his office in,"(he casually looked at his watch)"about five minutes from now." Skip turned and sprinted out the office door, running down the two flights of stairs, into Skip's 1970 Mustang Boss 350 parked on Griswold, and sped off to police headquarters. His drive to 1300 Beaubien was clearly short and very uneventful. Two gorgeous brunettes eyed him as he parked his car on Monroe and walked to police headquarters. He blew them a kiss as he ran up the stairs.

He was escorted into a very modest office occupied by the most respected chief in the city's history. Once inside the foyer, the innate artistry of the Albert Kahn designed building stood out with the architectural features that ordained the columns that circled the office. The connecting walls between the columns were of a dull gray, simple but carried a strong message of solidarity. The conference table sat in the front half of the office while the chief's desk sat along back wall under a long painting of Detroit by Diego Rivera shouldered by two 10' by 12' windows looking out at Windsor, Ontario. Detroit's dynamic P.I. was ushered into a meeting of suit-clad operatives and Chief Barney Nicholson.

"Nice of you to show up!"

"Would have been here sooner but Roy lost the tickets."

"Well, just sit down and let make some introductions." Barney looked to his left.

"You already know the feds that we deal with. The other members here are from Washington. To my left are Steven Marx of the FBI and Louise Crelly of the Home Security Agency. On my right is Louis Mullen of the CIA and Rose Hooper of the NSA. The President has sent them to bring us up to speed with what is happening here. Who would like to start?"

Director Mullen opened, "Mitchell, you have been asked here because of a very high recommendation. Here is the low down as we have know it. Marvelli Enterprises has been funding a build-up of arms with help from every Native American nation in this country. This big meeting is intended to be a ruse, while they facilitate a plan to remove every resident from the city. He has hundreds of Indian troops holed up at three locations; The Eight Mile Armory in Oak Park, the Detroit Salt Mine complex and three warehouses across from St. John's Hospital. We also know that he permeated a large quantity of the nerve gas, Varan, which we expect to see used within the next few days. This gas has the ability to incapacitate an adult within 15 seconds and kill in 25 seconds. Children are killed instantly. Our problem is that we do not have any idea what he is going to do with all of his weapons. That is where you come in."

"How?" Mitchell asked.

"You will be working with an agent that is well placed in the organization. They will have homing device so that a rescue attempt can be made if necessary. Tomorrow at 6 A.M., you will go to the basement delivery area of the old Book Cadillac Hotel and meet up with my man, Chief, who will equip you with state of the art tools to speed up your search. Steve?" The FBI Director looked at the duo with a stone face.

"I need not remind you the need for perfection on this mission. I have grave reservations about you, but I will hold judgement until the results are in. The President is concerned about this threat against the nation, especially where the Indians are involved. Mitchell, you will go undercover for the next few days. Stay in contact with us 24/7. Your instructions will arrive tomorrow. Contact will be made in the early A.M." Skip rose from the table and quickly left the room His gut told him that Tony had Wanda sucked in up to her pretty little neck.

Buzzing down I-75 at a bristling pace, the two undercover cops were completing their return of their precious passenger to Detroit. Wanda had slipped into semi-consciousness in the back seat the minute they hit the freeway near Pontiac. Her ears tingled as she listened to a conversation in the front seat of the car.

"In just a few short hours, we be on a plane for the Azores a very rich couple, tripling our wealth more than we could ever imagine," said Cindy.

"Yeah. We'll fly in there with our new identities that have been promised and build a whole new life away from this hell hole," her partner replied.

"For a city to pay one million dollars just to turn over a popular singer, she must have done something major to warrant this much interest," Bruce said. Cindy glared at him with a quizzical look.

"We are not to judge. Ours is only to perform our assignment and accept payment. Nothing more. We were already warned about any assumptions that we might make would be hazardous to our health. So shut up!"

Bruce closed his mouth tightly in a pout and turned his head back to the road ahead. Wanda cautiously opening her eyes to keep track of the landmarks as her captors traveled down the Chrysler freeway to her eventual destination. The Grand Boulevard sign sailed past, as did the Wayne State/ Warren Avenue and Mack Avenue signs. Somewhere downtown was to be the eventual destination she thought. The car slid off the freeway onto Lafayette Avenue, snaking through Greek town and Foxtown to reach the tallest building in the city. The car made a quick turn into the underground parking garage and pulled up in front of the elevator with a big Marvelli "M" on the door. He will stop at nothing she thought as her captors carried her to the lift and pressed the button for the 75th floor.

Vice Mayor Randy Meashon paced frantically across the thick, plush carpet of T.J. Marvelli's office. His bribed cops should have been here over an hour ago. Patience was the least of Meashon's virtues. His co-workers at City Hall considered him a loose cannon. His constant tantrums at council meetings, staff meetings and private meetings with the mayor would not help him win the Nobel prize. He never accepted any criticism well, leaving co-workers always walking on eggshells.

The door to the office burst open and the two cops dragged Wanda's sagging body, throwing her on the floor with a loud thud. The vice-mayor turned in character and faced the new arrivals.

"Well, it's about time. I expected you an hour ago. And what's wrong with her."

"She's been asleep since we left. She should wake up with a little nudge." Bruce proceeded to wake Wanda with his foot.

"Cut it out. I'm awake and I don't like being kicked." Wanda slowly pushed herself to her hands and knees before standing to face her new captor.

"And just who the hell are you? And where's Tony?" she exclaimed.

"Since you are obviously ignorant about city government, let me introduce myself. Randy Meashon, Vice-Mayor of Detroit. Mr. Marvelli is waiting for you down the hall. Come with me."

"What about our payment?" asked Cindy and Bruce in unison.

"Just wait right here. Someone will be here momentarily." Meashon shoved Wanda through the door closing it behind them. The couple paced nervously in front of plate glass window that faced the view of the river and Windsor, Ontario. Two men entered the room turning to face the other occupants. All eyes focused on each other as they waited for someone to speak. Finally, the silence broke.

"We have your money." His partner and he reached into their coats and both pulled out their 9mm Glocks and aimed them at the unsuspecting officers. The rapid discharge of the guns and the breaking of glass from the shells set the stage. The impact of the bullets on the two unsuspecting officers hurled them back towards the glass and crashing 75 floors to their death on the plaza below. Faint screams were heard from the ground below as the two assassins left the office. They climbed onto one of the elevators as police and paramedics arrived on the scene below. The clock moved closer to their date with destiny.

The Book Cadillac Hotel on Washington Boulevard bustled with activity as construction engineers rebuilt the forty year old structure from the inside out. Purchased by the Radisson Company, the hotel was being reconstructed to complete the hotel capacity the city promised The Democratic Party for their national convention in 2008, the city's first successful bid since the 1980 Republican Convention.

A solitary man walked around to the alley, eventually to the loading dock. A ramp leading to an underground garage sat nearby and the man walked right down to the overhead door. A small entry door was cut into the center of the overhead to allow single entry. He walked to the door and knocked twice. Like the speakeasies of the 1920s, a small flap opened. Two beady eyes peered out at the man and closed it quickly. The door opened and he was rushed inside.

"You must be Mitchell. We've been expecting you. Follow me."

Skip walked through what looked like a spy's Disneyland. Every covert contraption he had ever dreamed about was being developed- Rocket cigarettes, explosive carrying belts, laser watches and more. In the center of the room was a new Ford T-Bird. The noticeable icon of activity centered around what looked like an ejection seat like 007. A man with graying hair crossed right into his path, stopping him in his tracks.

"It's about time, Mitchell. I expected you over an hour ago. Follow me and we'll bring you up to speed." They walked through a mixture of explosive devices and fast-acting weapons greater than he had ever seen. Mitchell felt like he had finally raided the cookie jar. He snapped back to reality as they stopped before a rack of shoes.

"What size do you take?" asked the Chief.

"Nine and a half D," he replied. Reaching deep into the rack, the Chief pulled out a very stylish pair of shoes.

"This is your homing device we will be tracking you with."

Skip looked at him with astonishment.

"The device is wrapped in the laces of these shoes. The CIA has developed this as an answer to the box-like devices that MI-6 swore by for years. I hope you like the color."

Skip cringed at the two-tone shoes. He exchanged them for a pair of black patent leathers much to the chagrin of his guide. Chief frowned and moved on. Skip was amazed by the technology developing before his eyes. Flying trays that decapitate their victims, buzz-saw umbrellas and the sporty 2-seat Ford T-Bird. Chief noticed his eyes were glued on the hardtop and slowly moved towards it.

"I see you are an aficionado of good autos. Let me show you your car for the next few days. This model contains the same equipment that MI6 programs into their cars plus a few extras.

"First, you will have GPS tracking capability, instead of the usual radar. The homing device that will be in the vehicles you're tracking will be visible with this system. There are also two mini SAM heat seeking missiles behind the parking lights with warheads strong enough to knock out a city block. And yes, you will get a passenger ejector seat."

Mitchell stood stone-faced as he went on.

"Finally, we have installed a cache of grenades and land mines stored in a false floor in the trunk. The switch is on the instrument panel right here. Here is your Biretta,, your laser Rolex and a CO2 propelled line inside this belt. Now swallow this capsule and we can start tracking you as you leave."

With no questions, Skip popped the pill, put on the holster with his new gun and took off from the underground garage. The thousands of workers manned the floors above while they restored the old hotel to its once great French splendor. No one noticed as the shiny red T-Bird turned down the alley. A homeless man watched as Skip pulled onto Michigan Avenue. He talked to his glove as the car sped away. He turned and continued his trek elsewhere.

CHAPTER 9

Tony stood in the corner with a group of men, catching Wanda's eye as Meashon ushered her in very brusquely. The antiquated monstrosity he held in a case caught her eye. It looked like a dried up plant with two deep blue stones glued to it. It looked like the turquoise stones she saw when Wanda and Tony went shopping near Cortez. He turned towards her, anger filling his eyes as he walked closer. POW ! His fist connected with her right jaw sending her sprawling to the floor. Dazed and angry, she glared up at him.

"What the hell was that for!"demanded Wanda.

"No possession of mine just takes off for a jaunt cross country to see her ex and expect me to take it lightly, bitch. What did you tell that asshole? Tell me now!"

"Why should I tell you, you'd just kill me. I'm dead no matter which way I go. Besides, since when did I become a possession of yours. I'm a person, not a toy."

Tony was caught of guard. Her career was his meal ticket and he knew it. Her concert and nightclub revenues were laundered through banks in Mexico City, funneled back to the United States and distributed to his underworld empire. The arms he had purchased, the drugs he shipped all over the states that fattened his pockets were all thanks to her. A few months ago, she stumbled across an open telegram on the foyer table. It said money transfers to Mexico City were complete and the shipment was ready for the trip back.

When crates arrived from Mexico, she opened one while everyone was away from the ranch. Inside, under coffee grounds was the bulk of her last nationwide concert tour, all in unmarked bills. Wanda closed the crate quickly and shied away from Tony as much as she could, looking for her chance to slip away from his vice-like grip. Helford, his trusted aide, was sent back to watch over her while he was away. Marvelli covered all the bases his world revolved on. Patience became her norm in her drive for freedom

Two tractor trailers eased into the loading dock at the Detroit Institute of Arts under many watchful eyes. Back just a few hours from weeks on the Colorado plateau, Dr. Amy Mitchell stood beside her long-lost brother, carefully documenting the end results of their expedition. Crate after crate rolled off the trucks, placed in special displays stands for the opening the next day in the North American Hall of the institute Her caravan pushed the limit to get home to showcase the exhibit on time. The driver jumped out of the cab and ran straight up the ramp into Amy's waiting arms. She planted a passionate kiss on his surprised lips.

"I'll drive trucks for you more often if that's gonna be my payment," said Tim Moran.

"Well, if you like that, just wait till you see what's planned for you tonight at my place."

The hours passed by quickly as forklift after forklift unloaded each new treasure of the ancient Anazasi expedition. Amy, Tim and Drew were diligently directing the dock workers, preparing for the next day, that no one noticed a tall man dressed in black leather, come up behind them from the loading dock.

"I heard you had some fireworks on your trip," said the mystery man. A startled Amy whisked around to stare into a very familiar face.

"Daddy!" she cried, "what are you doing here?" She threw her arms around Skip, squeezing the air right out of him. As she released him, his eye noticed Drew standing well off to the side of the dock.

"Can that be Drew?" he asked.

"Yes it is. He worked with us for the whole expedition, but he only revealed himself a few days ago. He has been living on the Ute reservation since he ran away. The tribe took him in, sheltered him and taught him their ways. I might never have realized that it was him if he hadn't said anything. Especially after that ceremonial headdress was stolen."

"Why don't you have Tim finish up while you and Drew come with me so we can talk." Amy conferred with Tim as Skip took Drew across the dock to the supervisor"s office. Amy followed not far behind.

"I want to know everything you can tell me about this headdress that was stolen. Do not leave out any details." He sat down behind the desk waiting for one of them to speak.

Looking at his sister, Drew recalled all the reasons why he ran away. The turmoil was now the past. He took a giant leap of faith, detailing everything to his father. Mitchell sat spellbound as his son detailed the history of the ancient ones. When Drew finished, Amy spoke, "And Grandpa always told me stories that this headdress had something to do with our family."

Skip sat there, somewhat stunned by what he had just heard.

"So this thing can make anyone who wears it invulnerable. I know a lot of people who would love to have it. Right now, the objective is to find it. The Feds believe it is somewhere in this city connected to the American Indian convention happening this weekend. This is more than just coincidence."

Skip stared directly at Drew as he spoke watching for a reaction. Suddenly, the rapid fire of M1 carbines broke the quiet of the loading dock.

"Get down!" Skip yelled to his two kids as other workers scattered throughout the hallways, to get behind the desk. He quickly turned off the lights and cocked his Biretta. Ready to take on all takers, he cautiously moved towards the window to survey the scene. A dozen men in battle fatigues were lining all workers against the wall, searching them and escorting them to a waiting truck outside the building for transport. Skip watched with peaked interest as the squad ushered the dock workers into their transport to a "gathering place"as they were being called. He waited until the dock had cleared and told Amy to go somewhere safe. Drew, on the other hand, insisted on going with his father.

"I recognized some of those soldiers, sir. I could be of help." Skip reluctantly agreed and they skirted quickly down the dock to his waiting T-Bird. They caught up with the truck at John R and Warren slipping back to a four car length distance as they turned onto Jefferson.

Meashon was livid. Tony Marvelli was cleaning out Detroit neighborhoods like a vacuum. Over a third of the city was now a ghost town and no one seemed wiser to the

situation. The Indian troops had not encountered any problems with the roundup. Citizens left their homes quietly under the guise of protection from an approaching storm front coming west from the Mississippi, heading towards the city. Mayor Asher was asking questions at the council meeting this morning, very pointed questions about the appearance of recently abandoned buildings on the outskirts of the city. People were disappearing from neighborhoods without a trace. Police were baffled. The chief was up in arms because of the lack of clues. And most troubling of all for the vice mayor was that it was happening without his direction, which was promised to him by Marvelli as his stepping stone to becoming a leader in the Marvelli organization. Randy drooled over the endless possibilities he wanted to accomplish in a position of power. Meashon was known as an unscrupulous politician, unafraid to use dirty tricks to get his way while the public stayed ignorant of his methods. Today, though, he knew he was undermined by Tony in this situation and left to shoulder the responsibility. He sat back in his chair as the mayor finished his remarks.

"As I said, we have no clues as to the disappearance of nearly 40% of our population. Police are checking out possibilities of gangs on the warpath. Other than that, the chief may have something to add."

Barney Nicholson sat in the back of the room, praying that he would not have to speak before the council. His ulcers churned as he sat down in front of his captive audience.

"The mayor is right. We have checked out every possible lead. Federal agencies are also working on the case. The department has reorganized into two 12 hour shifts to facilitate maximum manpower during the upcoming convention and this ongoing crises. Mr. Mayor?"

"Thank you, Chief. Madam President, the administration has presented its case. I will leave the vice mayor to continue discussions with the council while I return to my duties. Let's go, Chief." Nicholson and the mayor quickly left the room as the council continued debate on the topic. They each jumped on different elevators going different ways.

The transport truck slid into the warehouse across from St. John's Hospital very quietly without anyone noticing. Skip and Drew saw them turn, parking their car on Moross and crossed stealthily to the warehouse. As they passed the alley, Skip heard the cries of little children, somewhat muffled, coming from an open garage door. Drew signaled towards the side of the building holding his hands together. Skip jumped up to the window and was aghast. In front of him were 50 canisters of Varan nerve gas all joined together to the sprinkler system in the main room of the warehouse. Skip saw several families with welts and bruises from apparently being beaten with the butt end of rifles. The sight reminded him of the Nazi concentration camps of World War II. The scenario was the same, only the players had changed.

Drew led Skip down the alley to the only open door. Clinging close to the wall, they slid down the docking bay out of sight from the rest of the building. Skip slowly raised his head over the edge of the floor to check out their location. Above the main floor were two catwalks hanging about fifty feet from the ceiling. The rusty supports and the deteriorating concrete told him that this place would not be safe if those nerve gas canisters ever got open. Windows were covered over in many cases with just plywood to keep snoopers away from the operation. Five guards armed with AK-47 rifles stood above the makeshift cage that contained the families. Another group, armed with AK-47's, walked around the main floor, keeping watch of the building perimeter. To the far left of the building sat what looked like a command post as two men stood hovering over something that he suspected were plans of something. Skip crawled out of the docking bay, scurrying towards a stack of boxes on the north side of the building. Drew flew right behind him a few seconds later. He tapped Skip on the shoulder and made a signal for him to stay put while he crept towards the office to find out what was going on. Skip objected but Drew took off anyway. He popped up behind the window of the office before anyone had a chance to notice him. Five minutes later, he reported back to Skip what he overheard in the office.

"The men in the office were talking about some operation. They said it is going along smoothly and should have their area completed by 1600 hours tomorrow. At that point, all of the troops will leave and the nerve gas will be turned on, killing everyone inside and making this building unusable for ten years. There was also something about other locations going smoothly too. Everything is set to cap off at the same time Sunday when the President speaks to the convention."

Skip stood frozen in his tracks as he listened to Drew's wild story. He looked around the boxes and saw that there were no guards looking their way.

"We have to get these people out of here right now. They are in danger if they stay here." They hurried towards the docking bay and jumped towards the door.

Two guards from the catwalks saw them and hollered, "STOP!"

Bullets began to fly towards the overhead door. They ricocheted off walls, barely missing Skip and Drew by inches. Drew took out two knifes and picked the two off dead center in the chest. Both men dropped like flies. Skip took his Biretta and pumped bullets towards the catwalks. The guards, caught by surprise, dropped where they stood, blood slowly oozing out of their wounds.

Skip motioned to Drew, "Go to the cage and release those people."

Drew flew over the floor in seconds, frantically working on the lock The two men from the office reached the floor, M1 carbines blazing away. Mitchell rolled onto the floor, firing from a prone position nailing the other two guards in the knees. Drew got to the cage door and beat the lock off the door, freeing the captive families. Drew grabbed an AK47 from one of the dead guards and began firing at the oncoming guards as the captive families escaped. Skip called for him to get out since the families were all outside the building. With one final burst, Drew sailed out the open door, running down the alley to their car and jumped in, speeding off towards downtown.

Skip was sweating buckets as they sped down towards Jefferson.

"Let's make a quick stop. I need to see somebody."

The main dining room was darker than normal this time of the afternoon. Mitchell stood at the entrance of the room carefully scanning the shadows looking for something or someone. Off to the right, his eye caught a slight of hand moving to light a cigar. Skip told Drew to stay put as he walked to the far side of the dining room. A chair was pulled out for him as he approached the table. The other occupant took a puff of his cigar and blew smoke right in his face. Mitchell sat, unflinching, as the obnoxious order swept past him.

"Still haven't changed after all those years in the slammer, have ya, Sammie G."

"It's always good to see you too, Mitchell. I know you didn't come to talk about old times. What's Marvelli done now?"

"It's more what his dad did forty years ago on his yacht. I thought you would enjoy filling me in on all the juicy details,"added Mitchell.

"Well, it's like this. Why should I lift a finger to help the man that got me put away. This information will cost you, big time."

Skip looked at the outlined face sitting across from him and said, "No price you could set would match the price of keeping my city alive. So, just spill the beans and I'll be on my way."

The two goons on either side of Sammie G began to reach for the weapons. Their boss raised his hands to stop them. He leaned forward towards the lit candle in the center of the table. Skip could finally make out the features of Sammie's ugly face.

"OK, I'll tell you. But only if you promise to put Marvelli away once and for all. He's been a thorn in my side ever since his dad died and I want him gone."

"I'll make that a high priority," said Mitchell.

"TJ's dad met with someone from the administrations of both the mayor and the president that year. They wanted to stem the tide of people leaving for the suburbs. Detroit had already lost 500,000 residents in the late fifties and the mayor didn't want to lose any more of his tax base. So they basically gave away the store. Marvelli was made head of a special committee to strengthen the city's industrial base, bringing in other manufacturers than just the auto companies. It made him in control of the city with the government nothing but a puppet to him. It is rumored that the CIA or one of the New York families put a hit on TJ and set up the apparent capsizing of the Montrose by that tug. To this day, no one knows the answer to that question."

"How does Tony fit into all this?" asked Skip.

"Young Tony, with the help of that guy Helford, searched the river to find the remains of the body. They supposedly came away with the agreement. Since that day, he has been at a frantic pace building his empire to be the richest ever in the Midwest. He even laundered Wanda's money to buy drugs and guns for some covert operation he has planned. That's all I know." Mitchell rose from the table and walked out to the parking lot. Drew noticed him walking towards the car looking like his world had just caved in.

"Well?" he asked.

"My gut says this is going to be worse than they thought. We have work to do. Let's go. Your mother is in grave danger." Both jumped in the T-Bird and sped off towards Michigan Avenue.

Seria Perez walked through her old neighborhoods now abandoned and desolate like much of the inner city. Since the explosion that killed her brother, she had been walking around in daze, knowing that her revenge will be carried out on whoever killed her brother, George. The man in the limo assured her that her chance was coming soon. But that was not enough for her. She turned the corner and was walking towards the ruins of the terminal. A long black limo crept up beside her, as quiet as a mouse. A passenger door opened and a long arm grabbed her dragging her inside the limo. As the door shut, the driver sped up and headed towards downtown.

CHAPTER 10

"Tony Marvelli, you are crazy. You order your little boy toys kidnap me twice in the last couple of years. You steal money from me to fund this little scheme of yours. And now you expect me to marry you on Sunday. I think somebody puts something extra in your corn flakes every morning." Wanda's eyes were hot with anger as she stared him down, waiting a reply. Tony stood there like a rock, not moving a muscle while he planned his reaction to her statement.

"Wanda my dear, I never said anything about marrying you. Tell me where did you get your information." A chill went down her spine as she worked on a proper reply to cover her fears.

"It was those two idiots who brought me here. They just didn't know how to keep their traps shut. By the way, I hope you paid them off well? I know they had big plans."

"They took a leap of faith and are now resting comfortably."

"You bastard! I'll bet you killed them!"

"Let's say that they tried to fly without wings."

"You must have the same planned for me. Will it be quick and easy or slow and torturous. Come on, stud, enquiring minds want to know."

"Your fate is undecided as of yet. For now, be thankful that you will live to be married again for life, dear Wanda." Tony picked up the air-tight case and punched the intercom right beside it.

"Come in, it's time to go." There was no reply. The doors to Marvelli's office burst open and Helford stepped forward with two goons right on his heels.

"Take her to the shipyard. I want her secure until day after tomorrow. Keep round the clock guards on her. If she tries anything, shoot to kill. Understood?" His long time friend and valet, Helford, acknowledged The two guards grabbed Wanda. She kicked Helford hard in the knee, making him cry out. Tony came over and slapped her, giving her an excuse to fake unconsciousness. The guards tied her up and dragged her to the elevator with Helford right behind them.

The trip to the shipyard was short, just a few minutes up Jefferson. Three state of the art dry docks were completing the hulls of two new cutters for the Coast Guard and a new super freighter for King Oil out of Houston. Materials for the upper super structure of each ship were carefully placed within reach of the many cranes around each dock. Helford ordered the limo to park at the freighter's dock, believing it was the most secure of all.

"Put her down in the bottom of the hull and remove the ramp. That should keep her occupied until Sunday," Helford ordered. He smiled as Wanda was tossed in the keel of the ship with the two sides of the hull surrounding her. She was too good of a person to receive the fate that was planned for her, he thought. She deserved better.

Rosa Parks Boulevard was once known as 12th Street, the hotbed of the 1967 riots that tore the city apart. Some rebuilding took place over the next decade, but not enough to make a significant dent into the damaged area. Unemployment still runs high with men in their teens and early twenties. Roving bands of gangs now roamed the streets enforcing protection payments from business owners putting some of them into bankruptcy from the severe loss of income. Many lots have stayed abandoned with no help of rebuilding in sight because of these gangs. It became an inevitable life for many of Detroit's youth. Spud Jones was part of that crowd.

On a hot night in July, his gang, the Young Knives were doing their patrols along Grand River and Rosa Parks when they spotted two army transports with soldiers forcing people from their homes and loading them into the trucks. These men all had one identifiable characteristic, they all had rapid-fire M16 rifles. Spud signaled to his boys to spread out and prepare to surprise these "soldiers" from their "roundup." A red T-Bird pulled in front of them slowing their progress.

"Yo, you're holding me up, man. Get the hell out of my way," said Jones.

"You're not going anywhere, Spud, not until you tell me what you are doing." Jones looked at him, recognizing the voice.

"Oh, the weatherman. Out trying to fight street battles again?"

"This one may be more serious than you and I have ever seen. There is a rumor that someone wants to take over this city. I've want to find out who and what is behind this. But I am seeking help. With your clout in the neighborhoods, we might stop this."

"You want me and my boys to help you honkies after all the hell you whites have put us through for years. Why should we help you now?"

"Someone needs to take a stand to get on the right road. Think you can handle the challenge?" The leader of the Young Knives looked at the others around him and they all nodded in agreement. Jones mulled over their possibilities.

"OK, Rainman, what do we do." Rainman was Skip's nickname from his day job.

"First, contact other gangs in the city. Tell them that someone is trying to kill this city. Stop anyone forcing people from their homes without getting killed themselves and report what they see to the chief of police right away. Any questions?"

Spud queried his gang, all nodding in agreement.

"The only thing I ask is can we jump these guys and take their guns?"

Drew answered him, "All of these men are experts in Indian fighting so to speak. If you do subdue them, turn over the weapons to the police as soon as possible. They will cause havoc in the wrong hands. Be careful."

"One thing further, Spud, all of these people are suspected to be part of this conference that starts today at four pm. It is apparently been well-funded and well-planned. Gather as much information that you can before noon tomorrow. I will handle the rest. Well, what are you waiting for. You've got a job now, go do it!"

The gang dispersed, heading straight up the street towards the unsuspecting trucks. Skip had worked with these kids before and had full confidence in them. He laughed at the thought of Barney's reaction when the calls started coming in.

On the other side of town, the newsroom at WGCB was buzzing with excitement. Crews were dispatched to search for missing residents. The continuing search for the rogue helicopter that destroyed the old station and the oncoming severe weather expected in twenty-four hours were filling the bill for the entire newscast. Bob Losin, news director, stood at the assignment desk, frantically moving his remote trucks from one location to another. *God,* he thought, *if they would only give me two more trucks, I'd be in seventh heaven.* But fantasy did not match with the reality of news. His people will earn something special after this mess was over.

Ron Firman sat thoroughly engrossed in his script on the severe weather on his computer that he was startled when his phone rang.

"Where's Mitchell?!" a voice said.

"Skip's on a medical leave right now. Is there something I can help you with?" Ron covered since he knew Skip was only on a personal leave, due back in four days. The throaty voice struck up his tune again.

"He is looking in the wrong area. Send him to City Airport and the Salt Mines. His answers are there. Transportation is waiting at Grosse Ile Airport." A loud click came from the other end of the phone as Ron punched Skip's pager number. Two minutes later, Skip called back on his private line.

"What's the matter, pal, lonely without me?" Skip said affectionately. Ron had been there for him through thick and thin. If there was one person in the world he could truly trust, it was Ron Firman.

"I just got a strange call from an anonymous source. They said you are looking in the wrong area. You need to head to the Salt Mines and City Airport. Also, something about transportation is waiting for you at Grosse Ile Airport. What do you make of it?" Ron paused awaiting Mitchell's response.

"Apparently, someone on the inside is having second thoughts. I'll call you later." Mitchell pocketed his cell phone and turned to Drew.

"When was the last time you took off from an airport?"

He floored the T-Bird down Jefferson towards the Grosse Ile Bridge, pistons churning like a stampede of Clydesdales pulling the Budweiser wagon. The twenty minute ride to the bridge went by quickly. A right onto River Road on Grosse Ile south towards the airport was accomplished without any effort. They followed the river down to Rea Road which led them straight to the tarmac at the airport. Skip instinctively hid behind the first building and he and Drew jumped out of the car slowly heading towards the far hangars at the south end of the island. With pistols drawn, Skip and Drew slithered from behind boxes and oil drums scattered throughout the hangar area. Slipping behind hangar #7, Drew opened the door and led his dad into the hangar. Skip stopped dead in his tracks. There, before him, was the rogue Cobra helicopter, thoroughly secured from the outside world. But apparently not good enough.

Drew ran towards the front of the hangar. He looked out one of the faded windows and saw three guards dressed in the same fatigues that the other Indian militia were wearing in the city. He slipped back to where Skip was hiding at the rear of the hangar.

"There are only three guards in front of this hangar. My plan is simple. We get the hangar doors open by using the automatic controls near the right side of the hangar. While the doors are opening, you and I will climb into the cockpit of the helicopter and prepare to steal it from these scum bags."

Skip looked at him with puzzlement. "I suppose you know how to fly that thing!"

Drew smiled. "The Great Spirit guides me through anything. You'll see. Just get in the back."

Skip carefully raised the side of the door, crawling into the rear seat. Drew slipped over to the door controls and pushed the open button. The huge door walls opened slowly but surprisingly quiet. Minutes later, the doors were completely open with the guards none the wiser. Drew slipped into the pilot's seat, studying the operation panels with the zest of a rookie. When the doors finally stopped, he said a prayer to his Great Spirit and flipped the switch. The overhead blades began to rotate with increasing speed. The guards were now aware of someone in the hangar and turned towards the revitalized chopper. Bullets began to fly freely at the two occupants in the cockpit. They bounced off the glass like rubber. Cockpit glass was bulletproof. This great spirit stuff must really work, Mitchell thought. Drew took the yoke and tilted it backward, causing the Cobra to rise off the ground. Once at a decent level, he tilted it forward and ran right over the three guards, who kept firing wildly as they laid on their backs. Only a few stray bullet holes pierced the rear fuselage leaving the gas tank unscathed.

"Well, what would you like for an encore?" asked Drew.

"Just get me a line to Selfridge. We need some help," said Mitchell.

Drew dialed up the military channel like a professional. Everything he had done was surprising his dad. Unpredictable just like his mother thought Skip. Just then, General Abraham came on the line. He had been the base commander at Selfridge for the last five years.

"Well, Mr. Mitchell. Why are you on a classified channel?"

"General, do you still have that helicopter gun squad at your base."

"Why, yes."

"General, why have reason to believe that there is a squadron of helicopters at City Airport that may have a stash of VARAN nerve gas on site. My authority to contact you comes from very high in the administration. We are on the way to the airport now. Join us when you clear things up. Your gun ships will be needed. These people are believed to be armed and dangerous." He cut off communications before the general's response.

The Cobra accelerated over the wooded neighborhoods of Grosse Ile, speeding up the river towards the Ambassador Bridge. Within minutes, they had passed under the bridge and came up parallel to the Cobo Convention Center. Helicopters from two TV stations were now in pursuit about a mile and a half to the rear. Drew increased speed, sliding over the river bank towards Gratiot Avenue. Mitchell looked towards the Marvelli Shipyards and saw suspicious activity. He made a mental note to check it out after this airport mess was wrapped up.

Drew flew the Cobra attack copter across Gratiot, aiming straight for the City Airport tower. As they got closer and closer to the tower, Mitchell's heart kept beating faster and faster. Finally, he banked left towards the hangars at the south end of the field. Airport security cars could be heard below, with sirens blaring, following closely behind them. They increased their speed as they swung over the hangars searching for something, one thing that would pop out loudly with a clue to this mess. Skip finally said, "Set down by the Marvelli hangar. We can start there."

The doors to the hangar began to open as they approached from the south. Blades from the two helicopters just behind the doors were almost at full power by the time the doors were fully opened. They sailed out of their confinement straight for the oncoming Cobra. Drew performed evasive maneuvers as the agile opponents strafed them with their machine guns. He pulled the stick back, throwing the copter into a climb. A yank to the left and he was right behind them.

"All right, Dad, you got the firing controls. Let 'em have it."

Mitchell frantically searched for the controls to disable the attacking Cobras. But he was not quick enough. The two copters regrouped and came straight for them. Fear began to engulf them. They had finally come to the end of the road. At least he got to see his baby boy again, thought Skip. Suddenly, a loud thunder began to approach from the north. The sky was clear but

Michigan was known for weird weather. More helicopters emerged from the hangar and began to surround the defenseless helicopter.

Drew shouted suddenly, "Look, the cavalry's here." Skip looked up and saw dozens of Hueys and Cobras descending on the enlarging entourage below. The General had come through. The calvary was here. The first few Hueys began to strafe the Cobras below. The lead Cobra suddenly stopped and issued a warning to the others below.

"This is the Air National Guard. You are to cease and desist. Stand down now or prepare to be shot down permanently."

The few outer helicopters began to set down, but the core ones would not budge. The Cobra AZK's fired on the remaining four, striking them all in the tail. The attack squadron converged on the now damaged attackers forcing them to land. The squadron leader landed beside them and jumped out from his Huey to control the situation. Skip smiled when he saw who it was. His older son, Ray, was leading this company. Drew set their Cobra down in the circle of enemies and opened up the cockpit. They jumped out, running over to the soldiers as they rounded up the renegade Indians. Ray met them halfway on the tarmac.

"We'll get these guys rounded up and take them back to the base." Ray looked at Drew, but didn't recognize his long lost brother.

"Listen, bring their captain over here. I want to talk to him." Ray signaled three members of his squad to bring the leader, Captain Ron Brewer.

"My God, man. What in blazes are you trying to do? Why do you have all these canisters hooked up to your helicopters?" Mitchell asked.

"That answer is yours to figure out. Mine is stay loyal to my brothers and right the wrongs committed against my people."

Skip looked at his impassive stone face, realizing another alternative is needed. He turned to Ray and Drew to talk privately away from the crowd. A few seconds later. Ray Mitchell emerged from the meeting.

"All right, men. We have some work to do. Get these birds back in the nest, ours too. Mr. Brewer, you come with me. The general has some questions for you."

Skip turned and grabbed Drew, running quickly back to their Cobra.

"Get this thing back in the air. There is something going on at the shipyard that needs my attention." They lifted off and glided carefully towards the shipyard.

The captain at the Salt Mine walked across the catwalk, viewing his captives much like the men of the Gestapo death camps of World War II. Families of all shapes and sizes were huddled into a fenced off area well within the mine itself. Suddenly, the phone rang. The captain picked it up and listened carefully. His face grew as pale as dust as he placed the receiver back in its cradle. He looked up at his men standing there, waiting for his orders.

"The day we have all waited for is now here." With that command, he took his Biretta and aimed it just above his ear, crumpling at the effect of the bullet in his brain. The men stood there as there world and everything they had worked for had suddenly derailed.

CHAPTER 11

It was a steamy, humid night in the Motor City. If steam wasn't escaping from the sewers, one could always find it hot on the streets in the form of hookers. Like any other large city, Detroit always had its share of prostitution. Since its incorporation as a city, police have fought an ongoing battle to keep the streets clean of ladies of the evening. The 21st century brought that advent of JOHN TV, a program to list all of the men who were arrested for solicitation of a prostitute in the last week. It grew to the most popular show on the city government channel. Still, the ladies continued as a thorn in the police department's side for nearly two centuries.

Seria Perez had lived a life on the streets since her high school days. After the tragic death of her parents from a car accident in the 1980s to her brother's death just recently, Seria had developed a clientele that rivaled some of the best call girls in Hollywood. But life for her was just a shell now. It meant nothing without her brother to talk to. Now, in the back of a darkened limousine, she stared out blankly at the passing street lights not caring what her destination might be.

They turned down Second Street and sped through stop lights until the limo rushed into the Cobo basement garage before it came to an abrupt stop before the elevators. The two henchmen grabbed Seria and took her into one of the elevators, pressing the roof button as they entered. The ride was quick and uneventful. She stepped out onto the roof and into a thick blanket of humidity. Her body wilted as she was forced to walk towards a solitary figure standing in the middle of the parking deck She summoned up all her strength to finish this journey as she approached the stranger. Her blood began to burn with revenge with every breath she took. The stranger raised his head as she approached, but the large Fedora on his head concealed his face from her again. She gave him the same blank stare that she showed in the car.

"Ms. Perez, how nice of you to come."

"Did I have a choice!"

"Well, I guess not. Tonight, you will see what the future holds for you. Your name will be etched in the history books. And your brother's death will be avenged."

"Just what am I supposed to do?" she asked.

The stranger looked at her and removed his hat for the first time.

"You have been selected to kill Mayor Kirkland Asher." Seria fainted from shock.

Guards stood above the prone body of Lieutenant George Red Feather in the control room. The remaining troops stood around waiting for guidance that would no longer come. Their training did not prepare them on filling the vacuums of command when they became empty. A tall, muscular man walked into the room with two men, equipped with black suits, sunglasses and 9mm Birettas. The man, George Tecumseh, stood staring blankly at the man on the floor.

"What is this mess?" asked the Seminole chief.

"He shot himself," said one of the troops.

"He was weak and ill-prepared. Remove him and clean this up." The squad snapped quickly together and removed the dead man to the nearest building outside of the cavern.

"Who is the next man in rank?" he asked.

The men hesitated in their response. A light skinned man stepped forward and walked towards Tecumseh.

"That would be me. 2nd Lieutenant Thomas Morning Sky."

Tecumseh responded, "You are now in charge of this phase of our mission.

You will continue to send troops out into the city and roundup as many people as you can fit into the trucks. You will receive further orders by 1400 tomorrow. Any questions?" A dozen heads nodded, acknowledging the order. Tecumseh walked over to the window and looked down into the cavern at the thousands of families now captive in the old salt mine.

"You will show them no mercy. For years, whites have degraded us and cheated us out of what was once ours given by the Great Spirit. For too long, we have been subjugated to lands of no value to us. Tomorrow we will claim a new nation for all the tribes to see."

Lieutenant Morning Sky barked out his commands and the response was quick and sharp. Tecumseh was proud with his men, coming through when it really counted.

"They will gain a seat of honor in their new order. It will be our ultimate revenge against this government that took away our lands. No law passed by this government can ever appease and replace the honor lost by their removing us from our homelands. The trail of tears shall be no more." With that, a large shout came from the troops in the cavern. It sent a chill of fear up the spines of the captive residents in their holding pen. No one saw two beady little eyes hiding behind the nerve gas canisters. They absorbed all of the events with reliable clarity for future use.

The red T-Bird raced down Connor to Jefferson Avenue. It turned right and then a quick left into the shipyard. Skip felt a knot of tension as they closed in on the dry docks. Suddenly, a white Mercedes-Benz limousine sped in front of them throwing the T-Bird into a tailspin. Skip got a glimpse of a woman in the back seat and hollered at Drew, "Get this thing turned around. Your mom is in that car."

Drew corrected the spin and floored the engine as they sped down Jefferson. Racing through stoplight after stoplight, they caused several cars to swerve to avoid a collision with the speedy T-Bird. The limo turned right onto Randolph Street. Two blocks down, they slipped into the Millender Center garage out of sight from their pursuers. Skip followed about two blocks behind them and missed their turn into the garage. Drew pulled up by the curb between Larned and Lafayette as Mitchell jumped out to get a feel for where they had gone. Suddenly, he felt the barrel of a .45 in the middle of his back. He froze instantly as he waited for the next move.

"Just walk straight into the garage. Someone has been dying to see you," the stranger said. He nudged Mitchell forward into the garage area and right up to the waiting limo. Two guards jumped out of the front seat, with one opening the rear door for Skip. Mitchell got a kick in the butt and tumbled into the back seat. Helford sat there with a wide grin on his face. He had a 9mm Biretta pointed right at a terrified Wanda. He pulled himself upright in the jumpseat.

"Welcome, Mr. Mitchell. Life at the TV station not exciting enough for you?" said Helford.

"And I want you to say hi to an old friend." He pointed forward towards the divider window as it was lowering. A face appeared from the passenger side of the window. It was his old CIA pal, Stu Watson.

"Long time, Skip."

"But not long enough. Roy enjoyed your warm reception from you."

"He was just in the wrong place at the wrong time," replied Watson.

"But you didn't have to hit him. By the way, the police are looking for you for questioning since you were smart enough to leave your CIA ID in his office after you clobbered him." Watson reached in his suit pocket and found nothing. He looked nonchalantly at Mitchell as he tried to sugar coat his mistake in front of his boss.

"Well, my future is locked in. So they won't be able to touch me. I have a job in the new order." Helford looked sternly from the backseat towards Watson. The divider was raised and Skip was alone with him and Wanda.

"So why am I here?" Mitchell questioned.

"My master is very concerned as to your intentions towards Miss Wanda. He intends to marry her this Sunday. He does not want anything to upset the ceremony."

"Is that what Wanda wants?"

"Why don't you ask her?" Their eyes met with an intensity felt only between them. She immediately knew what she had to say.

"If it will keep my family safe, then I want it." Her eyes stayed glued to Skip's before she broke contact. Mitchell looked carefully at Helford before he spoke.

"I am not sure what Tony is up to, Helford. But I will make you one promise. If you or anyone else harm Wanda, I won't rest till I hunt you down." He jumped at Helford, knocking the gun from his hand.

"And as of right now, I am not going to let Wanda do something that she doesn't have her heart in." He opened the side door, pulling Wanda out first.

"RUN," he hollered, "Drew is waiting." Wanda ran towards the garage entrance as Skip tangled with the bodyguards to give her time to escape. A tall figure stepped in front of her escape route. She stopped dead in her tracks. It was Tony.

"Going somewhere?" He grabbed her firmly by the arm, walking back towards the melee by the limousine. The two bodyguards were knocking Mitchell senseless with repeated blows to his belly. Blood was running out of the corner of his mouth. Wanda shrieked at the site. Marvelli held up his hand and stopped the fight.

"I think he has had enough," he said, looking at the disheveled detective. "Now get lost before I turn my boys loose to finish their job."

Mitchell crawled cautiously out the door of the garage. Drew spotted him and jumped out of the car to give him a hand.

Secure in the passenger seat, Skip picked up the phone. "Chief, I coming in. Have a doctor ready and call in the Mounties. See you in a few."

The T-Bird left with the speed of sound, weaving its way back to the Book-Cadillac Hotel.Marvelli watched them speed away,as the rush of victory against an old nemesis overwhelmed him.

"Now, I am going to put you someplace secure, so that you won't skip out before Sunday." Wanda bumped her head as he pushed her into the limo. It left the Millender Center towards Jefferson. They turned north and continued towards Belle Isle and the shipyards.

The storm front rolled slowly through the Mississippi Valley. The path of destruction was now as wide as a dozen football fields and long as Mt. Everest is high. Severe lightning and thunder led the front striking trees and houses with sheer abandon, burning them to the ground. Baseball sized hail followed reeking havoc with cars and houses that escaped the path of the lightning. Thousands of people lay dead throughout Oklahoma, Kansas and Missouri. The cities of Kansas City and St. Louis were laid to waste by super dangerous F-6 tornados that were at the back end of this front. Emergencies were declared in all three states. Emergency Alert systems were activated when power stations were demolished. As the last of the storm clouds rolled into Illinois, people began crawling out of the rubble to assess the destruction. The thunder heads continued to roll over the flat lands of the state, flooding rivers and destroying crops in its wake. The governor of the state ordered evacuations of every town west of Chicago. But the storm was just too quick. Many innocent people lost their lives on the highways from being overturned from the high winds or demolished by the hail. National Guard squadrons were ordered to open up old Civil Defense shelters to protect the people they could.

WAG-TV's newsroom became nothing but one giant weather center. Lucy Gillian was coordinating all the feeds from what was left of their affiliates in the Midwest. For the first time in their history, WAG was giving the weather 80% of the newscast. A total of ten feeds came into the tape room. Three extra satellite controllers were brought in to help make tonight a success. Correspondents from stations in Lincoln, Omaha, Topeka and Des Moines were covering the carnage. The clock clicked down to their 5 o'clock newscast. Feeds came as went as the anchors ran down the hall towards the studio.

"Twenty seconds, gang. Let's get in place," said Kris Johnson, the studio floor director. "Let's get some help to get these mikes on!"

"Ten seconds, stand by. And five, four, three, two..." Kris gave the cue to begin. Suddenly, everything went black. WAG was off the air. Mother Nature saw to that by demolishing their tower outside of town.

Richard Johnson and Michael Gibson of the Choctaw tribe pulled in to the parking lot of the 8Mile armory in Oak Park just as dusk was falling over the western horizon. A flurry of activity erupted as they approached. Squads stood as attention when they entered. The sergeant ordered parade rest as they walked by ignoring the troops. The remainder of the regiment was split between guarding the temporary holding pen with residents from the westside and the truck squads that were rounding up the people.

"The operation is flowing smoothly. By 1400 tomorrow, we will have detained over two thirds of this city as the conference progresses. The oncoming weather has provided us with the perfect cover of saving the people from the dangerous weather. Sergeant, how many transports are on the streets?" asked Johnson.

The sergeant grabbed his clipboard and quickly made his count of vehicles on the road. "We are sitting at thirty right now, sir. And we bring in about fifty people per truck."

A smile appeared across Johnson's face.

"The master will be pleased. The plan to reverse the actions of the Indian Removal Act of 1830 and the trail of tears experienced by the Cherokee and subsequent tribes after that. The Dawes Act that took away our lands struck a knife in our heart. Not even the attempt at reconciliation with the reorganization act of 1934 corrected the problems of equality on tribal lands. The time has come to create a new land for all Native Americans. And that will happened when the heir to the great Anasazi chief returns to lead us to new glory. Only then will we reclaim sacred lands of our ancestors." A loud cheer came from the remaining troops as they heard the speech. Johnson,

Gibson and their entourage stood at the front of the armory, acknowledging the cheers and adulation from the crowd unaware that trouble was brewing in the city.

The storm front passed through downtown Chicago. Uprooted trees in Grant Park was only the tip of the iceberg. Windows were broken on skyscrapers by either tornadoes or large hail. People were sucked out of the windows to their deaths several stories below. Those caught on the street died almost instantly. Mother Nature was hitting them so hard, no one could say what was the killer. As it crossed the shore into Lake Michigan, tornadoes destroyed the Navy Pier amusement area. Boats anchored at the marinas or in the lake were now part of the lake bed floor. Nothing could stop the onslaught that Mother Nature was raging against the people. Detroit was only eight hours away.

Mayor Kirkland Asher walked into the auditorium with Vice Mayor Meashon at his heels. Members of the news media were gathered together for a news conference, apparently discussing the on coming storm front. Questions began blurting out from everywhere, directed solely for the mayor to respond. He held up his hands to quiet the crowd as members of the city council gathered behind him as he prepared to speak.

"Ladies and gentlemen, I have a few words to say before I take any questions. As you all have been seeing over the news reports, there is a massive and very destructive storm front heading our way. Billions of dollars of damage has been reaped and over one million people have lost there lives. I just got off the phone with Mayor Drury of Chicago. He described the storm as 'hell unleashed' with hail, lightning, rain, and tornados, natures most destructive force literally raping his city. People were pulled to their deaths from the highest floors of skyscrapers as tornadoes ripped the windows from their frames. Torrential rains and hail collapsed the roofs of many homes and businesses either killing or injuring the people inside. High winds have hampered rescue efforts as emergency vehicles are being blown off the road on their way to help. He admitted to me that he might have been able to save more people if he would have ordered the civil defense shelters opened. So from Chicago's mistake, we are going to make it Detroit's finest hour. Through Mr. Anthony Marvelli, the security squad for the Indian conference is going to spend the next several hours gathering up people and take them to a place of safety. Mr. Marvelli, with this action, continues as Detroit's #1 citizen, putting his city first. This city needs more businessmen like him. I will now answer a few questions."

Chatter increased to a loud roar quickly as reporters tried to catch the mayor's attention. Ron Firman caught the mayor's eye. "Go ahead, Ron. What's your question?" Firman stood up and the rest of the room quieted quickly down.

"Mr. Mayor, as we have seen from St.Louis and Chicago, this very destructive storm is expected to arrive here within the next eight hours. Do you really think that this security squad is going to be able to accomplish what will be an almost impossible task. There are nearly a million people in this city and you know that not everyone will heed the warning you have given. Any comment?"

The mayor looked at his audience solemnly and said, "Then we will pray to God to spare this city from the hell heading for us." His eyes began to swell with emotion. "If you will excuse me, I have a city to protect." He turned and left the auditorium as the reporters clamored for more attention.

CHAPTER 12

The basement of the Book-Cadillac Hotel was abuzz with activity. CIA and FBI were mulling over maps planning a defense for the city. Skip sat in a far corner while doctors worked on his injuries from the fight with Tony. Chief Nicholson, Steve Marx of the FBI and Louis Mullen of the CIA were gathered around him for a debriefing of the past few days.

"First, Skip, who gave you the authority to give out my private office phone number. Every gang leader in this city has been calling me. We have collected a significant cache of weapons from the five trucks confiscated though. I haven't been able to concentrate on the department for two days."

"Well, Barney, someone had to do it. Tony is keeping Wanda under tight wraps. Even when I tried to free her, he had our escape blocked off. And then he gave me something to remember him by." He groaned and winced in pain as doctors wrapped his bruised ribs. Drew stood behind him with his hand on his shoulder, praying that his father will be blessed with a healing. As he opened his eyes, Director Mullen was grilling his father.

"Mitchell, we are fighting a losing battle. A major storm is heading this way that all but leveled Chicago. The Indians have a security squad that your mayor has given free run of the city. We have located two of the staging areas for Marvelli's operation. One is at an armory on 8 Mile and the is in a warehouse across the street from St. John's Hospital on Moross. We have discovered that George Tecumseh of the Seminoles just recently sent a lot of supplies to that location. We expect more nerve gas canisters have been placed inside since you were there earlier. We are running into dead ends everywhere trying to find the third site. That one, we believe, is the center of the operation." Skip looked calmly at Mullen.

"I got a tip from someone that there is something happening at the salt mines," said Mitchell.

"Maybe you should get someone staking it out before it's too late. And another thing, gentlemen, that helicopter show at City Airport has a whole slue of those canisters in their hangar. I have the Air National Guard squad holding them at the hangar for questioning. There is something planned for Saturday at four o'clock. What it is has yet to be discovered."

"Who is in charge over there, now?" asked Marx.

"My son Ray, who is an army Staff Sergeant in EOD and their Helicopter attack squad."

Drew came out of his silence and spoke, "We need to return. Ray is expecting us."

Mitchell, Nicholson and Marx followed Drew out the door and into their cars. *Answers will come*, he thought as they drove off to City Airport.

The Merchant Building was forever known as the jeweler's building since it opened its doors in 1925. Its ornate atrium with marble covering every floor except the top four made it a landmark of architectural greatness. First designed by Albert Kahn, it was going through remodeling as another venture of Marvelli Enterprises. Twenty-four of its twenty-five floors were getting spruced up for a new tenant within the next few weeks. The former jewelry shops were now giving way to rows and rows of major office space. The construction was on schedule, with no anticipated problems. Workers were tidying up as the afternoon was setting on the western horizon. Up on the twenty-fifth floor, a single figure stood sweltering as the sun's rays pushed through the unprotected windows. A group of men stood nearby discussing their situation with their captive.

Helford stood with a leather cat-o-nine-tails in his hand, the leather saturated with blood, waiting as his captive regained consciousness. He looked at the binds, tugging them to test the snugness of his work. He looked at the person whose clothes were shredded from her head to her waist. She was tied up spread-eagle between two pillars, her back bloodied from the beating she endured and head sagging from the exhaustion of her plight. Her exquisitely sculptured body, now battered and severely bruised, would not let her show any weakness to the man she considered her mentor and friend. Hatred burned inside her, one she would avenge even if it meant the rest of her life in jail. From America's Songstress to whipping post, Wanda Willington had now reached a level that was ten times lower than anything she had ever experienced. Tony Marvelli had reaped on her enough humiliation and degradation that payback would be her only satisfaction. Revenge against Tony would be sweet, no matter what it took.

"Miss Wanda," said Helford, "all you have to do is tell me what you know. Then Master Tony says I can let you go."

"Don't play dumb with me. You know as well as I do that he will kill me either way. Helford, for years you said you were my friend and would do anything for me. Tell me now what this is all about. It is the least you can do before I die." Her eyes glued on Helford as her pondered her request. Icy resolve showed in his eyes as the others waited for him to speak.

"Master Tony has been like a son to me ever since his father was killed. He was loyal to his father up to the very end. When he was ten, he participated in his first hit. He was the bait for a well known businessman in the area. Tony Sr. started training him to run the business soon after that. And Junior wasn't even his kid. He was adopted in 1955 from an Indian orphanage in Cortez, Colorado. It was there that he learned of a great chief of the ancient ones that started a lot of the rituals performed today. This leader, Amozeltec, created a headdress of Yucca leaves and placed Turquoise crystals over the eyes. Myths flowed that turquoise had the ability of seeing the future. Stories of the ancient ones also speak of similar instances. When Master Tony heard that your daughter was heading an expedition to the Four Corners area, he sent three of his best men from the ranch to join the expedition in Toweoac. The men were to capture the artifact when she discovered it. You see, Dr. Mitchell was looking for the same headdress as a remembrance of her great-great-great grandmother, Red Deer, the wife of Amozeltec. So Miss Wanda, you were a major player in this chess game with your career, whether you wanted to be or not. Now will you finish the job or do I have to continue your subjugation?"

A battered and bloody Wanda looked at Helford and said, "You tell that bastard that when I see him, I will spit in his face before I kill him." Helford put the gag backin her mouth and whipped more bloody welts on her sculpted back. She succumbed to unconsciousness as the beating continued.

Friday finally came. The army of buses descended on Joe Louis Arena with the advent of the Great American Indian Pow-Wow. Tribes from every corner of the country filled the hallowed halls of Hockey town with breakneck speed. Row after row filled with many different cultures that Native Americans were known for. Even with the Indian gaming act of 1988, many tribes still carried an axe to grind against the way their lands were stolen from them as they saw it. Every tribe had renegades that wanted all out war with the federal government take back what once was theirs.

The big Jumbotron clock clicked off the minutes to the 7:30 P.M. start. Buses unloaded tribal members like clock work. With the precision of a drill team, the Apache and the Sioux led everyone into the cavernous arena peacefully to their seats. By 7:25, the place was abuzz with excitement in anticipation of history in the making. The lights began to dim. The crowd began to applaud. A solitary spotlight appeared, shining solely on the empty podium. In the shadows lurked a tall, muscular man with graying hair on his temples. He moved towards the podium and the crowd began to stir with anticipation. Suddenly, a loud voice boomed over the PA system.

"Ladies and gentlemen. The City of Detroit welcomes you to Great American Indian Pow-Wow. This is the first one held east of the Mississippi. It is our hope to address major issues concerning every tribal nation within the boundaries of the United States. Though many of us are turning the tide, making major headway toward equality within our ranks, there are still are some things to resolve. And now, our keynote speaker for the night, Mayor Kirkland Asher."

Lukewarm applause fluttered throughout the lower bowl of the arena as the mayor carefully walked out to the podium from backstage. Members of the City Council were just taking seats in the front row as the applause died down. In a dimly lit suite on the fifth floor, a man showed a sinister smile as he looked over the beginning of a glorious coronation. He looked to his left and nodded. A man spoke the word "GO" into a walkie-talkie. He nodded back and the sinister one began to chuckle.

"Your ship has come in, Asher. Bon Voyage." A young woman began walking out on stage, very slowly with her arms at her side. She was halfway to the podium when two officers came after her. One had recognized her. It was Seria Perez.

Seria turned and fired on the mayor, wounding him in the arm. Shots began to ring out from the catwalks above, aiming right for the officers on stage. Detective Johnny Rood lunged for Seria to get her out of the line of fire and also check on the mayor. His partner, Matt Dungee, was calling for backup and SWAT to subdue the indoor snipers. Ten thousand people crouched low in their rows, afraid to move or even breathe for fear of getting shot. A sniper wounded Seria in the knee as she fell with Rood towards the podium. Once secure, Johnny poked his head over the podium searching for powder flashes from the sniper's guns. A bright orange flash appeared to his right. The detective pumped off two shots from his .45 automatic. Dungee called for the house lights. The arena suddenly became brighter from end to end. Dungee and Rood began pumping their pistols at the three snipers above them. The one on the right got up, trying to run from the scene. The two on the left kept pumping their Barrett .50 caliber rifles at the podium, whittling it to pieces. The closer one rose from the prone position to finish the job on Perez and the mayor. His laser scope lined up dead center with the mayor's forehead. A shot rang out from the shadows. The sniper dropped over the rail and into the crowd some three-hundred feet below, into the middle of the Chickasaw delegation. Chaos began on the catwalks. Members of Detroit's SWAT team landed on the roof, quietly made their way down to the cat walks. A second sniper fell over as he tried to fight for his freedom. The third was wounded and subdued to a solid round of applause from the crowd. An announcement came over the PA.

"Ladies and Gentlemen, due to the unexpected events of this evening, tonight's session is cancelled. We will reconvene tomorrow at 9 A.M. Please exit the arena quietly and safely through the provided exits. Thank you and good night." Security guards guided them up the ramps and out the doors.

The loading dock continued as a flurry of activity. Paramedics came off the elevator with the bodies of the two dead snipers. SWAT members brought the third member down with his leg heavily bandaged from a gunshot wound. Paramedics prepared to take him in an ambulance to Detroit Sinai-Grace Hospital in the Medical Center for treatment.

Mayor Asher lay on a table by the door as paramedics finished patching him up for transport. Chief Nicholson had just arrived on the scene. He walked straight over to the mayor to check on his progress.

"You just have to create excitement wherever you go, don't you, Kirk?" asked Barney.

"Well, I didn't make you chief of police just because you were a wall flower," replied Asher.

"Are you going to tell me what you know our do I have to fire you to find out what happened."

Barney pulled up one of the paramedic cases and sat on it while he talked.

"Seria Perez, a local hooker and also sister to George Perez, that homeless guy who died in the destruction of the MC Terminal, was hired by a man she never saw to kill you. They had programed her to think that you were responsible for the blast. One of our officers, Det. Rood, saw her and attempted to stop it. That's when shots were fired from the catwalks. The theory is that Indian Security would have laid claim to stopping her after she had killed you. But our one prisoner is not talking. A thorough search found two cyanide capsules in the heel of his shoe to use if he was captured. He must have kept an extra in case the first one didn't work." Asher grimaced in pain as he tried to control his laughter at Nicholson's joke.

"Seria asked me to ask for your forgiveness. The loss of her brother opened her up to the power of suggestion and the rest became history."

"Tell her I do forgive her but be careful about the company she keeps. By the way, has anyone found the Vice-Mayor? He was supposed to be here with me," said Asher.

"My department has been getting reports that he has been keeping strange bedfellows lately," said Nicholson. "We'll find him."

Paramedics loaded up the mayor in the ambulance and rushed him over to the hospital for immediate surgery. Nicholson stayed at the arena as the police wrapped up their investigation. The crime lab combed all of the catwalks upstairs, searching for any leads to who was behind this. A team down on the floor discovered a hand-held radio beside the body. Since it was programable, Barney suspected that the people behind this were working on the inside. It sure seemed to fit a espionage scenario.

Teams ran out of the elevator, splitting into two to search the thirty-five suites. In suite 520, Vice -Mayor Meashon was getting fidgety. He paced frantically between the door and the balcony. The lights stayed dim inside the suite. Movement remained undetectable inside from any one looking from the floor. The man in the shadows looked at the frantic politician. A bodyguard walked up and whispered in his ear. He could hear the searchers closing in on their suite. There was only one thing left to do. He pulled out his .38 Special, screwed on the silencer and planted one bullet into the forehead of Randy Meashon. The bodyguards opened a secret door and the man in the shadows led the way to escape down a stairwell. They exited into the arena parking lot and blended into the crowd.

The storm front rolled into Michigan like a freight train. Dozens of tornados and waterspouts tore through Michigan's wine country as it traveled along the I-94 corridor. Just like Chicago, thousands of houses and businesses were destroyed by the storm. Residents heeded the warning of St. Louis and Chicago by getting to shelters en masse. Abandoned cars on the freeways and streets were severely devastated and windshields broken by the baseball size hail. Lightning knocked out power from Benton Harbor to Kalamazoo. A tornado ripped the roof off the Kellogg plant scattering corn flakes for miles. No one could stop this killing machine, the worst in North America in over100 years. Its trail was clear as it left Kalamazoo. Mother Nature still held the best hand. And the storm just kept rolling on.

CHAPTER 13

The office walls blended in with the drab Army green of the fatigue uniforms as they sat at the conference table. General Abraham sat at the head of the table, his dress uniform cleanly pressed with medals shining, looking at the other members seated near him. On his right sat his Naval Reserve counterpart, Commander Paul Payne, fresh from maneuvers in Lake Erie with the Royal Canadian Naval Reserves. To his left was Master Sergeant Ray Mitchell, a career military man having completed ten years of service and receiving the highest honors the reserves could award. Sgt. Mitchell just arrived from City Airport where his squad had detained a squadron of Cobra attack helicopters loaded with canisters of nerve gas. Mitchell began the meeting with an update of the situation in Detroit.

"General, after interrogating them, I found some interesting things. At 4 P.M. tomorrow, helicopters are to begin flights over the city, starting on the eastside, and begin spraying VARAN gas over the neighborhoods. The goal is to kill everyone in the city. Detroit was chosen because there is so much abandonment in this city. They believe that no one would put up a fight to save it. They also admitted that this is only one part of a master plan to take over the city. After that, they started crying for lawyers."

Payne piped in, "Our reserve units stationed in Lake Erie near the mouth of the Detroit River are preventing any non- commercial vessels from entering. We have a list of everything in dry dock at Marvelli's shipyards and will stop anything that moves the wrong way."

"Intelligence from the CIA and FBI both show that this is just a small piece of a larger puzzle. They suspect Indian tribes are involved in this. Four renegade leaders have been meeting with someone, probably the financier of this operation, at the Yontodega club on Jefferson. The four leaders, Richard Johnson, Dan RuuningHorse, George Tecumseh and Richard NightOwl have been seen at three separate locations in the city, apparently coordinating activities of their so-called security squad. I think they are more like a goon squad." Sergeant Mitchell looked straight at the general's eyes. His voice remained very stoic as he explained his plan of action.

"Sir, you are probably aware that my father, Skip Mitchell, is working closely with the CIA on this. When we detained the helicopters at City Airport, he and I developed an alternate plan. At this moment, my squad is replacing the nerve gas canisters with nitrous oxide. The Indian pilots are being detained in a supply cage within the hangar. Tomorrow, with Captain Ron Brewer in my helicopter, we will fly their mission over the city minus the nerve gas. We must come up with a way to tell the residents. It would help the plan greatly." General Abraham looked at both the sergeant and the commander. He saw the intensity in their faces. Only one thing was left to do.

"Sergeant, get back to the airport. You have orders to carry out. Commander, get back to your fleet. I must report to Washington right away." The three participants rose from the table and left through different exits. None would foresee the calamity Mother Nature was sending their way. They had enough to deal with on their own.

Jackson, Michigan celebrated its 200th birthday with bicentennial festivities that rivaled Detroit's Tri-centennial in 2001. Parades flourished on almost every street in the city. Downtown had the annual Rose Festival parade with fifty intricately designed floats and talented marching bands from every school in the city, including one elementary school. The fourth and fifth graders practiced long and hard for their performance. The crowds gave them a rousing ovation as they danced their way into people's hearts. People enjoyed a grand time at local parties that never ended. Fond memories were all that was left for the residents as the "Devil Storm",as it was called, rolled through the city.

Abandoned cars littered the streets as the leading edge of the fury splattered the western suburbs with golf ball size hail. Scores of houses were flooded with hailstones busting through windows and into basements. Roofs were splattered with holes that resembled a piece of Swiss cheese. City officials reactivated old fall-out shelters and herded residents to safe havens. The second wave of the storm followed within seconds of the first. Bolts of highly-charged lightning struck trees, cars and houses, in random order. Fires blazed almost immediately as dozens of electrical poles and wires littered the streets of the city. After a few minutes, a hush fell over the city. Rain began to fall as Jackson's firefighters struggled to control the fires of destruction. Raindrops changed to torrents as thunderclouds clashed, drenching the city like a river flooding a canyon. Abruptly, the rain stopped and quiet fell upon Jackson. Winds began to pickup as the final phase of the "Devil Storm" passed through. A dozen funnel clouds appeared in the western sky, quickly touching ground and sending debris flying throughout the city. Animals, especially cows and horses from the western farms. Barns shattered like glass as shearing winds sliced through the farmland. As the twisters crossed the city limits, the destruction carried into residential neighbors, carving out paths one block at a time. Three twisters landed on Michigan Avenue, demolishing everything in its wake. Vegetables, fruits and other sundry items sailed up to join the debris cloud. Marshall's department store was reduced to a pile of rubble instantly and most of the inventory sailing down the freeway towards Ann Arbor. By the time the twisters reached the east side of town, the funnel clouds had retreated, sparing three thousand houses from destruction. Loss of life again was minimal. The few minutes of hell was gone, preparing to devour its next victim.

Her body ached liked it was beaten by 1000 baseball bats. The bloody welts on her back were a constant reminder of the pain she had endured. Her mind swirled with thoughts of her younger days with mom and dad in Colorado. Those were happier times for her. She worked hard to achieve the good life for her kids. As she laid here, wherever that was she thought, how could it end so soon. Thoughts of her mom and dad and her in-laws floated through her consciousness as she pondered whether to take that final step through the pearly gates. Just as she felt a peaceful resolution to her question, a voice abruptly brought her back to reality.

"Ms. Willington, it's about time you let us catch up to you." Her eyes slowly opened as she tried to focus on the nearest figure to her. Squinting, she could barely make out the figures of two men, one tall with salt and pepper hair on top and the other much younger and somewhat darker complexion but showed strong character, like her father. After a few minutes, she recognized them, Skip and her long-lost son, Drew. She looked around and saw that she was in some sort of hospital room.

"Now just where did you two come from?" she queried, looking half groggy from the her experience.

"And you, young man, you should let your parents know when you're taking off. I might have to ground you next time." She started to laugh, twinging with pain with every chuckle.

"Dad and I found you on the roadside near Comerica Park. You were left for dead, laying there with your back bloody and stripped of all your dignity."

"Why don't you just say I was naked. Or is that something too embarrassing to say to your mother?" Her mouth curved into a small smile as she awaited a response.

"The Ute people taught me one should honor and respect their parents at all times. I live by that code now and would not have it any other way. Now I have come back to show you how I have changed and what I can do to help make things better." Drew reached out and softly caressed his mother's cheek, wiping a small tear of happiness away.

"Why don't you start by telling me where the hell I am?" she asked.

"For starters, Wanda, you are in a high security wing of Henry Ford Hospital." The voice came from far across the room. Barney Nicholson strode into the room followed by an entourage of hospital security officers. They immediately took positions around her bed as the chief came beside Skip and Drew who stood there watching the show.

"We have put you and the mayor in the same wing to tighten security and give you a chance to get better. Doctors say you were pretty damn lucky the beating stopped when it did. Another half hour and you would have been a part of history. The Feds are in town to stop a mad plan against this city, but no one but Skip has been able to uncover any of it. What do you know that Tony wants kept quiet?" Barney looked coldly into her eyes awaiting her answer. She felt a hand slowly squeeze hers.

Wanda looked up into a pair of warm, brown eyes, ones that she hadn't seen that way in years. Skip gave her a quiet nod and she began unloading her chest.

"About six months ago, Tony started tightening the reins on his empire. He kept saying something about living his father's dream, whatever that was. I was spending more time at the Cortez ranch than I did doing concerts. If I wanted to go shopping in Denver or Phoenix, I had to arrange it with him so I wouldn't be noticed. Very cloak and dagger stuff. That started a year and a half ago, right after my visit in 2001. I was kept a prisoner at the ranch with Tony as my warden. A lot of construction also began happening. Warehouses and a new runway in the north pasture for starters. New people were coming to the ranch on a regular basis, especially four men apparently of considerable influence."

Skip briefly chimed in, "Do you remember any names?"

Wanda thought for a moment before she answered. "Only bits and pieces, Skip. I heard the names Running-Horse, Night Owl and George. Outside of that, everything else is just a blur." She paused to take a deep breath to ease the anxiety that was coming back to her.

"The more these four men came around, the tighter the cage around me became. Where I once had freedom anytime, I now had to have security clearance to walk out of my room." Everyone in the room stayed glued to her words.

"One day, I strolled into his office, looking for an antique plate that he kept in there that was his father's. It was then that I noticed the plans for a large arena filled with snipers. I know it was snipers because he wrote that word by every marked position on the paper."

Wanda paused a moment as her nurse gave her a shot of Demerol to ease her pain.

"From then on, I took off for Detroit to tell Skip what I found. The rest you already know." She squeezed Skip's hand tightly as she let the medication begin to relax her.

Barney replied, "Wanda, these six guards are going to be with you 24/7. You have been through enough. Besides, Mitchell would kick my ass if anything happened to you, so rest. And do what the doctor's say this time. I heard all about your last stay here." A sly smile cracked on his face as he turned to leave the room. Skip and Drew gave Wanda a quick kiss, rushing to catch up with Nicholson before he reached the elevators.

"That lady deserves more than this. I promise you, Skip, that I will personally see this case will end it once and for all. Whatever Marvelli is up to, he will pay."

The doors opened and the trio traveled down to their waiting cars and day two of the Great Indian Pow-Wow.

Tour buses blocked lanes on Jefferson a good four hours before the start of the Saturday session. Governor Gresham had increased security by calling in National Guard reservists. Mayor Asher was recovering well at the hospital after the attempted assassination opening night. The Detroit News and Free Press headlines for that day broadcast the mysterious death of Vice-Mayor Randy Meashon. His body was found floating face-down at the beach off Belle Isle with a bullet right through the head.

The 75th floor suite of Marvelli Industries was abuzz with activity. The four tribal leaders and Tony Marvelli were heavy into a heated discussion about events of the last twenty-four hours. Tecumseh, the quartet's senior chieftain, anxiously expressed concern over the success of the journey to take over the city.

"Authorities have both our eastside warehouse and the armory watched constantly. We can't make a move without winding up with someone tailing our people."

Daniel RunningHorse added, "Our helicopters are still safe at the airport. No one seems any wiser. Canisters are in place for their flight at 1600 hours. On my signal, they will takeoff from their hangar and position themselves parallel to the city limits to begin their clean-up flight. It will take only 45 minutes to engulf the city, leaving downtown area untouched. That is because the VARAN gas will seep through the concrete pores of the convention center buildings and risk killing us too. All we await is the word to be given, sir."

George Tecumseh spoke out, "The round-up has continued without a hitch. We have almost half the city in our detention centers awaiting their fate. And no one suspects what that might be." The Four Chiefs, now nicknamed the Apocalypse, sat glued to the dark skinned man behind the bar in the suite. An older gentleman leaned over and whispered something in his ear. Tony Marvelli turned to face his partners and uttered the words that everyone had waited for centuries.

"The word is given. Let the true Americans reap their revenge." Messengers left quickly to initiate the second phase of the plan and bury Detroit deeper than anyone thought possible. Marvelli turned to Helford and grinned, "Father's dream is about to be fulfilled. Chill the champagne. A celebration will be in order." Their grins erupted into raucous laughter as they realized their journey's end was near. But only one soul shared in the joy of the moment.

Mitchell carefully inserted the key into the main door of his Riverfront apartment. Since Wanda's return, he had only slept a few hours in the last three days. Having to rescue Wanda twice, lose her, and then find her again, was taking its toll on his psyche. Barney ordered Drew to take him home to recharge himself before this evening's meeting at the Joe. As he staggered through the door, the fresh scent of a two day old litter box reminded him of his little roommate who had gotten lost in the chaos; Maxwell. He felt the furry little feline rub against both of his legs, nearly toppling him to the floor. Drew grabbed him by the arm and carefully led him to the bedroom to get some rest. Maxwell was on the pillow right next to him before he even had a chance to close his eyes. His need for attention from his master was winning out over his master's needs. Skip began to scratch his cat's back while trying to sleep. The bedroom phone blared two quick rings before Drew answered it. The caller ID said "Unavailable" so he cautiously answered, "Mitchell residence," patiently waiting for a reply from the other end of the line.

"Hey yo, man, this is Spud. I've been trying to get through for two days. Your voice sounds different, Skip. Did Tony give you an alteration?"

Drew remained stoic at the feeble attempt at a joke. He calmly answered the question.

"I am his son, Drew." A bolt of pride shot through his spirit as he said that for the first time in over a decade.

"Well, that's fine. I need to talk to the Skipper." Spud's voice began to stammer as he continued. Drew sensed that something was going to happen and proceeded to investigate on his own.

"He was ordered to rest for a while. You can tell me and I can relay it to him when he awakens." His voice remained emotionless as he tried to scope out the caller.

"Well, I'm not supposed to but, since you're his son, I guess it will be OK. My gang is splitting up and getting on the trucks with the others. The few that have contacted me say that there is a big build up at the old salt mine near Melvindale. They were apparently caught by guards since there was a lot of shouting and gunfire after they called me. I've got Sanchez and his Latin Hitmen going down there to check it out. I am not sure how much longer we can do this 'cause these neighborhoods are getting quite spooky with all the quiet going on. From Five Points to Dearborn, there is not a creature stirring in the cupboard."

Drew gave Spud their cell-phone number. He quickly hung up and placed another call.

"The journey is almost done. The Sipapu will be permanently closed. Seek out the bowels of the city for the answer." He replaced the phone and jarred his Dad awake. They jumped into the T-Bird and drove off towards the sunset. A deadline was looming on the horizon.

The cool, crisp breeze turned harsh and humid in only a few seconds as the "Devil Storm" entered Ann Arbor less than an hour after destroying Jackson. People in the parks scattered as the winds picked up. Tornado sirens wailed urging the residents to safer havens away from the oncoming holocaust. Ann Arbor's penchant as a major sports town kept its residents in the open longer than they anticipated. Fear was now the driving force as the university town rushed to save itself from its short-sightedness. Rain and hail were making visibility almost zero. The twisters would not be far behind. Disaster loomed on their horizon. Detroit was now only seventy-five minutes away.

CHAPTER 14

Political factions have long held center stage in Detroit and its surrounding suburbs. From the French of the eighteenth century who made the inroads with the native Indian population to the dominant Germans of the nineteenth century, their numbers swelled to where for nearly a century they controlled economic and political climates of the region. When Henry Ford gave the auto industry its jump start in the early 1900s, an influx of immigrants descended on the Motor City, putting Detroit on the map, as newspapers referred to it, the "Best City in the Country to live and work in." Slums were non-existent. Good wages were paid by all employers and John Q. Public was content with the status quo of the 1920s. Japanese immigrants came to Cass and Canfield, near Wayne State, the Chinese opened shops near Third and Michigan and the infamous Greek entrepreneurs flooded Detroit's economy with fabulous restaurants and exciting enterprises to make Detroit the place to be in the early 20th century.

As the auto industry grew, so did the black population in the city. Centered in the Black Bottom area of the lower East Side, their community grew but suffered from the segregated view of their European descendants. The jobs they sought by moving to the city did not come as quickly as desired. The large influx caused friction at numerous public housing projects in the city leading to the riots of 1943. A few mayors like Albert Cobo and Jerome Cavanaugh worked towards repairing that damage. But the wheels of government slowed their efforts as well. Cavanaugh faced riots again in 1967 that led to an almost complete exodus of white residents to the new, less expensive suburbs that opened up during the post World War 2 boom that hit the country. During the 60s, 7 out of 10 blacks held unskilled labor jobs. Whites maintained healthy advantage in good paying skilled and supervisory careers. Native Americans, on the other hand, made up less than 1% of the workforce forcing a return to the reservation just to survive.

Political co-existence has never lived in Detroit. Many issues have always separated the people from those of their neighbors, mass transit being a major obstacle. Mayor Cobo spearheaded the construction of the current freeway system, creating an escape route to cheaper suburbs and racial segregation. Today, Detroit's system is considered the second worst in the country behind Los Angeles. Two brights spots have spearheaded the international flow of trade between the US and Canada for almost a century now, the Ambassador Bridge and Detroit-Windsor Tunnel.

The Detroit-Windsor Tunnel lies one block south of the Renaissance Center right behind the Old Mariner's Church on Jefferson. Some three to four million cars travel 80 feet below the river surface to Downtown Windsor, Ontario, Canada. The Ambassador Bridge is the most popular route for truck traffic and auto traffic, matching the tunnel does every month. Maintenance is constant since neither ever closes.

Kyle Lincoln, assistant administrator for the Detroit-Windsor Tunnel, arrived as usual, 1:55 P.M. at the tunnel offices next to The Renaissance Center garage. He always kept an airtight schedule, reviewing daytime logs on tunnel usage and maintenance to avoid duplication with the other shifts. Overlapping contractors were always an irritation to him. Repairs to their work always had to be done by his staff, since quality contractors were a scarce commodity in the metro area.

He parked his car in the usual spot, second from the left side just fifty feet from the stairway leading upstairs to the tunnel offices. Lincoln noticed a new air-conditioning contractor truck sitting in the space next to his, BILL'S AIR

CONDITIONING SERVICE, INC. from Port Huron was the name emblazoned on the side of the rear box behind the cab. Strange, he thought, must have an emergency. Normal ventilation repairs are done on Tuesdays. Lincoln made a mental note to find out why.

"Hi, boss," greeted his always voluptuous secretary, Anna Olsen. A luscious, Scandinavian with a body just made for his daily fantasies.

"Hi Anna. Why are contractors here on a weekend?"asked Kyle. "Don't they know Tuesday is the normal day for any type of emergency maintenance?"

"Normally, yes, Kyle. But these guys had papers from the Vice-Mayor ordering a checkup on the #3 work tunnel, the one above the US entrance. Things checked out so I gave the OK. Thought you wouldn't mind."

"You did make the usual copy of their papers I hope?"

"Of course. I always try to be efficient for you, Kyle," she said in her sultry, Scandinavian voice as she rummaged through the in-tray on her desk.

"Here they are!" Lincoln looked at the papers and his gut twisted into knots. Something was amiss. He quickly ran to dispatch and called his number two man, Chuck Caley.

"Meet me in the #3 tunnel right away. We may have a potential problem." He turned towards Anna. "Call the Canadians and shut this sucker down until you here from me. Call FBI and Border Patrol and have those contractors found and stopped. And put out an alert to the bridge people, too." Anna looked puzzled. Lincoln looked at her as her eyes began to swell from fear.

"Hopefully, this will be nothing. We will know in the next few minutes." He bolted out the door and down the catwalks towards the tunnel's main entrance. Abruptly, Lincoln stopped dead in his tracks. The ground shook like a 6.0 earthquake underneath him. Dust rose from the entrance. He regained his footing and ran back inside. Anna's look confirmed his worst fears.

"Both ends of the tunnel have collapsed. Hundreds of people are trapped with about 12 hours air. An explosion just happened at the bridge, too." She ran into Lincoln's arms quickly.

"Kyle, what's going on?"

He looked at her calmly, saying, "Call Homeland Security and the Red Cross. Have them get down here as well as FEMA. We've got an all-nighter ahead of us." Lincoln bolted back down the stairs to the entrance, praying that his good buddy, Chuck Caley, was not caught by the cave in. Searching for survivors was now the priority of the day.

The Twentieth floor suites at Henry Ford Hospital was once featured on "Lifestyles of the Rich and Famous/Detroit." Care at this level was considered second to none anywhere in North America. This was a true sign that someone had achieved the pinnacles of success. The best was yet to come.

Wanda Willington sat up in her bed, recuperating comfortably and fine tuning for her world tour next month, her first in years. Her broad smile shined towards everyone she met, always giving from her heart to brighten someone else's life.

Her doctors had already given her the word that she could go home in a few days, with the police commissioner's OK, too. A surge of anxiety swept over as she thought she saw a face from her past, right outside her window. After signing a few papers for the hospital, she said, "I'm feeling a little tired, guys. Can you come back later?" Obligingly, the room quietly emptied. Left alone, she snapped off her light and ran to the window, clicking it open. As she recognized the face, she asked, "Where the hell did you come from?" Climbing out the window, the two disappeared into the night.

A few miles away, at The Institute of Arts, Dr. Amy Mitchell stood watching the throngs of visitors admiring her work. The polished slate floor of the North American Exhibit Hall made the soles of the shoes sound like hundreds of shuffling sand crabs, each one taking in each and every ounce of history on display. The long awaited display of artifacts from the Mesa Verde Pueblos (the Anasazi) finally arrived. Family after family strolled the hall seeking a firmer connection with the past. Juan Martinez, with his daughter Sarafina, stood entranced by the showcase of dolls.

" Papa, what are these?" she asked.

"These dolls are what the ancient ones called Kachinas, representing souls of relatives who passed on to the underworld. They were also looked on as places where souls stayed until the flute-playing locusts led the way to the current world and their birth. The newborn and the dead would pass through to the new world through a passage called the Sipapu. Today, many use special places in the landscape or special bodies of water, as transportation and communication to the lower world. Many of our ancestors believe that one can float in eternity without a personal connection, through past relatives, to the Sipapu. Until that time, their spirits would remain inside these dolls until the gods opened the doors of the Lower World to them. Did that make any sense, honey?" She began to give him a confused look that was her trademark, when a chilled burst of air filled the hall.

A ghostly, pale aura began to float out of the doll showcase and hover above the crowd, absorbing the light as quickly as it appeared. Surprise quickly turned to fear as the ghostly aura began to take the shape of a face above the crowd. Juan held his daughter tightly as it began to speak.

"I am the last Great Chief of the Anasazi, as you call us. Our sacred burial caves have been desecrated and our god of the Third world seeks justice. Our people will not rest until our sacred tools are returned. Who is responsible for this violation?" Amy and Tim stood up from the crowd, ready to take any punishment that the spirits might shower them with. Protecting the visitors was first on their minds.

"My name is Dr. Amy Mitchell, a person who rebuilds the past to make the future better. This is my partner, Dr. Moran. We led the people to discover your caves, but someone outside of our group ravaged your caves. We ask your forgiveness, Oh Great Spirit, and vow to continue our search for the culprits who violated your sacred grounds."

A sudden flash of light and roar of thunder showed the anger of the willowy spirit. It spoke with a fierce vengeance, "Be aware. My people will return as the sun rises. The renegades will be turned over to us on that day or this land will be destroyed."

The ghost quickly left the hall before the crowds regrouped and left the building. Amy wished Drew were here to help her understand what was going on. Tim took her in his arms as they escorted everyone outside the hall, leaving the artifacts alone with the spirits. Their wonderful dream was quickly becoming a horrible nightmare. With a dazed stare on her face, Amy Mitchell locked the door on her crowning achievement.

Her hospital pajamas did not prepare her for the journey she chose with that mysterious face in the window. Though the face was larger and more mature, it still had eyes that would dance in the wind when they smiled. They were the eyes that lit up her heart on those dreary days when all she could do was fight for her life and family with Skip. The eyes showed a soul as pure as a fresh clean snow, unblemished from the corruptness of evil all around them. She always saw a strong, religious soul inside this person, one that she knew would be a leader of men someday, though she couldn't tell in what way. Those eyes had left her long ago, and she thought they would never return. Until now. Drew had come home.

Struggling for twenty minutes, Drew and Wanda finally reached the top of the hospital. He chose a route of drain pipes and ledges to avoid detection from the local constabulary. His Ute brothers taught him the fine art of camouflage, a tool that was said to have been developed during ancient times when competition was fierce for buffalo on the plains. As the white men traveled westward towards this new land, the art of ambush became the next step as native Americans fought to save their lands from the white invaders. He discovered his mission in life. A Journey that could cost him everything he had worked for and his family too.

Drew pulled his mother over the top rail of the main building, leading her to a bundle tied with twine near the heliport pad on the roof. He undid the package and threw Wanda a black jean outfit with a pair of hiking boots. She flung her hospital clothes off in favor of the new duds, accepting the new look enthusiastically. Grabbing him brusquely by his arm, Drew turned and gave Wanda his full attention.

"So now that you have so abruptly reappeared in my life after disappearing so quickly, how about some answers. Like why?" asked Wanda.

Drew looked at her with the same patient look she was accustomed too. He took a deep breath and sighed. "Really, Mother, we do not have enough time to give you all of the answers you want. Ray will be here with your ride in twenty minutes. We have a plan to get you to a safe place before anything else happens to you."

She looked at him, asking, "Just whose lame brain idea was this?"

"It was actually Dad's idea, but he is tied up right now. I have people working on those transport trucks. Ray is leading a squad of helicopters that your boyfriend, Tony, hired to spray the city with some deadly gas and take over the city as his own kingdom. Dad dropped me off at the hospital with orders to get you to safety immediately."

"Not until I start getting some answers!"

Drew looked at his watch nervously and checked the skies for any sign of their transportation. Reluctantly, he agreed to answer.

"Just before you and Father decided to divorce, there was the constant fighting between all of us, Amy and Ray included. I decided that I had to do something to change my situation. So, I waited one night and slipped out the back while everyone was asleep. After picking up a couple of scary rides on I-75, a trucker picked me up near Hazel Park and took me out west to Nebraska. From there, I stayed with some members of the Oglala Sioux near the Colorado border. They began to teach me the ways of the Native American Indians of the plains, their lifestyles and their beliefs. I became thoroughly entranced by the stories, told about wars and famines that soldiers put them through. Many women and children died while proud warriors could only stand by and do nothing. Some died from just losing their will to live.

"Listening to the stories stirred my memories about our ancestors that lived in the Four Corners area around Mesa Verde. As Grandpa Earl's tales rekindled my dreams nightly, I decided my answers would lie there in the sacred walls of the cliff dwellings. I met up with John Runningfox and Tisha Yellowfeather of the Ute tribe of western Colorado and they took me in as their brother. For years, they taught me every aspect of tribal life; from cooking through every tribal dance ritual known to the area. My expertise became the Snake dance, one that traced back to the Anasazi, during the final years before they left the Mesa Verde plateau for good. It was there that I first heard the name, Red Deer, from anyone other than you and Grandpa. It became my driving force to join Amy's expedition to the burial caves."

"My daughter led a group of people on an expedition in rattlesnake country?" replied Wanda.

"Yes and she braved many obstacles during her trip too. Once John and I led her to the burial caves of the ancient ones, some bad apples, as you call them, invaded the cave of great-great-great grandma, Red Deer and her husband Amozeltec, the last chief of the Anasazi, of sacred items that supposedly gave him supernatural powers. The theft devastated her to the point that I came out of hiding, letting her know that I was her missing brother. I know I put you through a lot. But the knowledge Grandpa Earl said I would gain from studying with them has been tremendous. How I wish he were here to thank. He sure would love to know that he is a great-grandpa now."

Wanda sat stunned for a minute before she jumped up, grabbing Drew and giving him a big kiss on the cheek.

"Enough of that," he said. "We need to stay close to the pad because Ray is due here any minute." They crouched behind an air conditioning unit to wait for their ride.

Mickey and Taylor McGee shuffled pedestrians off Ann Arbor's main streets into the protective shelter of UM stadium off State and Main. As the last few straggled into the concourse, the barrage of ice from the oncoming hail leading the "Devil" storm towards the university grounds.

Wave after wave of golf-ball size hail sailed through the foyers onto the concourse below. People screamed and wailed as fear began to engulf the hidden crowd. Taylor and Mickey, both Army veterans of the Iraqi Freedom War, took charge.

"Everyone, move back towards the rest rooms. We will find safety there from the storm." People crowded into the small area, literally shivering whether from the cold wind whipping through the stadium, their nerves or both.

Scurrying like ants running from an anteater, people searched for safe havens as the "Devil" storm took hold of Ann Arbor. Thousands became stranded by the sudden deluge of rain from the cumulo-nimbus thunderclouds that now stretched to nearly 60,000 feet high. The Huron River rose two feet over its banks, turning many neighborhoods into islands. Many lost their lives as they scurried too late to safety. NOAA weathermen at their White Lake, Michigan facility, issued warnings as far east towards Buffalo as Mother Nature's wrath intensified.

Sitting three levels below street level in the stadium, Mickey and Taylor felt their safety was now a given, though no one moved until they knew the impending funnel clouds had passed over them. Crash came the sound of a tractor-trailer hitting the southern end zone seats, destroying over half of them. Taylor rose from his hiding place. "Everyone, sit tight. I'm gonna check out the situation." Mumbles of "You're Crazy" came from his followers. Mickey remained quiet as her mate poked his out in the storm.

The play was already in motion. Seven F-3 tornado clouds had touched down on the field, ripping up turf and seats as they zig zagged through the 106,000 seat arena. The smaller funnels carved out many new aisles for the seats before they all merged into a gigantic F-5 tornado. The single funnel ripped out the side of the seventy year old stadium where the players tunnel was and ripped right through Crisler Arena and the Yost Ice Arena before leveling the nearly empty dormitories. Dead bodies floated through the water as overturned cars burned from exploded gas tanks. Busted gas mains roared with no end in sight as the lack of public safety equipment became more apparent as the storm moved on. Stations in Detroit broke in with reports that people evacuate to safety immediately. "This storm is a killer and is not taking any prisoners."

CHAPTER 15

Dust from the explosion stagnated in the uncirculated air of the tunnel. The ventilation system, once known for purifying the tunnel's 1.5 million cubic feet of air every 90 seconds, were now empty shells of steel. Large quantities of explosives placed near the system and the entrances caused the explosion and eventual collapse.

Chuck Caley was finishing up with painters near the border crossing when Kyle called him to the work tunnel on the US side. Halfway there, the explosion ripped his world apart. He dropped face down on the south walkway, waiting for the rumbling to stop. A heavy scent of gasoline met his nostrils. People staggered out of their cars to assess the damage while their engines still purred. Jumping down to the roadway, Caley went from car to car, finding survivors at every stop. A family, from Cortina, Italy on their way to Niagra, now sat in their car, frightened by the sudden darkness imposed on them. He climbed atop a tractor trailer cab to ease the increasing fears of the survivors.

"Gentlemen, right now we need to conserve air. The ventilators are probably destroyed, so we have about twelve to thirteen hours before the air runs out. We need to work fast. I need volunteers to go to the US entrance and help start assessing damage. And get those engines shut off too." Five hands immediately went up.

"Good. Then get going. And try to find a couple of workable two-way phones. We will need them." The men split up as Caley led a small group back towards the pillars to find a way out.

Long rows of fluorescent light cases cast a ghostly shadow over the disaster. Caley said a silent prayer for the safe rescue of the trapped people. He would not going to let this become a tomb for so many. There will be a way out of this mess and he was going to find it. Stress cracks were now his biggest fear. No visible signs appeared in the tunnel superstructure as he walked. His Canadian alter ego, Len Ottey, caught up with him as he reached the door to work tunnel #3.

"How's your side, old man," Ottey said. Being the younger of the two, Ottey always greeted Chuck that way, even though they were only two years apart.

"There is a crew shoring up the Canadian end before they start a rescue attempt. Should take them about five or six hours before it is safe for a rescue."

"So you have radio communications with the outside?" he asked.

"Never leave home without it." He pulled out his Nextel phone bringing a smile to Chuck's face.

"Len, take some of the men and quietly evacuate people towards the Canadian side. Tell them it is only precautionary. I want everyone in place for a quick extraction from the tunnel." Ottey sensed an urgency in Caley's voice. "And put a crew on checking the superstructure for any problems." A quick nod from Ottey and they were on their way.

Sixty helicopters lifted off from City Airport, splitting into twelve groups of five. Captain Ron Brewer looked at his watch. It said 1557, three minutes until zero hour and completion of this mission. His co-pilot sat unruffled with a Glock 9mm pointed right as his ribs. Sergeant Ray Mitchell watched every move Brewer made.

"Once the groups are in place, we will begin Operation Eliminate. Afterwards, rendevous will be at the old Tiger Stadium."

"Your bosses will never know what happened," replied Mitchell.

"Your intricate scheme could have worked if anywhere except the United States. Now you will find out why."

One by one, the squads checked in; four over the west at Five Points, four over the Melvindale border and the last four over the east side by Grosse Pointe. Each pilot was shadowed by a member of Mitchell's platoon. Ray said a prayer as Brewer gave the go ahead order.

"Alright, Eagle leader to all birds, time to leave the nest." Switches were thrown and an odorless gas began to leave the containers perched underneath the cockpit. Below, citizens began to drop like flies. Mitchell looked at his watch. It said 1600 hours.

He sat stiffly in a high back leather chair, resting his arms on the famous desk, made from the famous British warship "Resolute". Before him, a holographic image of Richard Johnson danced before him with an ultimatum. By the fireplace sat the chairman of the Joint Chiefs, Air Force General Tim Fouts, Secretary of Defense Garry Lawson and Interior Secretary Evan Birch.

"Mr. President," said the hologram, "the supreme council of Indian Nations is putting this nation on notice. By 4 P.M. today, every citizen of the city of Detroit will have been removed from their land. We intend to declare independence and form a new country called Karoenten. Our new leader, a descendant of the great Anasazi chief, Amozeltec, will receive his coronation at that time. You will not send in any troops to retaliate since the residents will have already been eliminated. Your government forced us from our sacred lands many years ago to land that offered nothing to our people. With the blessing of the Great Spirit, we now claim land abandoned by your people for ourselves as your people did to us." The hologram abruptly ended, leaving an eerie silence over the Oval Office.

After a few minutes, the President spoke. "Alright, General, give me military options," came the presidential order. Fouts stood and faced the President sitting behind the desk, a gift from the Queen of England, rapidly searching his military mind for answers for his commander-in-chief.

"Sir, the options are simple. Send in six F-18s armed with four stingers each and destroy the Joe Louis Arena while they are inside."

"Totally unacceptable, General. There will be no major loss of life between Americans on American soil on my watch. What else?"

"Secondly, we have the 82nd and 101st Airborne Divisions have been on ready alert for 48 hours. We would be over the city for an air drop in 12 hours, with four National Guard Armored Divisions as support by the same time tomorrow. General Abraham is implementing a plan to defuse this event as we speak. His men from Selfridge ANG base are currently working with FBI and local authorities to infiltrate the ranks of the Indians and a Detroit mafia don, Anthony Marvelli, Jr."

"I still can't understand what Marvelli wants with Detroit?" A voice spoke from the French Doors leading to the Rose Garden.

"I believe I can answer that for you, Mr. President." FBI Director Steve Marx stood solemnly in the doorway as the eyes of everyone centered on his presence.

"In 1962, Marvelli's father, Anthony, Sr. met with Bruce Hofen, then National Security Advisor and Darryl Carstairs, aide to Mayor Jewel Christie. They negotiated an agreement to stop an outward exodus of people to the suburbs. Right after the agreement was reached, Marvelli was killed when a freighter was rammed and overturned by a tugboat. His yacht was crushed. The captain of the tugboat lodged a complaint with the ACLU that was never heard by the courts that he was forced to ram the freighter by a mysterious stranger. After local police came to investigate, a gun battle ensued and many police divers were killed. It is rumored that young Marvelli led the raid with the help of his father's chief aide, a man named Helford. They left with a leather pouch under his arm that is believed to be the only known copy of said agreement. Young Marvelli also fancies himself descended from an ancient chief called Amozeltec. Junior was in a Pueblo orphanage in 1959 and adopted by the elder Marvelli a year later. His real father, a Zuni chief, John Runningfeather, and mother, Whisper in the Willows, were both killed in a bar fight when he was three. Junior waited a few years, studying under some of the great families of New York mafioso, eventually building an empire second to none. His flagship company, Renaissance Records, became his main front for laundering money out of the country. When he built his ranch in Cortez, Colorado for his lover, Singer Wanda Willington, it became obvious to us he was up to something. A large buildup of non-ranch buildings and late-night air traffic started and continued until two weeks ago when every one broke camp and came to Detroit. The rest you already know." Marx stood in front of the president's desk as his words took hold of his audience.

"General, what is this plan that General Abraham is working on." The President listened inattentively while General Fouts explained every aspect of Ray Mitchell's detailed assault on the city. After several minutes, the President looked at Secretary Lawson. His look was that of a father giving up on a lost son.

"Gary, I want you to keep both divisions on alert. I am alerting the naval reserve unit to redeploy into the Detroit River from Lake Erie. Send the 101st to a staging area at Selfridge immediately. Do nothing more until we hear from General Lawton. Well, gentlemen, you have your assignments. Get them done."

The President picked up his phone and buzzed his personal secretary.

"Sarah, get me General Abraham Lawton at Selfridge Air National Guard base in Michigan. Right away!" As he put back the phone, he turned his chair around looking out the windows at the Rose Garden. America was on the verge of a Second Civil War. It was now his job to prevent it.

Windows on the Eastern Michigan University shook as shattered as winds from the "Devil Storm." The campus was deserted as well as most of the city. Ypsilanti officials coordinated the most effective evacuation of their metropolitan area. All busses, both transportation and school, were taken over by the city emergency management team and used in a scheduled evacuation to the high school in Howell. Red Cross officials had cots and food prepared for them as they arrived. Nature was the only victim that day. Torn up grass, uprooted trees littered the streets with demolished bricks, broken glass and downed wires, both electrical and cable. Loose wires danced over the streets, sending sparks flying everywhere. The clouds frowned as they passed over downtown. There was no joy in Mudville tonight. Destroying nature was not enough. It wanted more. Detroit was now 30 minutes away. The lightning and hail rolled on.

Mitchell pulled up outside the Marvelli Dry Dock facility, on the end of St. Aubin at Atwater. All three dry docks will still full. A new destroyer would be finished in about two weeks. Junior would have more money than his father ever imagined. He stood looking out at picnickers on nearby Belle Isle. Their gaiety made him sick. Suddenly, the silence was disturbed by a loud chopping noise. One of the helicopters appeared over the island and the picnickers suddenly dropped. The plan was working. He saw the Cobra helicopter turn his way at the shipyard. It was flying low enough to see the face of the pilot and copilot. A look of stunned surprise hit his face as the eyes's of his son, Ray, met his. Consciousness slipped from his grasp. The sound of the rotors was the last thing he heard as he blacked out. Mitchell awoke about ten minutes later at the sound of a large truck braking to a stop close by. A few armed soldiers got out and lifted his body into the truck before continuing on. A couple of blocks later, Skip began to stir as the daze from the fly by wore off. Two men were chatting at the back tailgate of the truck. Mitchell laid still as he listened.

"Things are going like clockwork. People have been dropping like flies. Northern units have amassed nearly 5000 victims in the old armory. Southern units are boasting the same success. By 10 P.M., we will control Detroit and there is nothing the President can do to stop us."

"This government will still find a way. Some military attack, with tomahawk missiles with help from Canadian militia, would be the easiest way," said the second guard.

"Even with the casino laws, we are still considered non-citizens in this country. The Great Spirit will bless this operation. Our revenge will be sweet." Troops carried bodies from the trucks, placing them inside the wire prison inside the St. John's warehouse in front of scores of frightened faces. Skip laid prone on the ground, waiting patiently for the guards to leave the holding pen. His mind processed the situation as quickly as his computer in the office. Patience was not one of his greatest virtue.

The aura of the setting sun shifted the hues on the alabaster walls of Marvelli's office from azure blue to the royal lavender of a wine from southern France. T. J. sat in his high back leather chair, holding the mask of Amozeltec in his hands. A small vibration reverberated through his body sending his pulse rate almost sky high. The two turquoise eyes began to glow bright blue, shifting to golden orange and finally, a fiery red light shot out from the mask and formed into a sparkling apparition on the far wall. Tony sat in stunned silence as the ghostly guest began to take shape. The office walls became solid rock. His luscious blue carpet transformed to a gritty, rocky floor that spread out before his eyes. Women, dressed in leather buffalo skins, sat beating out a rhythmic beat for the warriors dancing the snake dance of celebration. Ornate turquoise jewelry accented their outfits as they held the rattlesnakes in regal positions to honor their leader, which appeared to be him. Children played with a leather ball and net-like catchers, like lacrosse, staying immune to a key component of Anasazi family life. The right of ceremonial rituals.

A young brave known as Jumping Wolf approached where Tony was sitting in the plaza. Jumping Wolf knelt at his feet with outstretched arms apparently wanting something. Instinctively, Marvelli held out the headdress and watched it gleam in the afternoon sun. The dusty old relic he held in his office now gleamed like it did in the hot Colorado sun. The relic was now transporting him back through the centuries, setting him at the center of the ceremonial kiva on the Mesa Verde. He handed Jumping Wolf the new symbol of leadership of the tribe.

"Go, my son. Honor the Great Spirit with our new symbol before I accept it as my crown. The people must accept it before they can accept me as their divine leader."

With that command, Jumping Wolf broke into a wild, animated dance, constantly holding the headdress towards the sky.

The people chanted, "Oh Great Spirit, bless this symbol of divine providence as we fulfill our ancient prophecy. Grant our divine leader the wisdom to guide our hearts and return our people to the prosperity of the ancient ones." The ceremonial drums began to beat louder as the dance frantically reached its climax.

A soft, but calloused, hand touched his right forearm. He turned and looked into the face of one of the most beautiful woman he had ever seen. His first reaction was shock. She looked exactly like Wanda. His words stumbled as he tried to speak to her.

"W-w-w-wanda, why are you here? Where are we?"

She replied softly, "My husband, do you feel alright? I am your mate, Red Deer. We met on the plains of the mesa when you saved those snakes from sheer death. We came to the village together to lead them to a rebirth and build a future on the plateau. Though my birth family has traveled to the land of the Rio Bravo, you are my family now. The Great Spirit has blessed our union. And the people have accepted you as their divine prophet." Marvelli took her hand and squeezed it tightly. Wanda was part of his destiny. Of that he was certain.

Suddenly, the drums stopped. All eyes in the plaza turned towards Jumping Wolf as he approached Tony. Marvelli rose as the leader of the council approached. The crowd hushed as he began to speak.

"Oh Great Amozeltec, divine leader of our tribe. We present you with this symbol of leadership to wear as the symbol of our faith and trust in you and the divine providence that brought you to us. May the sparkling blue stones grant you the wisdom to see our future and guide our hands to make our world grow and prosper." Jumping Wolf took the headdress and carefully placed it on Tony's head. The tribe jumped into a wild celebration as accepted his new place in their society.

Marvelli felt a warmth come from the two turquoise stones placed just above his eyes, stirring both hemispheres of his brain. His subconscious mind awoke with visions that boggled his mind. He closed his eyes and raised his arms towards the sky, chanting something in a language totally unknown to him.

"Mr. Marvelli, are you OK?" The soft voice brought him back to reality. He looked towards the door to his outer office and saw a young intern standing in the doorway.

"Come in and enjoy the seat of power." The naive brunette walked carefully to his side, flinching slightly as he put his arm around her waist. Minutes later, she laid on his desk, screaming as Tony exerted his power over the unsuspecting young lady. God, I deserve to be king, he thought. He pulled the girl up close to him to give her a passionate kiss. He pulled out his .38 special and shot her through the heart. *I have the power of life and death*, he thought. *No one can take that from me.*

And the "Devil Storm" just kept on rolling down I-94, hail and tornadoes wailing in its path. Total destruction was its ultimate goal. The clouds thundered with laughter as it created more chaos on its path. Father Time was unsure whose side to be on. Only "He" would know the answer. The Motor City was less than hour away.

CHAPTER 16

One by one, the helicopters landed on the outfield grass inside Tiger Stadium. Captain Ron Brewer, along with Sergeant Mitchell, hovered over the left field wall as each individual helicopter planted their stanchions on the freshly sculptured blades of history covering this famous landmark. Each pilot eased out of their cockpit as members of Mitchell's Army National Guard platoon, slid out the passengers' doors, M18 carbines still aimed at each pilot's mid-section. East side and West side squads had met above the State fairgrounds, finishing their routes straight down Trumbull. The southern groups followed the I-75 and I-94 corridors, watching people drop like flies as they passed overhead. To the east, in the Campus Martius, the 75 story tower of Marvelli Enterprises reflected the setting sun over the western horizon. Sergeant Mitchell felt the eyes of Tony Marvelli homing in on their arrival, gleefully enjoying his success.

A couple of miles away, two people waited patiently on top of the main building at Henry Ford Hospital. Wanda sat impervious to her surroundings, waiting anxiously for her rescuers to take her away from this mess she was in. Her son, Drew, hovered close to her constantly searching the skies, though for different reasons. A small, black speck appeared in the sky near the river. The constant whirr of the rotors increased as it neared the roof of the main building. Drew had said that Ray was going to pick them up. She couldn't wait to see him. It had been almost two years since she had been able to even just give him a hug. She raised up from her prone position underneath the heli-pad and nearly got her head knocked off from two other helicopters flying towards the old ballpark. She screamed loudly, falling back into Drew's waiting arms. Something cold touched her rib cage as she pulled herself together. Her son was pointing a 9mm Biretta right at her heart.

"So Tony got you too," said Wanda.

"You money hungry little bastard."

"There is more than just money here, mother dear," replied Drew.

"Power and revenge are sweet incentives, too. Tony planned this out to the minutest detail. In one hour, he will announce to his people at Joe Louis that Detroit is seceding from the rest of the country to become a new nation. The helicopters you saw heading for Tiger Stadium, have just layered the city with VARAN nerve gas, killing everyone from the city limits to the downtown area. His security forces are taking positions along all major thoroughfares to prevent any access to the city without his knowledge."

Wanda stood up and slapped his face twice, reddening both cheeks before Drew gave her a good knuckle sandwich in her left jaw, knocking her unconscious. He picked her limp body up and placed her in the seat of the Cobra helicopter. As it took off he jumped into a waiting Huey, rushing him off to the stadium and an inevitable rendevous with his brother.

Covered with dust and rolling in sweat, Kyle Lincoln ran down to the pillars entrance on the American side. Dozens of volunteers feverishly struggled to clear out a rescue hole for any survivors that might still be alive. His Nextel phone began vibrating severely as he stood there directing his troops.

"This is Lincoln."

"Kyle, it's Chuck. How does it look?"

"Not good on this end. Initial looks shows about three hundred feet of concrete between where you are and the main gate. Rescue operations will take some time. Ceilings on our side look very weak. We'll have to shore them up first before we can start digging you out."

"Well, that will take too long. Our air is beginning to stagnate and I don't think it will hold out any more than eight hours, long before you can get things set for a rescue. How's the Canadian side?" asked Caley.

"Anna is checking right now. Chuck, they took a chunk out of the bridge too."

"Figures. Kyle, Len got caught down here too. He's talked to his buddies in Windsor. Damage does not appear to be that severe, so they expect to have most of it cleared in three hours. About two hundred people are trapped with us, scared shitless. So pal, give me a plan."

Lincoln wondered how Chuck ever achieved his position in life. Common sense was not one of his strong points. He always had to be told the obvious in a situation. "Chuck, get everyone together and head towards the Canadian entrance. I'll call for some help. In the meantime, get the people across the border and prepared for rescue. Make sure you and Len check for any structural damage. Keep the info on a need to know basis. Got it?!"

Caley replied quickly, "Got it! Alright, people, let's go to Canada." The phone quickly clicked off, leaving a smile on Lincoln's face as he shook his head. He would never be able to understand his assistant, he thought, but at least he was a good change of pace to an otherwise boring job. Kyle turned and ran back to the office. Decisions had to be made. He needed Anna's help to save those people. The clock was now ticking quickly.

The storm reached the city limits of Romulus about 4 that afternoon. The thunder heads stood some 60,000 feet over the western horizon. Clashes between positive and negative energy started high above the wetlands of the area, building as the electricity traveled down the clouds. Severe lightning increased as the by-product of the extremely dense clouds. Several thousand people were now homeless in Westland. Twisters tore through neighborhoods, shredding them into popsicle sticks. Airlines at Rosa Parks Airport cancelled all outgoing and incoming flights. Crews frantically worked to drain fuel tanks from planes ready for take-off. Airport personnel hoped to avoid any destruction of materials, buildings and personnel from exploding because of a ruptured fuel tank. Winds now pushed the 65 mile per hour limit with no end in site. Four men were blown off airplane wings, two suffered fractured collarbones while the others fell into a coma from severe internal head injuries due to the height of the fall. Terminals were cleared off all passengers. Terminal basements overflowed with people thwarted from their everyday routines, shedding their confident demeanor, fearing that their end was near. Even two levels below the runways, people heard windows begin to rattle. Hail, the size of baseballs, rained down on the aluminum hangars with such ferocity, it shredded the metal like a paper shredder. Three planes, stuck in different hangars, exploded when their tanks ruptured. The hail attacked everyone, taking no prisoners. Airport personnel struggled to stay one step ahead of the "Devil Storm." The worst was only minutes away.

The T-Bird rolled off the freeway unencumbered by the normal traffic on I-75. Dozens of army transport trucks stood idle while security troops searched for unconscious bodies inside vehicles. No one paid any attention to the bright red car with tinted windows. His voice mail said, "Meet at the salt mine, right away. Answers will be waiting." Towering smoke stacks of the Ford Rouge plant loomed over the northern horizon as the mysterious car arrived at the mine. Mitchell stepped out into an almost eerie silence, a feeling he had not felt in years. He was reminded of all the many nights around campfires as a kid. The ghostly tales still haunted his psyche even as an adult. As he parked the T-Bird near the entrance, a flurry of activity approached from up the street towards the railroad tracks. Skip ran behind a row of boxes, loading a clip into his Biretta as he went. A half dozen trucks roared up to the gate of the complex minutes later, pausing as the remote control opened up the large metal gate. When the gate finally opened, the trucks rushed inside the compound. Skip saw many men in army chemical warfare suits. The new Thompson rapid fire M6 rifles were in the hands of most of the soldiers. He stealthily ran beside the last truck and crept inside the compound.

The lead truck slowed by the entrance to the shaft and cavern about fifty feet inside the compound. A small door opened and a very official looking person walked out. The guard chatted with the driver in the first truck for a few moments before two larger doors swung open and the trucks slowly disappeared underground. Skip crawled under the last truck, securing a hand hold on the frame as the last truck joined the trip below the surface. Five minutes later, everyone stopped cold. A flurry of feet appeared at the end of every truck as the lifeless bodies were unloaded. Feminine screams echoed throughout the salt cavern. Mitchell lowered his head to peer out from under the truck. Before his eyes was a cage holding thousands of people. These had to be the residents that were disappearing from neighborhoods, he thought. Two very long pipes stretched from one end of the cage to the other. The pipes were connected to a large tank, labeled VARAN gas, he had been hearing about. Something else caught his eye, too. The cage was wired with explosives, probably set to explode once the trucks were removed. Their clock was ticking away.

Soldiers laid out the bodies side by side, no spaces in between each one. Skip noticed a stack of barrels set a few feet away from his truck, but still close to the cage to observe everything. Whole families had been caged up by these people who were laying out corpses in front of the cage door. Two men stood on a catwalk watching the macabre scene unfold below them.

Lieutenant Morning Sky hollered, "Work quickly. We must prepare to leave in thirty minutes." Suddenly, a group of men rose from the dead and uttered a blood curdling scream. On cue, dozens of men rose up and attacked the nearest soldier. Skip sat there, awestruck with surprise as citizens began to fight back. Machine gun fire came from the catwalks above. Bullets ricocheted through the cavern, striking many of the security troops as well as innocent bystanders. But the people kept on fighting.

Mitchell grabbed a new clip for his Biretta from his belt and shoved it into the handle. He pulled back the barrel, emptying it into the bodies of three guards on the catwalk above. The bodies tumbled over the rail, landing right inside the temporary cage set up on the floor of the cavern. The men responded immediately. Hundreds of dead people came to life. Guards were attacked with short, inch wide pipes. The attackers bludgeoned their victims incessantly, leaving no skull unfractured and blood gushing from slashed arteries. Skip sat behind the empty drums watching the action unfold before his eyes. What seemed like hours only lasted a few minutes. Women picked up the guns left behind by the dead guards, taking defensive positions near the entrance. More trucks were expected soon, he heard them say. Skip decided to make himself known to the new shopkeepers. He raised his arms, Biretta in hand, walking towards the group's leaders. Two women quickly turned, aiming their rifles at right Mitchell's brain.

"Hold it, please, I'm on your side," said Mitchell.

"Who the hell are you?"said the leader.

"The name is Mitchell. Heard people were getting kidnaped so thought I would drop by."

"Vern, keep your gun on this jerk. Sal, check for his ID. I don't trust anybody farther than I can throw them," he said.

"Johnny, find out where all that dynamite went. It's got to be around here somewhere. I am not in the mood to let these people live."

"Wait!" yelled Skip.

"Revenge will not help. These people are probably just pawns in a bigger chain." He paused to catch his breath.

"You need to make a workable plan to deal with these people. Why don't you at least change clothes with these guards before they wake up."

His words echoed through the caverns of the mine like an explosion. "Then, lock them up in their own pen as bait." A couple of head nods by the leaders and the residents stripped their guards down to their skivvies. Women and children pulled the unconscious, half-naked bodies into the cage, locking them in as their groggy bodies began to stir alive from the fighting. One by one, the Indian guards awoke to rifle barrels aimed at their heads.

Twelve twisters swirled down from the low ceiling of the "Devil Storm." The destructive path stretched nearly five miles wide. From Michigan Avenue to I-75, the twisters tore through Allen Park, ripping up chunks of the freeway and dropping them on neighborhoods miles away. Two chunks, both about a half mile long, dropped through the roof of the Postal Service's bulk mail facility on Oakwood, killing everyone inside. Three funnels raced around the Ford proving grounds track like Formula One racers. Potholes developed where cement once laid. Large holes appeared in the tall Ford World Headquarters building, showing no respect for the ensuing life inside. Hail pelted museum goers at Greenfield Village with winds ripping the ancient, historical buildings apart, plank by plank. As the twisters crossed Schaefer Highway, alarms continued to wail at the monstrous Rouge Assembly Plant. Millions of dollars of new equipment quickly became obsolete. New models of the ever popular Mustang soon joined the swirling funnels of debris flying over Dearborn. Empty shells were left where buildings once stood. No house was left standing in its path. The Devil Storm was hungry. Nothing would stop it now.

People in the salt cavern stood there in their guards clothes, standing at order arms. Every member of the Indian security force now looked out from the inside the caged pen. Mitchell and the selected leaders took Lieutenant Morningfeather into the control room. They tied him to a chair and a canister of the nerve gas with a mask over his nose and mouth. Answers were going to come, even if he had to threaten death to the young Indian. Skip grabbed the young lieutenant by the shirt. He could feel the fear come through his eyes.

"Why are you doing this?" he asked. Morning Sky's lips quivered as he tried to talk.

"I know nothing of what you ask," the lieutenant stuttered.

"We are helping the mayor to save the people. I have no other reason."

Mitchell calmly asked, "Who is giving you your orders?" His eyes stayed glued to the young Choctaw Indian. Morning Sky felt a strong shiver travel down the length of his spine. Either way, he knew his death would be imminent. His voice cracked as he spilled his guts to his new captors.

"My chief, Michael Gibson, gives me my direct orders. I see him at times with Richard Johnson, Richard Night Owl, George Tecumseh and Daniel Running Horse. They are the ones that led us through tough times, also led the fight for our own casinos. With a constant source of money, these four have it coming out their ears. We get told that this conference would pay back for all the years this government oppressed our rights. Our ancestors owned this land. We were taught that taking back what was ours from God was the only answer. The four men, who we call the "Apocalypse", are not the type to organize a scheme like this. Rumors have floated about someone else helping them bankroll this operation." A young resident, dressed in fatigues, ran into the room, abruptly interrupting the interrogation.

"Sir, the winds are becoming evil. The Rouge River is turning the plant into an island. Dearborn neighborhoods are history. We are all going to die if we don't leave." He began beating the chests of the adults in the room, trying to get them to move. Skip grabbed him, swung his arm around and planted a knuckle sandwich on his left jaw. His body went limp immediately. Stars slowly drifted through his brain as he dropped into a deep sleep. Mitchell quickly ran to the entrance of the cavern. An almost black looking sky loomed over his head about 1,000 feet up. His meteorological training told him twisters would not be far behind. There were too many people inside to hide on the catwalks for safety. The metal would not withstand the weight of over 1,000 people. He turned back inside to formulate a plan.

The call came over the wristwatch comm radio.

"Take all squads to the convention site and land in positions to form a protective screen around the arena. The 'Apocalypse' will advise from there. Proceed immediately."

Ray Mitchell heard every word. His eyes met Brewer's. One look conveyed the message. The command went out, "All right. Mount up! Let's ride!" One by one, the Cobra helicopters lifted off the outfield grass, gliding over the third deck of the stadium on course for Joe Louis Arena through Corktown. The short trip took less than five minutes. Ray Mitchell saw a Huey transport join up with them, coming from the New Center area. He looked inside the cockpit, recognizing his brother Drew, riding shotgun up front. With a short wave of a pistol, Drew's copter banked left towards the Cobo Hall roof parking lot. Captain Brewer noticed the distraction and took advantage of the opportunity. He banked his Cobra severely to the right, hoping to throw Ray Mitchell off balance. He guessed wrong. Mitchell's reflexes brought his pistol right at Brewer's right eye.

"Level off right now!" he said calmly, cocking the pistol as he spoke. Brewer moved the control stick slowly to the right. The Cobra carefully leveled itself, with Joe Louis just a few blocks away. The squadron flew in low unaware of an impending holocaust just a few miles away.

The crowds inside stirred. The normal start time of four p.m. was switched to three thirty. National television networks were setup to cover tonight's session. Press releases stated a major announcement would be made by the tribal councils tonight. Restlessness pervaded the bowels of Joe louis Arena like a scorpion preparing to strike. A flurry of activity appeared on the podium as the house lights began to dim. A single spotlight appeared with a solitary figure. Silence fell over the crowd as the roar of helicopter rotors flew over head. The crowd turned its attention to the man at the lectern. A few tense moments went by before the hush was broken.

"My friends, welcome to day two of the Great American Indian Pow-Wow. I am Michael Gibson, Chief of the Choctaw Mississippi tribe. Tonight, you will have an opportunity to meet the man responsible for this great event. Then, without further adieu, hear is our sponsor and host, Detroit's most prominent businessman, Anthony J. Marvelli, Junior." Applause swelled to a dull roar as Tony walked to the podium. Cradled in his left arm was the missing Anasazi headdress. He raised his hands in response to the welcome. The cheers retreated as he began to speak.

"Brothers, I welcome you to the land of the Potowatami and the Ottawa. Over three centuries ago, our ancestors welcomed the white men to share the bounty of this land. Today, though, is a day of oppression and abuse by the government of this great land. This item next to me is the ancient headdress of the last leader of the ancient ones of the Mesa Verde, Amozeltec. With this symbol of leadership, he was empowered to see the future of his tribe and give them wise leadership. My father shared a dream with me when I was young, to do everything possible to help the people of his city. Today, Detroit struggles for a new identity after years of abandonment and despair. Everything is about to change. At this moment, our security forces are securing the city borders for our secession from the United States. Today, the nations of native American Indians will be under one banner, Karonteon, the coast of the straits. Upon this land we will build a new nation free from oppression. And once again with can live with the Great Spirit in blissful harmony." The arena echoed with cheers from the crowd. Marvelli reveled in the moment. He opened the antique headdress' case and put on the artifact. The dream was now becoming reality.

CHAPTER 17

9240 Dwight was a grand house built during the city's glory days of the 1920s. The original owner lost it during the Great Depression and it stood vacant until auctioned off to entrepreneur Alex Manoogian for $25,000 in the late 1930s. The 4000 square foot house was described as both Spanish and Italian design. With a terra-cotta tile roof as its trademark, the house was dominated by walls of windows-bowed windows, arched windows, leaded windows- that let light stream in and grant spectacular views of the city and the Detroit River. Three sunrooms were located on the downstairs level, all facing south towards the city and the river front. Since 1965, most of Detroit's mayors have made this their home, since the house was donated by the Manoogian estate as a thank you to his adopted city. A solitary man, with his arm in a sling, stood looking at the city he had loved all his life.

Jamieson, the mayor's valet, quietly walked into the room.

"Chief Nicholson is waiting for you in the library, sir."

Kirkland Asher turned from his view and directed, "Bring him in here, today." The valet turned and left, returning with the police chief in tow a few minutes later.

"Hello, Barney. Tell me what is happening."

"Kirk, it's a mess. The FBI controls our police. The Michigan National Guard controls our airspace with the 101st Airborne Division at Selfridge ready to strike at a moments notice. I feel totally useless. They have totally shut us out of the loop."

Asher looked at his chief pensively. "Barney, what do you think is needed here? Should we just sit back and let the Feds take over or do we take charge of what we have? Detroit has never backed down from anybody. Remember the '67 riots or the revolts against Martin Luther King's assassination in '68 and the Rodney King beating in the 90s. The city let off their steam and settled back into a tense calm, constantly looking for that magic formula to peacefully coexist. That is something that is always present in Detroit society and politics, whether it was the Irish against the Germans in the late 19th or early 20th centuries. Or the modern day battle between black and white that has torn this city apart since World War 2. We always come out with a better plan for the future, but never get solid backing between government and the people. I vow that these people will never be walked over again. Detroit will again become the epitome of cities to live in for quality of life. Get out of here and create a way for us to get control of this city back where it belongs, the people." Barney stood awaiting a further response.

Asher smiled. "You've got your orders, Chief! What are you waiting for!" Nicholson turned, slowly sprinting across the Italian marble floor. Ideas germinated inside his cunning little brain as he slid into his car. No one dared to get in his way

Trucks neared the salt mine complex loaded with bodies ready for cremation. Similar scenes were playing out simultaneously at the 8mile Armory and the St. John's Hospital warehouse on Moross. It had been one hour since the helicopters blanketed the city. Cleanup and elimination was moving along smoothly, remaining dead bodies should be cleaned up by 1600 hours. The leaders will be very pleased he thought.

Thomas Morningsky had never served in America's Armed Forces. He joined rebel Indian forces six years ago at age sixteen, leading the second riots at Wounded Knee, South Dakota, just a few years ago.

The wind blasted his face as he hung on the side runner of the lead truck.

The bumps from the Conrail tracks shook his insides like a paint shaker. The tacos he ate earlier felt like they were ready to regurgitate out of his stomach. It took all his willpower to suppress the urge to vomit. He hoped none of his troops saw his moment of weakness. He ordered the driver pressed a button and a metal gate began to roll back allowing entrance into the compound. The twelve trucks clamored to a rolling stop at the door to the underground cavern. The lieutenant jumped into action immediately.

"Corporal, take the second squad and secure the entrance before the storm hits. All right, driver, move in!" Morning Sky barked the orders like a boot camp drill sergeant. Troops emptied out of every truck only to be met by a platoon of M18 carbines aimed at their guts. Morning Sky met Skip's eyes as Mitchell burst out into a fiendish grin.

"Welcome to my parlor said the spider to the fly. All right, Sanchez, get their guns and start unloading these people. We've got about ten minutes before that storm starts bearing down on us. Move!"

The captive residents jumped in right away and finished unloading in eight. Suddenly, someone hollered, "Hey, these people are still alive!" An aura of shock fell over the mine cavern as the rows of dead people began stirring to life.

The Devil Storm was just seconds away from the salt mine compound. Hail began pounding the ground with the force of 100 machine guns fired from F18 Hornets. The roof of the cavern shook fiercely. Women screamed as children clung to their fathers. Rain pellets dropped from the sky like atomic bombs, so large they exploded on impact. Rivers of water flowed downward into the cavern, gathering as a little lake inside of the cage. Soldiers cried out in fear as the rainwater slowly creeping up their legs as they stood locked up behind the fence. The last of the bodies were helped off the last truck, sloshing through the murky water as it gathered in the mine. Skip stood for a moment, surveying the problem as chaos reigned supreme. A light bulb went off in his head as he quickly germinated another solution to their current dilemma.

"Sanchez, get every one out of that cage and put them in that elevated tunnel over there to your left," said Mitchell.

Sanchez looked stunned at Skip's order.

"These people were going to kill us! What are you thinking of doing, letting them go?" He moved to within inches of Mitchell's face awaiting his answer.

"Just do it! We don't have time for explanations. You'll just have to trust me." Mitchell held a cold look on his face, refusing to budge. Sanchez took his gang and emptied out the cage. Everyone quickly ran to the much drier cavern, screaming in fear as the roar of the tornadoes approached. Mitchell tried quieted the crowd to a dull roar.

"Listen, people, timing is critical. I need ten men to volunteer to drive those trucks. I want them placed into three rows of four, placed sideways in front of this cavern. The twisters will hit here in about twelve minutes. Moving these trucks will take about nine."

An unknown person spoke out, "How the hell are three rows of trucks going to protect us?"

Skip smiled back at him and said, "I am a weatherman. I do know something about these things." He quickly glanced at Sanchez.

"Get moving. Time is wasting away." Minutes later, the last of the trucks slipped into place between the storm and the sanctuary. Mitchell and Sanchez began herding the people further back into the cavern.

"When those tornadoes hit, the vacuum they create will probably suck out most of the trucks into the debris stream it creates. We should have three or four trucks left to get out of here after the storm passes. Everybody get down and hold on!" Skip grabbed four of the children and hid behind a large row of canisters for protection.

"And stay close, temperatures are going to drop drastically. You will need to keep each other warm till it's over."

The low grumble from the sky steadily increased as the clouds grew darker. Winds circled round and round grabbing everything from the ground that wasn't anchored deep below the surface. The whine of the wind screeched like a banshee in everyone's ears. Suddenly, the doors became a supersonic wind tunnel, probably category 5 or 6, sucking out everything in sight. Nerve gas canisters, pipes, catwalks and even the cage used to imprison the people. The first five trucks exploded as they flew out the doors, hitting the debris field immediately. The skies lit up like a bright orange sunburst, exploding like barges from the Freedom Festival fireworks on the river. But as quickly as it happened, it was over in the blink of an eye. The Devil storm had done its damage. It honed in on the center lane on Fort Street and Historic Fort Wayne. Downtown was just minutes away. Its hunger for destruction was insatiable. Marvelli's right hand, Helford, watched from Joe Louis Arena's roof with sadistic glee. Detroit was in the palm of his master's hands.

The Huey circled the oval shape of the ice arena as it prepared to place its stanchions softly on the tar covered roof. Drew could see two men covering their eyes, and shielding their faces, as the helicopter lowered itself to a stop on the roof of the arena. Winds buffeted the open sided helicopter severely. Temperatures had dropped over forty degrees in the last half hour. The "Devil Storm" was visible just over the southern horizon. Panicking, the pilot almost collided with the roof of the Cobo Hall parking lot, which would have scattered his occupants all over the asphalt surface. The gunman, in the passenger seat, pointed his .45 right at the pilot's temple.

"Don't even think about letting this thing crash or you will never see any of your family again." Drew Eaglewing carefully glanced at his passenger in the rear seat. His mother was still unconscious, but at least showing signs of breathing more on her own than when he had to hit her. A silent prayer came out of his heart for her. If only he could tell her the truth, she would definitely understand. He hoped that day would eventually arrive. He felt the power of the rotors begin to wind down as the Huey settled onto the roof by the elevator shaft. His seat belt was unbuckled and he was in the rear compartment covering Wanda with his coat before she woke up freezing. She always hated the cold, he remembered.

They carried Wanda, the pilot and Drew, with one arm each around her waist holding her up. The elevator ride down five floors was uneventful. On the first floor, Drew found a single flatbed cart to lay his mother on for the trip over to Joe Louis Arena. After hitting a few bumps on the sidewalk outside, Wanda began to stir. Drew jumped quickly into action, closely watched by the two men who met them on the roof.

"Lay still, Mom," he whispered into her right ear. "I need you to follow my lead. I'll explain later."

She cautiously opened her eyes, giving him a look of understanding that he had grown to know from his childhood. He turned to the pilot, who was pushing a cart. She obligingly laid on it with out a fuss.

"Be careful. Our orders are to take her to the master in good condition. The wedding is to take place in one hour." The pilot nodded and kept pushing towards the rear overhead door that faced the river front. The pedestrian walkway stood bare as people scurried for safety from the freezing cold and the oncoming storm. The guard at the gate acknowledged Drew's arrival and logged it in his duty log. He called on his 2- way radio to the guards inside. The overhead door began to rise and the cart carrying Wanda slid into the safety of the arena. They made a final stop at the door outside of the official's locker room where Marvelli had Wanda's wedding dress awaiting her arrival. She continued acting groggy as Drew and the pilot carried her into the room. As they placed her into a folding chair, she continued her reuse and began to act like she was coming to.

Stuart Gibson sat nervously at his desk at the Severe Storms Tracking Center in Norman, Oklahoma, watching the radar screens before him. A constant flow of satellite photos littered the usually tidy desk. Gibson hated messes. His wife left him for some sanity, she said, because he was such a stickler for perfection. No one could live up to standards. As he watched his monitors, Stu began to feel that his wife must have talked to Mother Nature as well. Destruction reports from the "Devil Storm" were piling up to where he couldn't keep track. His eyes and ears caught wind of a CNN report from Chicago. He grabbed the remote and turned up the volume.

"This is Lucy Gillian in Chicago. Power is totally out. The footage you are about to see will show you what this 'Devil Storm' has done to America's Heartland." The broadcast turned to a tape showing wanton desolation.

"Starting in St. Louis, the storm took out whole neighborhoods all over the southern suburbs, weaving a path through the city. The Gateway Arch barely escaped total demolition. Whole blocks are now nothing but mini lumber yards. You can also see that numerous volunteers are now combing the devastation for either survivors or to tally up the tragic loss of life throughout this holocaust.

"Here in Chicago, people from all walks of life are out in force, assisting in the rescue efforts. Millions of dollars of agricultural lands have been lost due to hail and flooding. Whole crops of wheat and corn are now waste by-products of the storm. Chicagoans have been trying to piece back together their once fruitful lives. For now, there is really not much more I can say about this storm. It is currently entering the Detroit area, leaving a long line of destruction behind. I want to leave you with footage that was shot by my cameraman, Mike Thompson, over the last 24 hours. I want everyone to see what has made this country great for nearly 250 years."

The image shifted to a tape that was being played out of a remote truck somewhere in the city. A crowd had now developed around Stu's desk as the tape began to play. Gasps of shock escaped people's mouths unknowingly. The entire Mississippi River extended four miles inland totally engulfing downtown St. Louis. People crawled out of their cars, swimming to higher floors of buildings not totally engulfed by flood waters. Police patrol boats circled abandoned cars almost totally submerged by the raging river. People from every walk of life, every race, color and creed were involved in search and rescue efforts. The scene shifted to the tall skyscrapers of Chicago.

Dozens of tornadoes clamped on to the sides of buildings, ripping out whole sides of buildings, sometimes three floors at a time. One hole on the 95th floor of the Sears Tower, took out whole offices with multiple workstations inside on at least two of the surrounding floors. Scores of people were sucked to their deaths while a small portion actually survived by being dropped in the Chicago River. The Magnificent Mile laid in ruin from Grant Park to North Shore Beach. Gates Planetarium and the Natural Science Museum showed roof damage from an attack of hail stones. Undamaged exhibit halls served as a triage center for emergency services, already overflowing their capacity.

The Ferris wheel at the Navy Pier stood as a modern Picasso, a tower of twisted metal with cars hanging by a thread. Restaurant row was now a distant memory. Mother Nature had invoked her wrath on her subjects for not taking care of her world. But the aftermath was still the same. One after another, people rose to the occasion. Gang members helping rich people, police rescuing would be looters only to lock them up later and even a teenage boy helping a woman deliver a baby on top of a stranded car. Gibson sat there thinking that there must be a way to slow this storm down before it hits Canada, which would be its next stop after Detroit.

"Todd, get me Zachary Air Force Base in Cedar Rapids, Iowa. I need to talk to the head of the high altitude weather plane team." Moments passed before the phone buzzed.

"Captain Will Strasburg, sir. What can I do for you?"

Gibson cleared his throat. A wave of nervousness started to overwhelm him.

"Listen, weren't you guys involved in that plan to seed clouds to try and avert disastrous storms in tornado alley?"

"Well yes, that is true."

"OK, Captain. Sit back and listen. I may have a plan for you. Do you have any of that equipment left?" Gibson's voice fluctuated with a bit of hope. He began to explain his idea as the captain sat at the other end of the phone. Finally, the captain's voice piped in.

"Say no more, sir. The equipment is already loading as we speak. Just tell me where we gotta go." Gibson grabbed his maps and quickly blurted out the coordinates, a smile of hope rose on the face of everyone in the room. The plan was simple. Seed the thunderclouds with the titanium chemicals and diffuse the negative electricity within the cumulonimbus water factories in the sky. I will get you orders momentarily." As he hung up the phone, Stuart said a silent prayer. Everything was now in God's hands.

A fully-equipped C-130 barreled down the runway to begin its race against time. Captain Strasburg and crew pushed the bird to its limits. NOAA scientists busied themselves with satellite data tracking the "Devil Storm." Everyone was oblivious to each other as they began their race to save the world. Time was now their worst enemy instead of their best friend. The race was on.

CHAPTER 18

She sat is the back of the SWAT van. Her breath came in short, staccato strokes as the lungs she depended on for air daily, struggled to overcome the tension building in her gut. A veteran of Operation Iraqi Freedom, Reese Watson joined the Detroit Police reserve unit just a few months before after her honorable discharge from the Marine Corps. Her ex-husband, now on his way to becoming a lifer in the Corps, had forced her to seek a better way. She choose to start over and raise her two kids, a boy and a girl, on her own. The marriage dissolved after he began seeing his family as merely another troop under his command. With the love and passion gone, she returned home to mom and dad in Whitmore Lake, searching for a foothold in a new career.

Detroit Police were the first to respond. After months of testing and a tough academy stint, she was accepted in the reserves and placed in the top five candidates to join the force. Two months later, the call came and a new chapter in her life began.

Reese Watson achieved a Master's in Forensics and a Ph. D. In Criminal Psychology before her tour of duty in the Corps. While in Iraq, she worked at training an elite police squad as they struggled to achieve independence from dictatorial governments. After surviving two car bomb attacks from terrorist organizations, she came home. Returning home to her abusive husband, she requested an honorable discharge and immediately flew to Reno to get a quick divorce from the asshole. Abuse was not something to be tolerated. It became her mission in life to teach her kids how to avoid that in their future.

As a last minute addition to the SWAT team, on loan to the FBI, Watson excelled as she fought for a permanent place in a team of men with ten to twenty years on the force. She was listening to Lt. Williams talking with one of the senior members about a mafia madman loose in the city. She began to prepare herself for their quarry as the team approached the shipyards.

Chief Nicholson was half way down Jefferson when he spotted the van as he passed Erma Henderson Park towards downtown. Listening to the local news radio station, he began to clear his head of all the bullshit the Feds had brought him and come up with a plan to save the city he grew up in. When he reached the MacArthur Bridge, he saw the SWAT team van turn onto Beaufait towards the dry dock shipyards. His car followed them as if it were already programmed to.

The van arrived at the old dry dock canals, now refitted to handle newer, super ships being built worldwide. It stopped just short of the river front fence, a stone's throw away from the old Rivertown warehouse district. The ten team members jumped out and deployed along the perimeter fence, led by a lieutenant whom he did not recognize. But there was one member who stood out in his eye as they deployed. He kept a close eye on them as they worked.

Watson led part of the team through a hole she cut in the fence with wire cutters. They searched high and low for any evidence to this plot, but found nothing but an empty shell. Warehouse after warehouse lay completely bare before their eyes. She reported back to FBI Agent Obo in the command truck.

"The place is quiet as a church mouse, sir. Either nothing was here or they knew we were coming."

"Secure your area and return to base." Obo turned as the door to the van flung open and he saw Barney's smiling face burst into the control center.

"Well, Cliff, what are you guys up to now?" asked the chief.

"Following reports about a weapons cache stored at the shipyards. The director wants every lead followed up on to build up a case against Marvelli," he replied.

"So why are you here?"

"Nothing better to do, Cliff. I'm just keeping tabs on what's going on."

Suddenly, the clouds began to darken to th west. The Devil Storm was closing .Obo ordered the team members back to the van.

"May as well stick around for the ride, Barney. I hear this thing packs a wallop." The chief strapped himself in with no questions asked.

Miles away, Skip's T-bird raced up Fort Street at blistering speeds, unrestricted by normal Saturday traffic. Mitchell left Sanchez and his gang in charge of the Salt Mine with orders to wrap things up and meet him at Joe Louis. The asphalt was slick from the heavy rains from the storm that now crossed the international boundary with Canada. He raced towards the arena at speeds close to +100 miles per hour in his government issued toy.

Mitchell began to encounter remnants of the storm scattered across Fort Street. Uncontrollable donuts and fish-tailing became everyday occurrences as the car slid on the ice. The computer spoke, "Initiating super traction," located in the center panel of the console. Flipping open the cover, Mitchell hit the button and the car did an abrupt stop, throwing him into the steering wheel. With his nose now bloody and broken, Skip ignored the pain and reached behind his back for his.45 caliber pistol and popped the clip. It was still full. He reached for the glove box for the Biretta Chief gave him. Still fully loaded. It was time to kick ass, he thought as he sat in the middle of Fort Street. Immediately, he pressed the accelerator, pushing headlong into the storm and his date with destiny.

The "Devil Storm" lingered over the Detroit River as it slowly advanced towards the now empty Ambassador Bridge. The broken roadway, in the center of the span between the arches, looked like the wounded eye of a cyclops. The roadway now rested sixty feet under the surface of the river. Rescue divers from the Coast Guard and both Detroit and Windsor police departments, worked feverishly attempting to rescue survivors from the two cars seen plummeting to their demise from the explosion. Tornadoes from the storm turned to waterspouts as they reached the river. Whirlpools enveloped any and all living things above and below the water. Sailboats, fish and even underwater litter disappeared in a flash.

The core of the storm passed over Zug Island, center of Detroit's steel industry. A swampy marshland, once owned by Samuel Zug in the late 1890s, who sold it to a steel company at the turn of the twentieth century. Today, the silent factories were about to get an unexpected facelift. Hailstones dropped through skylights like anvils falling from the sky. Broken glass scattered across the bubbling smelters and glass-like floor of the factories.

A skeleton crew of maintenance workers scurried for safety as the rain of debris littered the plant. The plant was closed so no lives lost. The storm wanted more. All but 500 feet of the 9200 foot bridge hung precariously in the storm's path. The divers below were aware of the rapidly darkening skies to the south. A bolt of lightning raced from the clouds, striking the radio antenna on the Coast Guard cutter, shorting out all radio and sonar equipment inside. A 5K electrical charge traveled through the bodies of the operators killing one and leaving the other unconscious. Captain John Stansel, a twenty-year veteran in the service, turned and stood in shock at the aftermath of the incident. A few miles away, six waterspouts swivelled and twisted towards the unsuspecting ships up from the southern end of the river.

Up the shoreline at Joe Louis Arena, Sergeant Ray Mitchell stood outside, assessing the situation as the Cobra gun ships enforced a security ring around the arena. The other members of his platoon, part of the 758th Air National Guard unit at Selfridge, stood ready to implement the next step of his very simple plan. Replace all of the deadly nerve gas canisters with less dangerous nitrous oxide and temporarily put the city to sleep was the essence of the scheme. It was like asking the whole city to play dead while the wolves danced around their victory fire. Part two was the hardest part; have local authorities convince every gang in the city to convince the citizenry to go along with the plan. It was risky, but he prayed that it would work. If it did, the apocalypse would be in their trap and vulnerable for the kill. Little did he know that it was already working. Sedated citizens began to awake some forty-five minutes later, ready to kick some butt Detroit-style.

With his .50 caliber, M18 rifle pointed at the rib cage of his captive, Captain Brewer, Ray Mitchell whispered an order into Brewer's ear. Within minutes, every crew from the helicopters were on the street with their M18's cocked and ready. The final phase was about to begin. With a wave of the hand, the platoon advanced into the arena.

Turning under the Veterans Memorial Building, the SWAT team passed under the viaduct at the rear of Cobo Center. Officer Watson hollered, "Lieutenant! Stop the van!"

"All right, Watson. What gives?!"

"Sir, wouldn't it be more in our favor if we advance to Joe Louis from above rather than ground level like from the roof of Cobo?" The lieutenant paused a moment, giving his brain a chance to catch up with Watson's. He reached out and slid open the door to the driver's compartment as they went past Cobo Center.

"Stop the van here," barked Lieutenant Williams. "Everyone out! I want a command post at the roof top elevator in five minutes. Let's move!"

Watson was the first one off leading the team up the stairwell to the roof. The first thing they saw was the abandoned Huey. Watson signaled two other team members to secure the Huey and make sure it was operational. A double thumbs up came from the advance team. That was good, she thought, now does anyone know how to fly that thing. Without asking, Officer Parish jumped up and ran to the cockpit. Within seconds the rotors began to turn. A few minutes later, Parish gave a thumbs up also. Watson smiled and signaled the rest of the team to follow, the chief and her lieutenant included. They boarded the Huey transport and took off in a circle around the roof garage. In the co-pilot seat, she directed Parish to fly directly to the center of the Joe Louis roof. Their touchdown went unnoticed.

Sanchez and his gang left the salt mine with a convoy of vehicles on the trail. With the help of a portable blow horn, he began traveling through neighborhoods echoing, "People, defend your rights. Follow us to Joe Louis and kick some Indian ass." Convertibles from Mexican Town, stake trucks from Japan Town, even a few rickshaws from China Town, all stepped in line with the remaining transport trucks heading down the Fisher Freeway towards Downtown Detroit. Hoppin' hydraulics from Mexican Village led the convoy.

"Spud" Jones followed his lead on the north and west sides of town. His gang took a bunch of residents and overran the 8 Mile Armory.

A great white roostertail mushroomed from behind the rear spiked tires of the T-Bird. Skip pushed the 5.2 liter engine to its limits. The body was shaking from the stress the car was being put under. Buildings whizzed by nothing but a blur to his peripheral vision. His concentration was only on saving Wanda from a fate worse than death itself. Faster and faster he sped down Fort until he came upon the Postal Service building. Less than a mile away, stood six armed guards and two Cobra helicopter gun ships. He popped open his drag parachute and slowed to a quick stop just a few blocks away, taking a few moments to assess the situation.

The lights were now dimmed inside the arena. A single, solitary drum began to beat a slow processional rhythm as four elegantly dressed men, with full Indian headdresses walked onto center stage at the open end of the arena. The men of the apocalypse, Running Horse, Tecumseh, Night Owl and Johnson, took their places as the wedding procession began to start. The event was moved up 24 hours.

Tony Marvelli walked out first, with Helford following close behind. In his hands, the air tight case that held the ancient headdress of Amozeltec. They approached the men of the Apocalypse and bowed in reverence to their title and position in the Indian world. Chief Johnson touched Marvelli's shoulder as a signal for him to kneel before them and the 60,000 onlookers in the arena. Chief Tecumseh was the first to speak.

"Oh Great Spirit of our people, your humble servants assemble before your mighty sword to crown a new leader. We have traveled many moons to reclaim this land once inhabited by the great chiefs, Pontiac and Tecumseh. Before you we present a man who, with your wisdom, will lead the creation of Karontaen, our new promised land. The descendent of the great Amozeltec, the last great leader on the Mesa Verde plateau of the ancient ones, kneels before you now to accept that role for the future of your people, bringing us together again as one people under one spirit." He stepped back in line as Dan RunningHorse came forward.

"A chief's headdress is a symbol of regal leadership in our peoples. To become a chief, one has to show that he is a man of the people, who is respected, trusted and worshiped by all. One who can take the advice of others and apply it for the good of all. A man who, above all else, is a man of compassion. That brother kneels before us today to accept the role of divine leader." He stepped back in line as Richard Night Owl stepped forward.

"The ancient ones of the Mesa Verde and the Rio Bravo are gone now but their legends live on. Through many tribes, our cultures flourish, but our people suffer. But tonight, all of that will end. A new day is dawning for the American Indian." He stepped back in line as the final chief, Richard Johnson, stepped forward.

"In this box is the restored headdress of the last great leader of the Anazasi, Amozeltec. With the psychic powers that this headdress possesses, I place it on the head of our new leader of the new home of our tribes. Anthony J. Marvelli, Junior, rise and take your place on the council as Kapoteantec, leader of all Indian tribes."

Marvelli rose and turned to face the multitudes. The ancient headgear now shined from the restoration and polishing that was done since the theft a week ago in Colorado. The crowd rose and gave their new leader a rousing ovation. A sadistic smile slid onto his face as he soaked in his moment of victory. The chicken was ready to be plucked.

CHAPTER 19

Barney Nicholson sat watching this petite little tiger order around a bunch of hyenas like she was cutting Swiss cheese slices. Four men spread out to the perimeter of the roof, setting up sniper positions over each entrance to the arena. Watson took the rest of the team down an access stairwell onto the arena catwalks. Damn she's good, he thought. He looked at Lieutenant Williams and said, "Give me that .45 and let's go kick some ass before we miss this party and she get's all the fun." The chief and the lieutenant jumped out of the Huey and followed Watson down the stairwell to join the action.

As the door to the roof opened, the afternoon sun burst through, into the arena, casting shadows as the SWAT team deployed into strategic positions above the crowd below. A stern look from Watson made the chief feel like a rookie again.

"How long have you had her on your team, Williams?" he asked.

"She came aboard a couple of months ago when Fitzgerald got bumped up to detective. A solid career in the Marines with a tour of duty in Iraq during the occupation and transition. Excellent marksman. Can hit a fly dead center at forty paces."

"And she is only a junior member of the staff?" questioned Barney.

"In name only, sir. She has led the capture and rescue efforts in at least twenty different efforts so far. Every one here has complete trust in her as a leader and strategist." A smile began to emerge from his sorrow puss face. His brain was germinating ideas like his office computer.

Barb Cook opened her eyes carefully feeling completely rested after a good night's sleep. She looked at her clock. It said 5:00 P.M. She couldn't have slept the whole day. After all, she still dressed in her leotards that she always wore for her senior citizen sex therapy class at the Coleman A. Young community center on Chene. Her students were still there with her, also beginning to stir. She looked at her two regulars, Ira and Verna Levine questioningly.

"What happened?" she asked.

Verna gave a quizzical look and said, "Don't know, dear. Took a breath and fell asleep. Must have cut off my oxygen. My nose must be plugged."

"Can't be, dear. You just smelled my cologne and gave me a big kiss. In fact, we were still kissing when we woke up from this nap," replied Ira.

He turned as a gaggle of noise began outside of the center. Barb flung the door open and found hundreds of people stretching as they also from a deep sleep. The crowd seemed restless and jittery. Verbal jousts were bandied about like rubber balls. Ms. Cook hollered, "What's going on?"

"Those darn Indians are trying to take over our city. We're fixin' to go down and set them straight. I hear other people are doing it to from every part of the city. Wanna come?" Barb looked at her students and they all agreed.

"Why not!" They joined the crowd and took off down Chene towards Jefferson and Cobo Center.

Ouellette Avenue in Windsor was now a military pedestrian mall. In the last few hours. Canadian armed forces were called into action by Prime Minister Charles Auger when terrorist bombs hit the bridge and tunnel. Crossing the international border in the middle of the river, Kyle Lincoln sat in the back of the Detroit Police Harbor Master's boat, anxiously awaiting arrival at the tour boat docks in Riverside Park. Coming across to supervise the rescue efforts for the people still trapped inside the tunnel 100 feet below the shoreline. A very tall, muscular man of German and Scottish descent, Lincoln graduated from Michigan Tech in the Upper Peninsula in the late

80s. His major in structural engineering led him to a 8-year tour of duty with the Army Corps of Engineers at the Soo Locks in Sault Saint Marie, Michigan. Supervising the reconstruction of the Poe lock secured a place for him in the engineering world. Offers landed on his doorstep the day he got discharged from the Army. To be able to supervise the maintenance of one of the world's greatest international wonders and get paid well too was too good to pass up. He joined the Detroit-Windsor Tunnel Corporation five years ago unprepared for what would be the greatest challenge of his life.

The boat drifted up to the beautiful new metal docking facility, built by Great Lakes Cruise Lines for their river boat cruises, with both bow and stern lines flying simultaneously into the hands of waiting Mounties enforcing security on the river front during the crisis. Lincoln was ushered into a military HumVee and swiftly traveled the three blocks to the Canadian entrance to the tunnel. An angry mob met his car as he pulled up in front of the administration building. His Canadian alter ego, John Clark, grabbing him by the arm immediately, walked straight to the rescue effort in full swing at the entrance a few hundred feet away.

Deep under the flowing waters of the Detroit River, Chuck Caley took his rag tag crew of volunteers towards the American entrance, some 400 feet away from the entrance to service tunnel #3. A cold, damp mist began permeating the atmosphere inside the connected cement cylinders that were now almost a century old. Each man, of his team, spread out from each side of the tunnel inspecting its structural integrity. A sudden attack of water droplets hit the young engineer like a Chinese water torture. He looked up in shock, hoping his worst fears would not become reality. A big round puddle of water, about three centimeters in diameter, was now forming on the ceiling. A terrible chill ran through his spine as he reached for his phone.

The damaged span of the Ambassador Bridge shook violently as the "Devil Storm" passed over head. The cables, recently replaced during refit of 2004, snapped with the ease of a twig. Three hundred feet of roadway dropped like honey oozing off a spoon. The center arched support cable dangled lifelessly from the support towers on each side of the border.

Captain Stansel, still reeling from the lightning bolt that struck his ship, stood awestruck at the massive destruction Mother Nature was sending his way. Another crackle of thunder rolled through the heavens, shocking him awake.

"All hands, this is the captain. We have about ten minutes to do this so listen up. Seal all water tight doors. Anchor both bow and stern some how, some way. Chief, lead the crew to secure the police boats to ours before this storm hits. So get moving!"

Men started swarming all over the decks preparing for the impending disaster just moments away. Twenty miles to the west, Will Strasburg and the crew of his C-140A High Altitude weather plane, were busy plotting their plan of attack against the "Devil Storm."

"Radar, time to the center of the storm?" he asked.

"25.7 minutes, sir," replied the radar operator.

"Johnson, do we have enough titanium sulfide to slow this storm down?"

Specialist 4th class Rip Johnson was due to be discharged in a week from the Air Force. He had twenty loyal years serving his country, developing new ways to alter the weather. He was minutes away from his greatest challenge ever.

"Yes, sir. We can put that baby to sleep without a whimper."

Stu Gibson sat in front of his NOAA monitor watching the destruction of the storm as he listened to the cockpit chatter from the plane piped into his speaker. He pulled a rosary out of his desk, holding it in his hand and reciting the prayer of St. Francis of Assisi to guide the crew as they flew towards their destiny or their death.

Drew led his mother up the wooden stairway to her date with history. Marvelli, proudly wearing the ancient headdress, achieved roars from his captive audience as he laid out his plans for the new nation. Wanda shook violently as a cold shiver sailed through her spinal cord. Her ears burned with horror as Tony described the macabre scene he planned for the city.

"As security forces travel through the city, residents bodies and disposed of as fertilizer to enrich the soil of this wonderful land as our forefathers did centuries ago. We shared with the white man as they came to our land. They took from us that which the Great Spirit provided, that which put the food in our bellies and saw us through many harsh winters. We were forced to live on land they gave us to live on so that they could absorb our tribal lands into their new country as they advanced westward. We are now striking back. We will no longer be dictated to buy an inconsiderate, dictatorial government of white people. We, the people of the land of the Sun, will never shirk our responsibilities to our peoples. As your new leader, I will protect this land with my life and soul as will my wife, the lovely descendant of the famous Queen of the Anasazi, Red Deer, Ms. Wanda Detroit." He turned and looked to his right as the spotlight swung over to shine on Wanda and Drew.

"Don't worry. I got your back."

"You think I would trust you, leading me to what will ultimately be my death sentence!" she replied. Drew gave her a quizzical look, wondering what she meant.

"This marriage is a ruse, son. He knows I can spill the beans on him and this is his way of keeping me quiet. Your dad couldn't keep me quiet, turned into a dictator and I kicked him out. Tony was raised with delusions of grandeur. He thinks he is the supreme ruler and will stop at nothing to keep that reality. So, once this wedding is over, I will disappear quietly probably at the bottom of Lake Superior. At least it was nice to see you one last time." A small tear began to trickle down her heavily made up face as she turned to look at the thoroughly intoxicated crowd. The lust for power and glory now reigned throughout the arena.

The podium was now removed from the stage. George Tecumseh, senior member of the Apocalypse, now stood with Marvelli as they awaited the procession bringing Wanda to her date with history. Ceremonial drums beat out a tenor to the pace of the processional march. Quickly, she sped her pace to hurry up the ceremony. Chief Tecumseh called for quiet from the audience. A deafening silence fell over Joe Louis Arena. The future of America's Motor City now laid in the hands of America's singing sweetheart.

She walked to center stage as the drums dolled out their slow methodical beat. An impatient Tony walked over to Wanda, grabbing her hand and pulling her to his side. Marvelli nodded to the Seminole chief and the ceremony began.

In the catwalks above, the SWAT team deployed stealthily behind every spotlight perch that hung from the roof. Beside each light lay a heavily armed sniper with a rapid fire M18 with a telescopic laser scope from the Indian security squad. Officer Reese Watson stood on the center walkway some two hundred feet over the center of the stage. The chief and the rest of her team were positioned, as well, ready to pounce on their unsuspecting prey. Ropes were uncoiled and secured to the iron railings to repel them to the floor when surprise was in their favor. They laid in waiting, preparing to strike in a moments notice.

Far below, George Tecumseh of the Seminole tribe gave the marriage incantation to the two participants at center stage. Marvelli, stood with arms raised, proclaiming loyalty to the Great Spirit.

"Oh Great Spirit of the mighty Indian nations, I commit my spirit to be subject to your continued guidance as the nations of our ancestors unit under one banner. Together, the ancient nations will rebuke the yoke of oppression thrown upon us by the evil ones. My queen and I promise to lead with authority and compassion as we knit the threads of our tribes into one. I accept this woman and this duty as my spiritual mission. To this I pledge my troth."

Wanda looked at him and exploded in a rage.

"You damn bastard! If you think I am going to roll over and succumb to your every whim, you have another thing coming, you bastard. I will never marry you even if you were the last man on earth." She turned to storm of the stage. Tony grabbed her arm severely. She screamed in pain as he pulled her back to within inches of his face.

"No one embarrasses Tony Marvelli and lives to tell about it, bitch. You will pay." He led her to center stage, relishing the thrill of power over the cornerstone of his underworld empire. The time to put the final stone in his foundation arrived. Wanda was now excess baggage.

The water was now sloshing around their feet almost ankle deep. Seepage from the overhead cracks increased from a slow drip to a steady trickle. Caley felt the chill of the damp air seeping into his bones. Over a hundred people stepped carefully through the murky floor following his carefully placed. Many of the little children were now in the arms of their parents, their chests heaving heavily as the damp atmosphere of the tunnel began to lose its fresh air. The ventilation fans no longer changed the air at the rate of over one million cubic feet every ninety seconds. Stagnation settled in as he analyzed his situation. A light bulb turned on in his heads. There is almost 1000 feet of fresh air ducts just past the international border line. Could they use it to escape? Caley picked up his Nextel phone and called Len.

"Len, are you getting stress cracks towards the American side."

"Yeah. It's turning into Soak City down here. Just arrived at the pillars area, Chuck." He added, "Whatever caused this or whoever did this certainly did a thorough job. There is a good quarter mile of concrete blocking our way." A fearful air fell over his voice as he described the horror he saw.

"It looks like maybe twenty or thirty cars were crushed in the explosion. They didn't have a prayer." Ottey held a moment of silence before he spoke again.

"So what's the situation on the other side, pal?"

Caley turned to look at the others in his group as he talked. "Len, are you close to any of the fresh air ducts of the ventilation system?"

"Uh, yeah. Why?"

"Go to the entrance nearest you and call me back. I may have discovered a way out." He clicked the phone off and looked at the rest of his troop.

"Keep pushing on, people. We've got about another two hundred feet to go till we will be in a safe zone. The sooner we get there, the better." The survivors followed obediently.

Twenty-two feet below the surface of the river, a lone diver in a thermal wetsuit settled down into silt of the riverbed. He unhooked a package from his utility belt. Removing his right glove, he touched the package and it began to light up. The diver punched in a time: 6:45 P.M., just twenty minutes away. He set the package down on the river bottom, directly 20 feet above the damaged section of the Detroit-Windsor Tunnel. Like a speeding bullet, he swam away from the bomb he had just planted. A boat waited for him on the surface. It retrieved him from the water and sped off towards Belle Isle.

Chuck and Len found their respective entrances to the fresh air ducts. After removing the covers, volunteers went through to check for damage. Both came back with all clear reports. One by one, the survivors began their crawl to freedom. Women and children went first on the Canadian side since they made up over half of the group. Some thirty feet above them, a bomb, made from C4 plastic explosives, quickly ticked off the seconds till an earth shattering explosion shook the now fragile superstructure of the tunnel. A few of the stress cracks became fissures gushing silt and water into the tunnel. The small group of men on the American side were inside the duct about halfway up to the surface. The people on the Canadian side were not as fortunate. Twenty men, including Caley, perished as the wall of silt and water swept through the tunnel. Water pushed into the ducts, bringing screams from mothers as they reached for their children. The force of the torrent pushed them through the ducts and out of the shaft on the Canadian side. It was a fountain of people raining on the city of Windsor. Out of the 80 people that came out the shaft, twenty died from concussions suffered when they landed on top of the building. Sixty people were taken to Windsor hospitals. The more serious were airlifted to Toronto or Cleveland. Sixteen people popped out on the American side, another shower of people. This nightmare was only the beginning.

CHAPTER 20

Crowds were beginning to gather around Joe Louis Arena. Angry protesters advanced on the circle of Indian security forces standing guard around the arena, M18's ready and armed with bayonets. Over on Fort Street, Skip Mitchell slammed on his brakes as he passed the Detroit Newspapers manufacturing plant. Black streaks burned into the unsuspecting concrete as the all-wheel drive brakes of his T-Bird screeched to a grinding halt behind the ever increasing mass of flesh. Jumping out through the open convertible, he pushed through the crowds as he hurried to rescue Wanda. Mitchell had only one mission on his mind; to make Tony pay for using her, even if it meant killing him.

Abruptly, a heavy chopping noise appeared to his ears some distance away. Skip looked around the area, hoping to see a familiar face. Striking gold, he bolted towards someone near a Cobra gun ship amid shouts of, "Halt or I'll shoot!"

"Ray, what's going on!" A puzzled look besmirched his otherwise stoic features.

"Hello to you too, Dad," replied Ray.

"The plan is working. And the 101st Airborne is on its way from Selfridge to help contain the situation."

Skip threw him a quizzical look. "What are you talking about?"

"Four hours ago, we came up with an idea that I suggested to my commanders at Selfridge. Within an hour, we received orders to commandeer these helicopters and fly them according to their original plan. One small change though. We replaced that nerve gas they were going to use with nitrous oxide. We only gave the city a little cat nap."

A smile began to surface on Skip's face.

"It's nice to see your mom and I taught you well," he replied. The sergeant let a big smile of pride shine from his face. His father ignored it, responding with a question.

"Have you seen your mother lately?"

"No, but I saw Drew land on Cobo roof in a Huey. He might be inside," he added.

"There might have been someone else also in the copter. Couldn't really see all that well at 2,000 feet."

"Thanks, son. Can I get around to the loading dock entrance?" Mitchell added.

"You will be cleared to get around the building. The rest is up to you." Ray gave his dad a big hug.

"Give that to Mom. Good luck." Sprinting like a gazelle, Skip raced to the river entrance of the Joe hoping to save his only true love.

Well north of the city, thirty transports loaded with regiments of the 101st Airborne Division of the U.S. Army. Led by Colonel Mick Lutz, the Air Rangers' consisted of 300 soldiers, specially trained in riot containment, were deployed just hours ago to capture and contain any participants at the Joe. A tall man, over 6 feet in height, Lutz entered West Point at the age of 18. With the recommendation of his good friend and United States Senator, John Gillis, Lutz breezed through the Academy with the highest average since MacArthur. His rise to Colonel took only five years, the fastest rise of any officer in military history, outside of Ulysses Grant. His division included the finest soldiers ever trained in counter terrorism and riot control. From the 2001 attack on the World Trade Center to the 2004 Olympics, Lutz and his men earned respect and honor from every level of government, the President on down to local officials. With the best men trained in counter-terrorist tactics under him, the 101st could stop Saddam Hussein from taking over the world. As they approached Joe Louis Arena, Lutz barked out orders over the inter-squad radio.

"Fix bayonets to your rifles, men. We will be entering the arena from the ground zero." As his men did a final check on their weapons, connecting their bayonets, the drivers of the transports trucks enclosed a circle around Joe Louis Arena, slowly stopping near the Indian Cobra gun ships. As they touched down, local officers from the police department, arrived and took each Indian pilot into custody. With Marvelli's security force neutralized, the Army Rangers secured every exit door to the arena. Not even a cockroach could have escaped.

Inside, a tense crowd watched as their newly selected leader held the woman, his bride, on stage at knife point. Marvelli now held the crowd of over 60,000 Native Americans totally speechless in awe of the ongoing spectacle at center stage. After learning that their tribal leaders conspired to take over land that was not theirs, creating a new country called Karontaen and eliminating the residents of this fair city that had been so hospitable to them drew nothing but astonished stares from the masses.

From the depths of his now half-crazed mind, Tony whispered softly into Wanda's sweat drenched ear, "I have been wise to you for a long time, my lovely squaw. Your efforts and those of your father's supporters in the tribes to keep me from assuming my rightful power as decreed by the Great Spirit will now see their fruits. For as you have already assumed, since you have insulted me in front of my people, you must be sacrificed as a casualty of war."

At that moment, the end of a rope slapped Tony on the curve of his bony forehead. His eyes looked up too late and caught the boots of SWAT officer Watson as she repelled down from the overhead catwalks. Her boots hit Marvelli square in the eye sockets, knocking him off his feet, writhing in pain. Wanda fell abruptly to the stage, bruising her left hip as she crashed into the hardwood flooring. With his CIA issued Biretta drawn, Drew rushed to her side immediately.

Mayor Kirkland Asher visited Washington D.C. many times, but never as a politician. After twenty years in the political arena, it took a band of renegade Indians to get him an invitation to the Oval Office. He sat there on one of the two center sofas in awe of the history that surrounded him. Being a veteran of the U.S. Navy, Asher stared intensely at a sword and part of a flag encased on the wall to the right of the president's desk As an Academy graduate, Asher was required to know his naval history backwards and forwards. He recognized the exhibit as something that belonged to Commodore John Barry, the "Father of the American Navy. A smile broke free on his face as he beamed with pride at the heritage and history he realized he has been a part of.

The grandfather clock now showed twenty minutes passed since he had been ushered into the Oval Office. With utter secrecy, the mayor was flown to Selfridge, in Mt. Clemens, and flown to Andrews Air Force Base in Maryland an hour after he ordered his police chief to get control of his city. Outside of his family, Detroit was the only other thing he cared about. He promised to guard it with his life and heart as long as he lived. Today, he began to have doubts about his abilities to continue that promise. Casually, he continued his personal tour of the most powerful office in the world. The walls began to glow a bright pinkish red as the summer sun continued setting over the banks of the Potomac River.

Asher walked over the Presidential Seal, boldly emblazoned into the carpet between the two sofas, ending at the fireplace mantle. On the walls hung three paintings of some of the most memorable battles in naval history. These were the centerpieces of an already grand salon. Above the fireplace hung a painting of the Bon Homme Richard and the H.M.S. Serapis just off the coast of England during the War of 1812. Commanded by the famous naval hero, John Paul Jones, the Richard totally destroyed the flagship of the British fleet. Asher admired Jones' leadership skills and courage in battle. Those examples became a foundation in his political career. To the left hung the battle painting between the U.S.S.

Constitution, "Old Ironsides", and the Guierriere, of the coast of Virginia. To the right was the battle painting of the H.M.S. Branch and the same French frigate, the Guerriere. All three evoked memories of the fight for freedom, the destiny of our country and the courage it took to get there. Asher turned, walking towards the now famous presidential desk. Made from oak timbers from the salvaged HMS Resolute, it was a gift from Queen Victoria in the late 19th Century. Behind it stood a table of souvenirs from an illustrious career of the first popularly elected Jewish president in American History. Asher turned as he heard a door open. A small group of men entered led by his old friend, President Gordon Berkowitz.

"Well, Kirk, been out to see the Rose Garden yet? I'll let you take some home to Yvette." He shook the mayor's hand vigorously as the rest of his entourage took their places on the sofas.

"Gentlemen, this is his honor, the mayor of the City of Detroit, Michigan," said the President.

"Our objective today is this: find out the problems that his city has and fix them. In other words, help rebuild his city. With what has been happening, we will need a plan of action to avoid this type of situation in the future. The floor is yours, Kirk." With that, the words began to flow freely from his mouth, detailing every last problem his fair city suffered from. There is a pot of gold at the end of the rainbow he thought as he spoke to his captive audience of presidential advisers.

The winds whipped the C-5A like a bouncing ball. Captain Strassburg fought hard against the extreme wind gusts the "Devil Storm." Hail pelted the fuselage like a Gatling gun, damaging the wing flaps to the degree that altitude control was becoming a major problem. Pilot and co-pilot used every muscle of their well built bodies to keep the Weather plane on an even keel at 30,000 feet. They had achieved their objective. The center of the "Devil Storm" was now all around them.

"Radar," the captain hollered, "how long does take to pinpoint a storm's zero point? You've never taken this long before!"

Perry Butler, Air Force specialist 4th class, sat in front of the radar screen. Just under 6 feet tall, he stood out in the squad because of his similarity to the character "Radar O'Rielly" from the TV show M.A.S.H. With his wire rim glasses and uncanny knack of tracking down epicenters of major storms, he alone had made this weather control program a success.

"OK, Chief," he always called the captain Chief.

"Two minutes to zero point." The term Zero Point was similar to Ground Zero, which was used heavily during the War against Terrorism to describe the point of attack. The Zero Point in a storm is the point of weakness that would also give maximum dispersion to the chemicals used to break up the threat of a natural disaster. With the discovery of Titanium Sulfide, NOAA and the Air Force were achieving success with minor storms throughout the Midwest. Tornadoes rated as high as F3 on the Beaufort scale were breaking up before they ever caused any physical damage to the people or the land. Crop production was on the rise. America again was the bread basket of the world.

Stu Gibson sat at his desk at the National Severe Storm Center, in Norman, Oklahoma, watching the satellite photos track the storm. To the right of his monitor sat a smaller monitor, showing a radar screen with a big red blip in the middle of the storm. Strasburg's plane had made good time and was now in position to save millions of lives. He closed his eyes and said a little prayer. It was all in God's hands now. The time truly test his weather control idea was about to happen. The future of his career laid before him as a little red blip over southeast Michigan.

Captain Strasburg could hear the hail pelting the fuselage of his airborne weather station. The fury of the storm pushed his plane like a rocking chair, sending the wings on a constant roller coaster ride. Stability was becoming a mere memory because of the strength of the "Devil Storm." He pressed his intercom button as he approached Zero Point coordinates.

"Bombadier, are you ready to drop your load?" he asked.

"Package is ready for delivery, sir," he said.

"It's your call."

"Navigator, time to Zero point!"

"Ten Seconds." Strasburg counted to himself quietly.

"The order is given. Deliver promptly." Within seconds, a door opened on the underside of the fuselage. Tiny grey pellets rushed out at a lightning pace into the surrounding clouds. Their pace increased as the funnel clouds approached the Ambassador Bridge. Hail clouds were less than a mile away from the Joe, throughly pounding the Detroit Newspaper Agency's printing plant. As the winds increased, the titanium pellets swirled round and round disappearing into a complete blur in the condensed air mass, absorbed completely by the menacing storm. Strasburg banked his plane towards Canadian air space to await the outcome.

The President stood in front of the French Doors, leading to the Rose Garden and the South lawn of the White House, looking pensive as he listened to Asher discuss his city's problems with his chief economic advisors and high ranking senators from Congress. The meeting had lasted over an hour. My God, he thought, I knew Detroit was bad but never to this degree. The president heard the mayor and the advisors begin to wind down as they arose to shake each others hands. He turned and faced them, his faced wrinkled and worn, as they started to file towards the door.

"Gentlemen, tomorrow I am committed to addressing the Indians in Detroit. When I get there, I will need your plans for the city of Detroit on paper so that I can deliver it to the people in my speech. You have 18 hours. The Blair House has been set up for your discussions and your families have been notified. I will not accept anything less than a workable reconstruction plan for this city. We must put it back on the map as the "Motor City." Good Luck and get to work."

The Secret Service detail entered as if on call.

"These men will make sure you will not be disturbed." The advisors walked single file behind the lead agent. Two agents brought up the rear as they crossed the foyer of the office into their inevitable all night session for the president. Mayor Asher turned to shake the president's hand before they flew back to his besieged city. The president grabbed his friend's hand like it was the last time they would ever see each other. Their eyes exchanged woeful glances as the two men for their trip to Detroit.

The storm felt something enter its space. Thousands of little buds, it thought, had been sucked into the body of its destructive soul. The strength and power it had developed slowly seeped out of its watery body into the surrounding atmosphere. Hail storms developed into rainstorms. Funnel clouds dissipated into high winds. Thunder and lightning withered away to sounding like a hungry, growling tiger. The Devil Storm felt its fury beginning to weaken. The force of its thunder broke to a mild roar. The central brain that produced this disaster was weaker. Time would be the final judge. Thunder clouds were breaking. The light was finally at the end of the tunnel. In Norman, Oklahoma, for the first time in days, a smile appeared on a man's face.

CHAPTER 21

Her head throbbed like someone was beating her with a baseball bat. Consciousness returned slowly like the tuner of a satellite radio. Nearby voices were mere mumbles to the constant ringing in her ears. Her eyes were still very out of focus as she opened her eyelids to the noises surrounding her. Bright lights. Many bodies. Faces staring at her. Police in Army uniforms. What was this place? Who are these people? Will they affect the plan she was to carry out per orders from the Caliph of Basra,. Her name eluded her brain. She no longer remembered the two kids who were the reason behind her life, career and her future. Reese Watson now experienced a hidden identity engraved in her psyche by terrorists during her two month captivity in Iraq. On a routine patrol towards the oil fields on the Gulf of Aqaba, Watson and her platoon were ambushed and captured by Iraqi Muslim insurgents. Taken to an abandoned Republican Guard base, they suffered through torture and degradation. But the captain of the guard thought Watson would make a brilliant subject for the ancient mind control techniques never before practiced on Westerners. Stripped to just her Marine skivvies, Watson was tied spread-eagle over a hot fire pit. As flames flickered across the slim, taught physique, terrorists carefully indoctrinated her with their mission against America. Through the distraction of constant pain as the flames licked her body, Reese slowly accepted their beliefs and their mission as her alter ego, set to trigger at a moments notice. The fall from the catwalks triggered her evil side about two months too early.

Wanda recovered from the fall, running over to the down officer immediately after she knocked Tony flat on his keister. Marvelli laid in a ball at the feet of the men of the National Tribal Councils. No movement was seen stirring from his seemingly lifeless body. The ancient headdress still remained in place on his oversized head, as if cemented with super glue. A heavy silence floated throughout Joe Louis Arena as the delegates tried to figure out the events happening at center stage.

"Are you are alright? That was a very nasty fall from the end of that rope," said Wanda.

Reese looked at Wanda quizzically. Her brain began to click off answers to her question. Words began to formulate into sentences at a rapid fire pace. Her eyes formulated shapes and outlines as her brain began to focus on the events in front of her. The woman seemed to be a very caring person, she thought. That will be her downfall.

"I am fine. Where am I?" she asked.

"In Joe Louis Arena in Detroit, Michigan," Wanda said

"So I am in America?"

"Yes."

"Then you are my prisoner, woman."

"What!" exclaimed Wanda.

"I am the daughter of the great leader, Mohammed Zaraqwi, and you will provide me an escape from this prison." Mouths dropped in surprise as Watson unsheathed her knife. She grabbed Wanda by her right arm and whirled her counter-clockwise. The razor sharp edge settled on the jugular vein on the right side of Wanda's pearly white neck. A gulp of fear settled in Wanda's throat, lodged just above her Adam's Apple. Her rapid breathing echoed through the caverns of ear canals as her heart raced at breakneck speed, pumping adrenaline at record levels.

Mitchell sprinted past the security guard at the Atwater gate. The old man in the wooden gatehouse, was dozing off again. One more time security was lax at the arena. Barney will have to address that after this mess is resolved.

Bursting through the entry door beside the overhead garage door, Skip saw hundreds of people running through the walkway behind the backstage entrance to the floor of the arena. Fighting his way through the stampede, Skip got his jaw socked, kicked in shins twice and one good swift kick in the groin just before he broke free on the other side. Rolling in pain from side to side, he began to open his eyes to survey the area while seemingly distracted by the attack on his family jewels. A feeling of shock and surprise overcame him as he looked towards at the stairway leading to the stage. At least a half dozen men stood with rifles at position ready to shoot on command. As his pain subsided, he cautiously stood up and stepped lightly towards the wooden stairway. The screams of the crowd muffled his steps as Mitchell walked through large puddles of water from the Zamboni storage area. Zamboni machines keep the ice fresh during events. It was stored in a small garage-like room just under the lower bowl of the arena

The drama at center stage was escalating. Watson held Wanda at knife point, slowly edging towards the back stairwell. Dozens of M18 rifles stayed aimed on her forehead, ready for that opportunity to save the queen of their new nation. High above, on the catwalks, armed snipers aimed telescopic, laser guided Abrams rifles on all the players on the stage, Watson and Wanda, the still prone Tony Marvelli and the four men of his Apocalypse group. Watson, with Wanda in tow, slowly backed across the stage towards the exit stairway. Every member of the security force on stage carefully turned, keeping the SWAT officer completely in their sights. Drew stood off on stage right, looking for an opening to use his CIA training and save his mother. For years, Drew Mitchell hid from his everyday world, living off the street till his sixteenth birthday. It was when he was hitching hiking along I-80, outside of Lincoln, Nebraska, that he met up with a family of Ute Indians from western Colorado. Yellowfeather was their name and they had a daughter named Tisha. They were returning from a visit to their oldest son as he prepared to leave for an overseas tour of duty in Korea.

For the next several hours, Drew poured out his heart to them, detailing the problems his mother and father were having. The pain of his hurt echoed through their souls as he revealed the mental abuse his parents were throwing on each other as well as his brother and sister. They were older and found their escape through careers. He was a dozen years younger and did not have that privilege. One day, after a big fight with his mom and dad, he packed his stuff and left the old fashioned way, hitching a on railroad box cars heading westward to Omaha, Nebraska. Once in Omaha, he sought work any where to be able to start a new life. But his age created walls of impassable height. After a few weeks of soup kitchen food and hand me down clothes, Drew offered to drive a car to Ogalala for a friend, knowing full well he did not have a license, just for the money and to get closer to Colorado. Aunt Cindy and Uncle Bill lived just outside of Denver and would give him a place to stay. By then, he would know how to put his life back in order.

After meeting the Yellowfeathers, Drew began to see that their way of life could be an answer to a prayer for him. Living on a reservation would give him a great opportunity to hide from his world and discover who he really wanted to be. That was five years ago. Three years later, a man approached Drew and several other Indian boys about doing covert work for the United States Government. At 15, he jumped at the chance to play spy, every kids dream, like James Bond 007. One of his favorite childhood memories was sitting with his parents, watching 007 drive those cool cars with camouflage, missiles and ejector seats. So he jumped into his training and learned the art of espionage.

Behind the stage, Skip slowly crept up the narrow staircase, .45 caliber drawn in his left hand, assessing the situation as he went. On one side was the four Indian chiefs he had heard so much about, Tecumseh, Johnson, Night Owl and Running Horse. In front of them laid an unconscious Tony, Jr. To his left was his son, ready to pounce on someone like a mountain lion. His gaze move to the center of the stage and he froze in disbelief. There was this police officer holding something to Wanda's throat, though he could not see what it was. Skip looked back at Drew to get his attention. Their eyes met briefly. A slight nod of his head was enough to let Skip know a distraction was needed. As they approached the stairway, Mitchell carefully put his gun in the middle of Watson's back. A look of surprise came across Watson's face. Drew hollered the cry of a banshee as he flew across the stage with blazing speed towards the knife being held at his mother's throat. The cry startled Skip and he pulled the gun away, expecting an attack from someone very near to him. In the click of one second, the bayonet slid across the delicate flesh of Wanda's neck, slicing the carotid artery. Blood gushed out of the gash with each pump of her heart. Drew hit Watson with both fists, knocking her right into the arms of his father who was standing right behind her on stage. Wanda collapsed like a lead weight on the stage, her life withering away. Her long lost son held her in his arms crying while his father held her killer in his. A stunned hush fell over the capacity crowd in Joe Louis Arena.

"Call 911, now! Get me paramedics! Get a chopper outside now," yelled Drew.

"Hang on, Mom. You will be OK!" Wanda looked at his face, unable to make out his features. His voice triggered her memories and she gasped as she spoke her last words to him.

"I love you, son." With one last loud groan, Wanda Willington, alias Wanda Detroit, America's Sweetheart, rolled her eyes back into her head and died. Nevermore would the world be blessed with the wonderful voice and most giving spirit ever to grace the earth. Every head bowed and prayers were mumbled for the soul of the woman considered the Soul of Detroit. Fifteen minutes of silence passed without the slightest whisper.

Abruptly, Watson shook herself towards the stairway only to be clubbed with the butt end of Mitchell's .45. She dropped to the floor like a rock. Skip made sure she would be out for a while before he walked towards the lifeless body of his only true love. She was still in Drew's arms as he cried his eyes out, apologizing for staying away stubbornly for so long. Mitchell knelt down beside his son as Drew carefully caressed his mother's cold body. Neither saw a body stirring back to life about 100 feet away from them.

The men of The Apocalypse stood transfixed at the scene before them. Their leader, Tony Marvelli, laid either unconscious or dead. No one dared to move to find out, fearful of death or punishment from Marvelli's spirit. Their souls trembled as they watched the next act of this ongoing play unfold.

Tony Marvelli, the youngest mafia don in the history of the United States, sprang back to life as if he hadn't skipped a beat. With the newly restored headdress still clinging to his over-sized ego, he began preaching about how Wanda had angered the Great Spirit by denouncing his right as leader of the Ancient Ones. He turned to point his finger at her. As he saw Drew Eaglewing holding her lifeless body, Marvelli stopped in mid-sentence. His movements became rote as he slowly walked towards the dead body of the woman who helped him build his empire with her voice. Tony noticed that Skip was kneeling right beside Drew while the boy was shedding his tears. Tony stood, looking puzzled at Drew. He wondered why an Indian would be so emotional over someone he barely even knew. His eyes moved from Drew to Wanda's face to Skip. There was a similarity with the three of them. He could see it, but how. His brain lit up like a light bulb. Drew must be Wanda's son that ran away some years ago.

The men of the Apocalypse, Tecumseh, Johnson, Running-Horse and Night-Owl, followed Tony as he walked across the stage. They watched cautiously as he moved closer to the body of the woman who would have been their new queen. With blank minds from the shock of the events happening around them, their movements were very slow and zombie-like. Marvelli's mind, though, began to race. Wanda was now gone. No one could squeal on him about his plan to create his own country.

The Indians, having pledged their allegiance to him, were now his servants. On his command, they will give their lives for him. A sinister smile reappeared on his face as he returned to the podium.

"Brothers," he said. "your queen has been taken from us. Again the great white father in Washington, (he loved to talk the way Indians were portrayed in the movies) who stole our rightful lands that the Great Spirit gave us, now take away our rightful leaders. I command you to take up weapons, anything you can find, and scour the streets of our new land to find our people a new queen. The future of our country depends on this." With sadistic glee, he hollered, "Go with the blessing of the Great Spirit!"

The people began to rip apart Joe Louis Arena, creating weapons with anything they could get their hands on. Pieces of chairs. Utensils from concession stands. Pipes, wood from broken benches and glass liquor bottles still full of booze from the Olympia Club to use as Molotov Cocktails were now in the hands of the half-crazed mob. The bloodiest battle in the history of the city was about to take place.

Ray Mitchell felt the wind increasing for the last 15 minutes. His platoon of National Guardsmen held to their positions around the arena, keeping the ever growing crowd at bay. Spud Jones, Sanchez and several other gang leaders worked to the front of the crowd, throwing insults at the squadron before them. Sergeant Mitchell could see the "Devil Storm" creeping up behind the unruly crowd. Safety was becoming the priority for the moment. The raging mob was vulnerable he thought. He looked around for a protective site that he could get to quickly. Only one thing came to his eyes. The Joe Louis parking garage. One problem solved. Now how to convince this angry mob to go. He noticed Jones, Sanchez and a few others acting as instigators. Leaving his post, he approached the gang leaders, praying his plan would work.

"Gentlemen, please! We have a crisis coming and I need your help," he said.

"Who would want to help you! You is keepin' us from killing off the bastards who are trying to kill us and take our city," said Sanchez.

"Just get out of our way and let us do what we come to do."

"Well, would you rather die in there or at the hands of the thing coming up behind you?" said Mitchell.

"I think these people who like to live to see how this turns out. Help me get everyone into the parking garage before it's too late." The gang leaders turned around and stared at the oncoming storm. Sanchez, having seen the storm's fury was the first to speak

"Si! We will help. I seen what this storm can to do people. We take them to safety. Let us take them to the garage safe."

Sanchez and the others turned and began hollering at the crowd in Spanish, bringing them under control. Other leaders did the same. Little by little, groups of families rushed to the parking garage's lower levels. The men kept it orderly. These men would make great leaders one day, Mitchell thought. When the last family entered, with at least ten elderly people in tow, Ray Mitchell breathed a sigh of relief as the local people were swiftly herded into the garage, hiding behind cars for protection. His men would not be so fortunate. Their training required that their posts be manned in any situation. They would not budge under any circumstances. The President would be proud of this platoon, he thought. At that moment, something about the storm caught his eye. The sheet of hailstones and lightning abruptly diminished. The tornadoes that followed vanished. The dark storm clouds gave way to a calm sky. God does answer prayers, he thought. A heavy rumble came up behind him, startling the sergeant as he watched the fury of Mother Nature dissipate before his very eyes. Turning quickly, he watched the rest of the101st Airborne Division pull up behind him from Jefferson Avenue under Cobo Center. Reinforcements had arrived.

Thirty miles north of Windsor, above the mouth of the Detroit River at Lake St. Clair, Captain Will Strasburg and his crew sat in utter amazement. The first official trial of titanium sulfate crystals on weather phenomena had worked beyond expectations. History books would list him with the crew of the Enola Gay over Hiroshima in 1945. Weather One would forever be etched in the mind of future generations as the instrument that saved the earth from global warming. All he had left to do was to call Stu Gibson at NOAA. With microphone in hand, he flicked a switch.

"Zachary tower. Connect me with the NOAA Storm Center in Norman, Oklahoma. I want to talk to Gibson."

Theories don't of become reality. It happened for Darwin, Einstein and Galileo. Diligence and perseverance always prevailed, turning dreamers into thinkers, philosophers and even scientists. Stu Gibson sat at his desk, mulling over the data returning from the Weather One on-board computers. The sight was amazing, ultimately inspiring. A dream had finally become reality. The future of the earth could be in the balance. He picked up the phone and dialed the White House in Washington, D.C.

"This is Stuart Gibson of the NOAA Severe Storms Center in Oklahoma. Let me speak to the President."

CHAPTER 22

In every household in the 7 county Detroit Metro area, men sat in front of their wide screen TVs, beer in hand, watching the Detroit Tigers get devoured by the New York Yankees 17-6. In the beginning of the 7th inning, veteran Dimitri Young had a count of three balls and two strikes with the bases loaded when the game was abruptly interrupted by the Channel 30 News Team. The taped announcement played before turning it over to Adrian Markell in the newsroom.

"Good Afternoon, everyone. I'm Adrian Markell. TV30 News has just learned of a plot to take over control the City of Detroit by the Native American Indians who are currently holding their convention at Joe Louis Arena. Four members of the national Tribal Council have been implicated in this plot. Richard Night Owl, current chief of Michigan's Chippewa Tribe, Richard Johnson of the Atpasca Apache Tribe, George Tecumseh, Chief of Florida's Seminoles and Daniel Running Horse, chief of the Sioux in South Dakota. The four are known to be involved heavily with underworld connections. Sources have confirmed that a fifth man is involved in this attack on the city, but his identity is yet to be confirmed. Ron Firman is on his way in Sky30 to give us a birds eye view of the situation. Reports have been confirmed that citizens of Detroit are surrounding the Joe while National Guardsmen and members of the 101st Airborne from Fort Bragg, N.C. maintain a protective perimeter around the arena.

"Beginning our coverage, Bob Stepanski is high above I-75 freeway in Troy, reporting on a major procession towards the city. Bob, are you there?"

"Yes, Adrian. Below me is a monstrous caravan of cars, SUVs pickups and tractor-trailers. Led by Michigan State Police and Oakland County Sheriff's Deputies, from orders of the Governor, these people are flooding the city with both physical and moral support to help save and rebuild the Motor City into a thriving metropolis again. Over 70 years ago, before the depression, Detroit was considered the place to live, a city with no slums. Anyone could get a job with a decent wage and live in good housing. Fifty years ago, Detroit was the Arsenal of Democracy, building much of the armaments and vehicles used during World War 2.

"The people below me are plumbers, carpenters, electricians and laborers prepared to fight and die for the city as well. Citizens of Oakland County are not going to sit back and let someone dictate the future of a piece of their history. Let's go to Ron Firman, who is high above Joe Louis Arena on the riverfront. Ron?"

The camera quickly switched to an overhead wide shot of Jefferson Avenue North towards the Joe Louis statue and Hart Plaza.

"A large, very angry mob is swarming down Jefferson, heading towards Cobo Center. As you can see below me, the city is preparing for a fight. I see people with 2x4's, baseball bats, lead pipes and even a few with boxing gloves. Detroit has a reputation as a city that refuses to fade away. We are flying over Cobo Center now to check out the situation on the other side." The view of the crowd disappeared as the helicopter flew over the blacktopped roof of the Cobo garage. Within seconds, the red letters of the arena appeared as the helicopter passed over the south wall of the convention center. Around the outside, hundreds of fatigue-clad soldiers stood with bayonets ready. Firman described the scene below as it opened before his eyes.

"There are at least 200 soldiers below me surrounding the arena. Sources have confirmed that troops from the 101st Airborne and the 758th Air National Guard at Selfridge make up the squad below. The citizens, I am assuming are unaware of the military prescence that awaits them. We will stay on top of this Adrian as the situation develops. Back to you in the studio." A camera shot of Adrian Markell jumped back onto the screen, replacing the overhead shot of Joe Louis.

"Thank you, Ron. Please stay tuned to TV30 for further developments. We now return you to the ball game." The feed from Yankee Stadium returned showcasing the box score. Tigers 18, Yankees17. The switchboard at the station lit up with thousands of irate calls.

The White House Press room is like a beehive during pollinating season. A dull hum was constantly heard reverberating through the walls, whether reporters occupied the seats or not. Secret Service agents constantly joked about foreign termites hibernating in the walls to steal any secrets they could. This years press corps was the most vindictive ever, attacking the President any chance they could through a multitude of accusations and scandals sparking another independent Special Prosecutor.

Today, the press corps was abuzz about the rumors of a terrorist attack on the Motor City. Theories bounced off the bulletproof windows and insulated walls as the branch of the information super highway tried to decide which direction the country would go before it was ever announced. They didn't have time though. President Gordon Berkowitz stepped briskly into the room.

"Good afternoon. An hour ago, at the Great American Indian Pow Wow in Detroit, an attempt was made by Native American Tribes to murder the innocent citizens of that great city. Four men have been identified as masterminds behind this nefarious plot; Richard Johnson, George Tecumseh, Daniel Running Horse and Richard Night Owl. All maintain ties with a known Mafia Don named Anthony Marvelli, Jr. Their attempt at killing the civilians was to happen at 4 pm this afternoon. With the help of the Michigan Air National Guard, that plan was thwarted. At this moment, the 101st Airborne and the 758th Airborne National Guard Unit have established a perimeter around Joe Louis Arena, the site of the 1980 Republican National Convention that gave us Ronald Reagan as President. Detroit's Mayor Kirkland Asher will be returning to the city as we speak on board Air Force One to take control of the situation. The authorities in Detroit are carrying out my directives. They are spelled out as follows:

1) The people maintain order and let the military and the local police contain the situation.

2) The people refrain from looting and rioting because of the threat. The following has happened:

A) The Governor and County executives have instituted martial law and empowered all skilled trades contractors to report to designated areas to assist in reconstruction of abandon homes and manufacturing plants. I have ordered the US Army Corps of Engineers to Detroit to oversee this rebuilding effort. I have asked Congress for an emergency allotment of $3 billion dollars to pay for this massive reconstruction of one of our most famous cities. This plan will start when the situation in Detroit is contained. I will take no questions today. Please take the press releases for any further information that will be presented in my speech in Detroit tomorrow." The president walked out of the press room, down the hallway to the Oval Office briskly. Time was now a precious commodity. His mind raced as he entered the Oval Office.

"I have Mr. Gibson on a conference call from NOAA in Oklahoma, Mr. President," said Libby Kennedy, his personal secretary.

"Good. Hold all calls until I'm done with this call," he replied. His feet flew across the embroidered Presidential seal, grabbing his phone scrambler as he abruptly came to a halt at the antique desk by the Rose Garden french doors.

"Stu, is that you?" asked Berkowitz.

"Yes, Mr. President."

"Give me your report. Make it short. The Japanese Emperor will arrive soon."

"Yes, sir. The experiment worked. The titanium pellets destroyed the nucleus of the storm in record fashion. Within seconds of the drop at zero point, the tornadoes fizzled, hail changed to rain showers and lightning stopped all together. I have Captain Will Strasburg on the line from the weather plane over the Windsor skyline to give you an on the spot update. Go ahead, Will."

30,000 feet above Windsor, Ontario, Canada, Captain Strasburg looked out the windshield of his C5-A weather plane, observing the desolate landscape that the Devil Storm had raked through the Motor City.

"Mr. President, our weather project finally paid off. The storm had torn a path up I-94 about 5 miles wide through Dearborn and Detroit. When we reached the storm, it had passed over the international boundary with Canada creating water spouts and destroying the Ambassador Bridge. I took the plane immediately into the storm's central cloud. My navigator and radar operator had calculated the zero point of the storm during our approach and we were able to get the latitude and longitude exact enough for maximum effect. As I look out my window at the city, most of the clouds have disappeared. Sporadic rain clouds are traveling through the city, crossing over the border into Canada as we speak. There is no destructive power left in the storm. The weather control experiment worked like clockwork, sir."

"Thank you, Captain. You have just done your country a great service and maybe the world too." The President took a deep breath and relieved a heavy sigh as a great weight was lifted off his shoulders. After pausing for a moment, the President directed a final comment to his friend at the Severe Storm Center in Oklahoma.

"Stuart, my friend, you have the go ahead to produce more of these pellets and inform the Vice President and Secretary of Defense when they are finished. Then select new sites throughout the world and see what good American technocracy might do towards ending world hunger."

"Yes, sir. I'll get on it right away. You will have the report in 24 hours. Goodbye." Gibson clicked the receiver silent, leaving Gordon Berkowitz alone in the rays of the setting sun, beaming through the thick windows of the Oval Office. His greatest challenge was about to unfold.

The doors to the arena burst open. Thousands of screaming Indians rushed onto the concourse stairways unaware of the members of the Michigan National Guard and the U.S. Army were waiting their arrival. Hundreds of pipes, seat backs, arm rests, etc. were being waved by every red man and woman. With a blow horn in hand, Colonel Mick Lutz issued orders to his men before he addressed the raging crowd.

"Load with the plastic bullets, men. The President does not want another Little Big Horn in reverse." The colonel then turned towards the on coming crowd.

"By order of the President of the United States, I order you to cease and desist immediately. Or you will be fired upon." The crowd refused to slow down.

"Open fire!" Bullets rained throughout the enraged crowd. Wave after wave of people fell across the concrete walkways. Soldiers responded immediately arresting and corralling the dazed crowd. Sanchez and the other gang leaders came out from their hiding places in the parking garage. They formed a support line behind the soldiers, using pipes, windshield wipers and loose boards from the parking lots next door, herding the dazed crowd into one of the fenced parking lots on Atwater. The men eagerly guarded the gates to prevent anyone from escaping. The blood thirsty crowd lost its fire. Roundup started early this year in Detroit.

Ray Mitchell led his platoon herding the last few hundred people into the two fenced parking lots under the People Mover station. This was too easy. Almost liked they were trained to do this, like playing a role in a play. His instincts were on high alert. The smell of a rat traveled through his nostrils. Danger lights went off like skyrockets. His Mom and Dad were in danger. He approached the Colonel.

"Sir, I believe we have people still in danger inside. Permission I take my platoon and investigate. Situation is secured by your men sir!" Lutz thought for a moment before he spoke.

"Take your platoon only, Sergeant. I realize you have family in there. Go assist the police as they mop up. That's an order." The National Guard platoon followed Mitchell up to the concourse entrance, changing their magazines as they went. As they reached the bottom of the stairwell, a Detroit Fire Department EMS vehicle turned down Atwater heading towards the river front gate. Mitchell flagged the driver down. When the truck stopped, most of his platoon piled into the rear of the vehicle. The rest redeployed with the 101st outside the arena. The sergeant now had an element of surprise. *Don't worry, Mom,* he thought. *I'm on my way*. The EMS truck sped off around the bend as Mitchell said a quiet prayer for his family.

Tony Marvelli relished the power he absorbed through the mystical headdress. He watched gleefully as the thousands of crazed Indians blindly obeyed his command to avenge their new queen's death. This stupid police officer had given him the perfect excuse. Killed by a member of the Great White Father's own tribes. Hollywood could not have done better themselves. Papa would have been proud. Helford would be just as proud. The thought of Helford reminded him that he should have returned from the bombing of the tunnel under the river. That happened almost an hour ago. As he looked around the stage, a familiar face appeared to his eyes.

Skip Mitchell was standing beside the unconscious body of the policewoman and Wanda's now blue, lifeless body. A small movement caught the corner of his eye. It was the policewoman. She was beginning to wake up. With his Apocalypse in tow, Marvelli slowly moved over to Wanda's dead body, pretending to pay his last respects to his empire's money tree. Drew and Skip did not notice Tony creeping up behind them. For once, they had committed the criminal sin of letting their guard down. Marvelli stood between the two of them, waiting to be noticed before he finally spoke.

"She was a good woman, gentlemen. But not good enough to survive in my world. Her demise was doomed to happen. You just helped expedite it quicker." Skip jumped up and turned to face Tony, pulling his right fist back as he grabbed Tony's shirt. Immediately, the sound of rifle bolts being pulled back put him on notice. Skip slowly released Tony's shirt, lowering his arm.

"And I'll take your gun, Mitchell. And your son's too." A look of surprise hit both of their faces at once.

"It was so easy to figure out that you were a plant, Drew, especially after the way you reacted to Wanda's death. So who is it you work for, FBI, CIA, DDS? Tell me, son."

"I will see you rot in hell before I ever tell you anything."

"Well, I'm afraid you will be there before me. Boys, take them away." At that moment, Watson moved to try and get up distracting Tony and the other chiefs from carrying out the orders. Skip and Drew took advantage of the distraction and began wrestling with the chiefs that allied with Marvelli. Up in the catwalks, the other SWAT team members maintained their sights on the stage to shoot to kill when they got a good shot. Time was of the essence.

One by one, the members of Marvelli's Apocalypse dropped like flies, each screaming like a child. Their right legs were bleeding profusely from gunshot wounds inflicted by the SWAT team. Only Tony was standing between Skip and Officer Watson as she struggled to regain her footing. A now panicky Marvelli pushed Skip away, grabbing Watson's gun and immediately held it at her head. The familiar sadistic smile came back as he boasted to Mitchell.

"Never underestimate my abilities, Mitchell. I always have alternatives. Now order every one to back off or I'll shoot her and as many others as I can for my worthy cause." He slowly backed down the stairs. Mitchell waved the crowd away as Tony and his captive made their way to the loading dock door of Joe Louis.

"You'll never catch me, Mitchell, 'cause I'm too smart for you," he said as he slipped out the overhead door into the bright sunlight of the setting sun. Skip said a quick prayer for the young lady. Up in the catwalks, the chief ordered the men back on the roof. This man was not going to get away from him again.

CHAPTER 23

Tony Marvelli kept the 9mm Glock pointed straight at her right temple. Droplets of sweat rolled off both his and her foreheads like raindrops from a hurricane. Watson's pulse rate was at about 185 beats per minute. Security officers stood within 3 feet of them forming a protective circle for their escape route. She felt Marvelli's hot, foul smelling breath on the back of her slim, taught neck. What a repulsive person! she thought. She did not dare move a muscle the wrong way. Her gun had a hair trigger. Slightest movement would mean her kids would be motherless. She swelled with guilt for not keeping the family together. Second guessing herself would not do any good now. This man is a maniac and will do anything, short of mutilation, to get what he wants. She turned to God, reciting the prayer of St. Francis of Assisi, to give her the strength to forgive the poor soul who threatens her soul. Her life clock ticked in her mind with every step she took

Skip stood at the edge of the stairwell, watching the man who led his Wanda to her demise. His shoes now drenched in her blood, Mitchell watched in awe as Tony, again, manipulated the world to his advantage. *NO MORE!* he thought angrily. The pedestrian walkway, under the stands, was very congested. Security from the arena and Detroit Police cleared off an area 10 feet wide so that Marvelli could walk to the outside overhead door, at the loading dock, unobstructed. He glanced at Drew, looking for signs of support. With a slight nod of his head, Drew slipped off into the crowd. Skip admired that aspect of his son. A quality he wished he possessed. Cautiously, he slipped into the crowd on the opposite side of the arena. His own time with God took precedence as he followed his nemesis.

As Mitchell was following Marvelli, Chief Barney Nicholson stood in the catwalks above the 5th floor as the events unfolded before him. His mind was a fast mind, known to analyze situations and create an action plan in mere minutes, without perspiring. People stood in awe as he performed this feat time after time. He earned his money as police chief. That was why Detroit's crime rate was close to one of the lowest in the nation. His decision today would dictate the future of his political career.

"All right, men. Back to the roof." The command resonated through the ears of the SWAT team. They broke position and regrouped on the roof of Joe Louis, awaiting further instruction.

Kirkland Asher sat in the office on board Air Force One. He had never been a guest of the President before. Reveling in the moment was all he could do to keep his sanity. President Berkowitz was in the press section, giving a briefing on his speech to be given tomorrow at the Indian convention. The phone rang. Asher jumped. He wasn't expecting such a shrill ring. Anxiety entered the mayor's stoic demeanor. What was protocol? Should he answer the President's phone? Oh hell, the worst they could do was shoot me, he thought. His hand stretched out to grab the receiver when the outer door burst open.

Asher looked like he was caught with his hand in the cookie jar before he let out a big sigh of relief.

"You could have been wrestled to the ground by the Secret Service if you had picked up that receiver, Kirk. They guard everything of mine very carefully." The President was ready to roll over in a barrel of laughter. He had never seen his old friend so embarrassed.

"Just trying to help out a friend. Can I ask you a very personal question?"

"Shoot. Not literally though." They both chuckled as they settled onto the couch in front of the TV. Asher pondered for a moment, then spoke.

"Why, after all these years, is the Federal Government now pushing to rebuild a city that people have basically left for dead for decades?" He searched his old friend's eyes as he awaited his answer.

"For years, Detroit has dealt with strife in their political system. As people began to leave during the Roman Gribbs era, the system became even more polarized as the city focused on the needs of survival rather than constructive growth. Coleman Young fought it during his tenure. Dennis Archer and Kwame Kilpatrick too. Everyone, including you, Kirk, have dealt with uncooperative political factions in the southeastern Michigan area that have road blocked any federal aid. Whether mass transit aid for a subway or just help to rebuild houses, the independent nationalities that lived in the city built walls that created friction with the surrounding suburbs. This attack on the city has given me a forum that I am taking advantage of; to bring Detroit back up to the level of other cities in the country, rebuilding its tax base and make it the manufacturing center of the world once again. Does that answer your question?" Asher began to crack a smile as the president was speaking.

"I guess you could say I have no more questions. Let's go rebuild a city!" The president poured two glasses of champagne as they prepared to commit to this new adventure for the country. Air Force One cruised at 30,000 feet crossing the Pennsylvania-Ohio line. A sense of revelry began to infiltrate everyone as they flew towards a date with destiny.

A small Chris Craft powerboat sat anchored just outside of the shipyard's dry dock. Helford, Tony's long time aide, stood looking at his watch. He had synchronized with Tony early this morning as they left the mansion on this glorious day of victory. In a few hours, he would be sitting on the right hand of the most powerful man of the new Indian nation. Together, they would control the port of Detroit, rebuilding every decrepit factory into a drug refinery. It was now almost 6:30 in the evening. The boss should be done by now.

"All right, Captain. Head to the Joe louis dock. The boss should be waiting."

With a nod of his head, the boat captain turned the key. The powerful Allison turbo-charged engine roared like a charging lion after his prey. Pushing the throttle to its limit, the powerboat pushed nearly 15 knots as they raced down the Detroit shoreline.

People backed away as Tony and his hostage crept towards the outside gate of the arena. The sweat rolled into his eyes like water from a shower head.

He struggled to maintain his eye sight as he took Watson to the dock on the other side of Atwater Street. His grip on Watson remained strong, muscles unflinching as he walked along the gravel covered loading dock. The over hang from the Cobo Center roof lot shaded them, adding a sharp chill to an otherwise warm day. A shrill siren startled came around the curve from Jefferson Avenue. The fire department EMS truck whipped into the parking lot, almost striking Marvelli and his hostage. The ambulance came to an abrupt stop. Doors flew open and the National Guardsmen jumped out into a ready arms formation. Tony moved the gun from the side of Reese's head to the middle of her back. He squeezed her left arm tighter, letting her know he was still in control. Sergeant Mitchell gathered his troops and rushed inside the building, totally oblivious to the hostage situation taking place behind him. Marvelli smiled devilishly. No one will ever be able to touch him. He took Watson and turned, running towards the dock quickly before the troops returned.

Running down the stairway into the great hallway under the lower level concourse at Joe Louis, Skip and Drew nearly stumbled over themselves. The father came out in him as he turned to give his new found son some parental direction.

"You stay here with your mother till paramedics get here. I will take care of that maniac." Skip raced towards the open overhead door. The milling crowd began to separate again. As Moses parted the Red Sea, a team of Detroit Paramedics parted the crowd rushing to save a life already lost to the ages. A little prayer escaped his lips as he watched the team race to the stage where Wanda's lifeless body lay.

"We'll be together again. Be at peace." He wiped the moistness from his eyes as he turned to continue chasing Tony. Just as he took a step, two hands grabbed his shoulders.

"Dad, are you all right? Is Mom OK?" Ray stood with a worried look on his face as he awaited his father's answers.

"I am all right. But your mother is dead. And the man who caused all this is getting away. Come with me." He led the platoon back outside, like a good son, right at his father's footsteps. Mitchell rushed to the guard house by the outer gate, panting when he arrived. Ray was right behind him.

"Do you see any sign of Tony, Ray? Be careful. He does have a hostage." Ten pairs of eyes began searching like radar for any sign of movement. One member of the platoon hollered out.

"Sir, over there by the pedestrian walkway. Getting into a boat on that dock. And he's got something weird on his head." Skip quickly glanced towards the river front. There he was, standing out like the sore thumb he always was. The boat began to pull away from the dock. Tony turned and caught Skip's eye. He smiled like the Cheshire Cat from Alice in Wonderland. The sun reflected brightly of the pearly white enamel as the boat's pilot roared the engine, pushing out to the middle of the river channel. The setting sun shone into Skip's right eye. As he raised his hand to protect his eyes, Skip noticed a long cylindrical black tube with a blade on the end.

"Ray, is that a helicopter?"

"Yes, sir. We captured a whole squad of them. And they work pretty good too."

"Can you fly one?"

"Is that a rhetorical question? What do you think I have been doing for the last 6 years!"

Ray ordered his men to reposition on the dock. Skip ordered the guard to find Barney and have him call out the Coast Guard. Doing that, the two took off to the near Cobra. They climbed into the cockpit, secured themselves into their seats and began an accelerated take off. With a slight flick of his wrist, Ray and Skip lifted off Atwater, banking left towards the river. The chase was on.

Helford stood next to the pilot, radio mic in hand, definitely talking to someone over the radio. The helicopter crossed over the river bank, carrying a full armament of missiles and machine guns on board. Ray Mitchell flipped every necessary switch to arm themselves to cover every possibility. Skip sat in the rear seat, looking through binoculars, and occasional glances at the radar screen, when he saw something begin to bubble near the US-Canadian border. The radar screen showed the small powerboat was sitting still in the middle of the river. Just south of them, a long, tube-like boat came closer to their location. Skip's mouth dropped.

"Ray, I think Tony is being picked up by a submarine."

"Are you sure, Dad?"

"Just look out your window." Ray looked. There it was. A submarine was coming up the river, already beginning to surface just north of the Ambassador Bridge. Alarms went off in Skip's head.

"In need to get on that boat before that sub gets here. Get me down there now! Hey, how do I get out of this thing?" Mitchell searched for a lock to let him out of the cockpit.

"Hold on, Dad. Let me get down to less than 100 feet so that I can release the window locks. Only then will you be able to unstrap and climb out onto the runners. So hold tight."

Ray pushed the control stick forward, sending the Cobra downward to almost water level. With a quick flip of a switch, the latches on the rear window released. Skip undid his buckles and climbed out onto the right runner. Ray slowed the Cobra until it was nearly hovering over the rear of the power boat. He could see the glare in Marvelli's eyes. His left arm was raised to protect from the windy backwash of the helicopters rotors. No longer being held, Reese Watson moved quickly forward, shielding herself near the front windshield away from her captor. With one great leap, Skip jumped off the runner, crashing into Tony and the rear deck of the boat. Skip grabbed the dazed Mafia don by the leather straps of his Indian costume. He clenched his right hand into a fist and planted it squarely into Tony's nose, sending him reeling into the pilot. The boat careened sharply to the right, almost throwing Skip into the river. Noticing the change of fortune, Tony jumped up to throw Skip off the boat.

After a few steps, he stopped. His eyes rolled under his upper eye lids. His knees grew weak, collapsing on the deck of the boat. Behind him, Officer Reese Watson stood with the butt end of a flare gun sticking out of her hand. Her breathing was rapid from the adrenaline rush it took to take care of that jerk. As she pulled herself together, a smile bloomed on her face.

"Would you like a hand?" she asked Mitchell.

"Only after you put that thing down," he said. She laughed and through the gun in the river. With her right hand, she grabbed his left one and helped him stand up. Their eyes met for a moment, locked in a deep, thankful glance. She broke the stare and walked to the front of the boat.

"Turn this thing around and take us back to the dock," she ordered the pilot. With a quick turn of the key, he pushed the throttle forward. The boat banked to the left, heading back to Joe Louis Arena. In their wake, two shrill whoops of Coast Guard cutters sounded as the submarine surfaced in the middle of the American side of the river.

"Stop your engines. You are violating American waters and we are placing you under arrest. Everyone has ten minutes to report on deck." The sub slowed to a stop. Skip smiled. This nightmare was over. The maniac, Marvelli, lay unconscious at his feet. His son waved from the Cobra gun ship, shifting to high gear as he raced back to the mainland. His city was safe. Most of his family was safe, too. The loss of his precious Wanda was now beginning to catch up with him. There would be days of debriefing to follow. Especially for the lady beside him.

"Can I ask you a question?"

"Sure, just so long as it's not too personal."

"What do you remember about the assault on Joe Louis?"

"I came down the rope, kicked some guy in the face. The next thing I knew I was waking up and held hostage."

"That is all you remember?"

"Yes. Why?"

"We're almost at the dock. Let's wait till we get to the dock." He looked away. He did not want her to know what was about to happen. The Chris Craft power boat coasted up to the side of the dock. National Guardsmen grabbed the bow and stern lines tying them to the posts at the side of the walkway. Chief Nicholson, Colonel Lutz and Sergeant Mitchell walked over from the street to meet Skip and Reese as they stepped off the boat and onto dry land again. Barney sent the SWAT team onto the boat. They threw a pair of handcuffs and a kevlar jacket on Marvelli, whisking him off in their paddy wagon to the federal penitentiary on 6 Mile for holding purposes. Nicholson turned and started walking towards Watson. As he reached for his handcuffs, Skip jumped in front of him.

"Barney, let me talk to you a minute." He turned him away from her view as he talked softly in his ear.

"I don't think she remembers anything about killing Wanda. Get her some hypno-therapy, or something like that. I think she might have been brainwashed or something." Skip's face begged for mercy from his old friend.

"I'll keep that in mind. But I still have to take her into custody. The tapes from the arena may jog her memory. Until then, there is nothing more that can be done." The chief turned and walked back to Officer Watson. A few seconds later, a shocked Reese Watson mouthed the word help as she passed Skip on her way to a waiting police car. A cell was waiting for her at police headquarters.

Mitchell watched from the dock as Barney and Reese drove towards the RenCen and out of his sight. He was unaware that Drew and Ray were right behind him. Ray placed his hand on his shoulder and said, "Come on, Father. It's over. We have a funeral to plan."

CHAPTER 24

The remaining conventioneers were released after the capture of Tony Marvelli and the four members of his Apocalypse. Choctaw tribal chief Michael Gibson was elected the new head of the National Tribal Council. His first two decrees were immediate investigations into all tribal affairs of every tribal nation within US borders. The second was to move the final day of the convention to Comerica Park, the home of the Detroit Tigers. Mr. Ilitch offered the stadium to give the President a chance to speak to the tribes. Brown accepted and now patiently behind the podium, preparing to introduce Michigan's Second President of the United States, Gordon Berkowitz.

"My fellow Native Americans. We have now turned a major corner in our lives. Never have some many been so stripped to the bone to benefit so few. The perpetrators are now on their way to permanent residence behind bars. It is the dawn of a new day. And what better way to start it than a welcome word from the leader of the free world, President Gordon Berkowitz."

Applause rose throughout the 55,000 seat stadium. There were no security forces present other than Secret Service and Detroit Police. The President walked out of the Third base dugout, jogging to the microphone and podium that stood in front of pitcher's mound. He raised his hands to quiet the crowd as he reached for the speech in his pocket.

"Ladies and gentlemen, thank you for such a warm welcome. Today, we are here to establish a milestone for this great city and this great country. Two centuries ago, my forefathers took away lands given by God to your forefathers. Lands that you used to feed your families, to hunt for food and skins to make clothing. But they were taken away and, in return, you were given barren strips of worthless parcels under government supervision. Yes, things have changed. You are now permitted to have casinos on your land to fulfill the financial needs of your tribes. Well, that was still not enough.

"Yesterday, I sent to the Congress a presidential decree for their endorsement. That decree states that as of today, all restrictions that the Bureau of Indian Affairs has enforced throughout the last two centuries are now lifted. Any member of any tribe may come and go as they please and still maintain their sovereignty as an independent entity. All government programs that help improve the lives of Indians and their families will remain in place.

"In regards to this great city, I offer this. With the advent of the cooperation of the local and state governments for the first time in Detroit's history. As skilled tradesmen start their own make overs in the residential areas, National Guardsmen will be leading demolition crews to tear down the most degraded buildings by age. In their place, the Army Corps of Engineers will be creating farm areas inside the city to help diversify the economy." Cheers erupted from the crowd. He waited before he continued.

"With donations from all over the country, new housing will be going up, adhering to stringent building codes. Their will no longer be any slums in the city, just like it was before the depression." Again, cheers interrupted his speech.

"The housing will be near the farm areas to assure consistent and available work year round. There will be dairy farms too, with dairy manufacturing centers within a half-mile of every farm. Detroit again will soar in the manufacturing arena also. The Corps will also rebuild main of the currently abandoned factories and restore them to maximum efficiency. And best of all, Mayor Kirkland Asher has asked me to invite any of you, even with every thing that has happened over the last week, to make Detroit your home. Your efforts will be welcomed, especially in the area of the 4 major subway routes that are starting construction in 3 weeks." A standing ovation erupted throughout the stands. The field of dreams was blooming. Visions of many years were finally beginning to happen

The funeral for Wanda Willington, a.k.a. Wanda Detroit, was massive. It rivaled the funeral of President John Kennedy. Businesses shut down on the Friday of the funeral after a week of people filing through the Detroit Institute of Arts to pay their last respects to America's Sweetheart. On Friday, the funeral procession traveled slowly up Woodward Avenue to the Cathedral of the Blessed Sacrament, the home of the Archdiocese of Detroit. There, the Archbishop of Detroit presided over her funeral. A devout Catholic, she felt most at peace with God as a. Catholic. The day ended, after a three hour ceremony, with a long funeral procession to White Chapel Cemetery in Troy. 75 cars followed behind the hearse as row after row of people lined the I-75 freeway as the procession traveled up to the Rochester Road exit. Thousands of people lined both sides of the newly shut-down freeway, to pay their final respects to the woman who touched their hearts with their voice. The sun was setting when the final person from the procession arrived at grave site. The casket was draped with an American flag because of her years of service to the troops overseas. The Federal government picked up the tab.

Skip sat in the front row with Amy, Ray and Drew by his side. The archbishop recited a piece in Latin from the Catholic funeral book. He took the incense burner and swung it from side to side at all four corners of the casket. He, then, grabbed a water shaker, sprinkling it over the head of the casket.

"Ashes to ashes. Dust to dust." With that, the military band struck up a coronet solo of "Taps" as an honor guard removed the flag from the casket. They sat in reserved silence as the honor guard finished folding the flag. With TV cameras rolling, the sergeant of the guard turned and walked over to Skip. He bent down and handed the flag to him, speaking the customary words, "Thanks from a grateful nation." The sergeant turned and walked back to the casket. He barked out two orders. The honor guard turned, began to march and slowly left the grave site. The archbishop followed. Row by row, the funeral goers filed back to their cars. Skip and his kids stood at the casket with single yellow roses in their hands. One by one they placed their roses on Wanda's casket and walked away, knowing that her soul was finally at eternal peace.

Construction flew by. The Corps of Engineers kept a tight schedule on contractors, holding everyone to their commitments. It was like watching an "*Extreme Makeover*: City Edition." Even the crew from ABC came in and built a very special house for a totally handicapped family. The father had a heart condition. The mother suffered from seizures. And each child had some form of birth defects. Downtown was now a bustling metropolis. The Woodward and Gratiot links of the subway were complete to Pontiac and Mt. Clemens respectively. The elevated railways that ran from 8 Mile to their respective cities with artistic flair. Creative construction led to a newly reinforced titanium alloy, made to last forever. It could be shaped into any design before being finally put into place on the structure. Critics raved that the Detroit subway was the most efficient and artistically creative designs in the history of subway construction. The area wide fleet of buses was split in half, with most being sold to Buenos Aires Department of Transportation. It was being billed as an "All-American City" and slum free for the first time in 90 years.

Six months after Marvelli's arrest, he was convicted of High Treason and sentenced to death by lethal injection at the Indiana Federal Penitentiary. The four chiefs of the Apocalypse, Tecumseh, Johnson, Running-Horse and Night-Owl, were sentenced to consecutive sentences of life without parole. The National Tribal Council requested the President's permission to administer their own brand of honorable judgement to the men. To the world's surprise, the President consented. With military observers watching, four braves, one from each of the respective tribes, sat astride white stallions with spears in their hands. A hundred yards away stood the four chiefs, bound by ancient vines used by their forefathers. The four braves were dressed in their respective war paint, distinctive for each tribe. With a bloodthirsty cry, the four took off at breakneck speed towards their prey. Within minutes, each brave struck their targets in the heart ending their earthly life in the blink of an eye. A new era in Indian-American relations began that day.

It took almost nine months to clean out and rebuild the tunnel. But under the leadership of Kyle Lincoln, his expertise cut the reconstruction time in half. Again, titanium alloys were used to strengthen the inner tunnel walls. On top of the tunnel cylinders, a one foot thick alloy wall topped off the construction. Impervious to any known explosive, the new construction was to protect the tunnel for millennia, not just centuries. The bridge had been finished six months before, reopening the US-Canadian border to trade again.

The estate of Wanda Willington was finally settled just before February. Some $2 billion dollars, after court costs and taxes, was divided up among the three kids. She left Skip a stipulation that the $500,000 dollars left to him, if she passed away early, was that he use it to do something he always wanted to do. She always knew his needs. He immediately left his broadcasting job, jumping full time into work as a private eye. His partner, Roy Maxim, passed away a couple of months earlier from complications from his injuries during the office break-in. At least, it happened peacefully in his sleep. Amy gave most of her money to her alma mater and current employer, the University of Michigan, setting a portion aside for family use. Ray left the National Guard, becoming a major contractor in the rebuilding effort in the city. Drew choose to further his mother's legacy. When Renaissance Records went on the auction block, he was able to pick it up for a mere $100,000 dollars. He immediately turned it around as a money maker for him and the city.

A Yellow cab pulled up to the M&M Detective Agency on Griswold. The slim, petite woman got out, paid the cab driver and walked inside the revolving door. She walked up to the marquee, looked for the agency's floor and got on the elevator. Within minutes, she was standing outside the office door of the man who saved her life. After six months of military reprogramming, Detroit Police dropped all charges of manslaughter against Officer Reese Watson for the death of Wanda Willington. Because of Skip Mitchell's suspicions, enough doubt surfaced to lead to the discovery that she truly had been brainwashed during her tour of duty in Iraq. For that, she owed him her eternal gratitude. Her only consequence was to be forever banned from police work forever. The third floor office seemed dark to her as she walked up to the frosted glass door. The name of Roy Maxim was partially washed off the door. Mitchell's name still stood out below the agency header in the middle of the door window. She turned the knob and slowly opened the door. A loud creak erupted from the rusty hinges that had not been oiled in six months. The Penobscot building tenants were moving up Michigan Avenue to the newly rebuilt Michigan Central Terminal Building. The Corps of Engineers were scheduled to gut the inside of the interior walls in three days. All of the file cabinets in the front office were sealed shut with combination locks. Watson slowly walked towards the empty, dark office on the Fort Street side of the building that belonged to Roy Maxim. That too was packed away. The other office door was cracked open ever so slightly. She walked over and cautiously pushed it open. There stood Mitchell hovering over boxes piled on his desk. He appeared to be lost, looking for something but not knowing what.

"Mr. Mitchell." A startled Skip looked up at the person in the doorway. He recognized the soft features of her face.

"Oh hi. Barney told me you were being released. How was the reprogramming? I hear the Army has made the process a lot easier on the participants." She smiled a sheepish little smile as she walked in towards the well lit room.

"It wasn't bad. I spent most of my time in regressive hypnosis reliving what I went through in Iraq. The doctors fixed it to where I will be able to remember and taught me new methods to fight that type of torture in the future. Like I will ever go through that again, I don't think so. Did the chief tell you that I might stop by?"

"Yeah, he casually mentioned something."

"Well, then you know that I am eternally grateful to your perception and your influence to get me the help I needed and keep me out of jail. My kids even made you a thank you card." She pulled a folded piece of paper out of her purse and handed it to Skip. He opened and read it aloud.

"Thank you, Mr. Mitchell, for saving our mommy and making her better. Signed, Michelle and Bertie. That's cute. They sound like sweet kids."

Watson replied, " They're my pride and joy. Well, I just wanted to thank you personally. I'll be on my way now."

"Don't go. I really could use some help right now. Movers will be here in an hour." She turned and smiled.

"Sure, why not," she said. Throwing her purse on a chair, she dove in with duct tape sealing packages under Skip's directions. The movers came and left. Skip looked around at the office that was part of so much history. Life changes and if you don't change with it, you are left behind, he thought. Times never stands still for the future. After one last look, he let Reese out and locked the door.

Walking to the elevator, Skip was very pensive. He knew Reese's situation, not having a job anymore. He, too, was in a need. With his cases, he could use a new partner. It was worth a try, he thought.

"Say, have you had dinner?"

"Not really. Spent most of the last two hours cleaning out my locker."

"Want some? Maybe we might even consider this a business dinner. I've got an idea I would like to throw at you. Interested?" Sensing something good was coming, she showed that sheepish, pearly smile again.

"Sure, why not." The elevator door opened and they walked into the parking garage.

The alarm beeped off as they approached his 1970 Boss Mustang. He opened the passenger door and let her in. As he jumped in and buckled, he asked, "What do you like? Steak or Seafood?"

"I'm a steak fan myself. By the way, nice car." They drove out onto Fort Street, opening up a new chapter in their lives. Life does go on.

SKIP MITCHELL WILL RETURN

Printed in the United States
77044LV00004B/106

9 781424 162604